THE DEPTHS

LUCY BANKS

www.bloodhoundbooks.com

Print ISBN: 978-1-916978-63-8

CHAPTER ONE

I t's been a while since I've been on a rural coastal road. Right now, we're driving through tree tunnel after tree tunnel. Winter-stripped branches, hedgerows high and dark to either side. Narrow, sunless routes with bumpy surfaces. Vinnie hasn't said a word for about half an hour now, and the radio went off when we stopped to fill up with petrol. It's been a long journey.

The road feels alien, though it shouldn't really. It's not so different to where I grew up. Seaside village. Quiet beach. Crumbling old cottage on the outskirts, Mum decked out in dungarees, Dad in a wetsuit. I can't picture him in anything else. Me too, clad in neoprene from top to toe. All that endless diving, out there in the water with him until my skin puckered like crumpled fabric. I never wanted to go back to that, but here I am. New home. New life. Vinnie's idea of a good place to live, not mine. That's what love is, I guess. Letting the other person bob to the surface, breathe and be free. Even if it means holding my breath for longer than is comfortable.

I tap my nails on the dashboard. They're long, royal blue, with a wave-line of red across each one. My last treat before we left Clapham, a final trip to the manicurist. God knows what state they'll be in after a few weeks of living in the middle of nowhere, let alone the rest of me. What a pair of idiots we are, giving up the life we worked hard for. But we had to get away.

Vinnie's frowning. The tapping's annoying him. I'm past caring. He's packed too tight into the driving seat, a folded-up version of his usual six-foot four self, bearded and big as a giant. His body's looser these days. He's baggier and hairier since he quit his job. Back when we worked together, it was always tailored suit jackets, open-necked shirts, hair wax-styled in a smooth quiff. Now he's a man of corduroy and woollen-wear, comfy jeans, slouchy boots. It makes a mountain of his already big frame. Reminds me of how strong he is. I should try to remember how much I used to like that about him.

He glances across. I stop tapping.

'Are we nearly there yet?' I ask.

'Believe me, I hope so, Heidi. I'm done with driving.'

'I said I was happy to take a turn.'

'You don't know the car like I do.'

'This looks different to when we last came down.'

He shakes his head. 'It's the same. The trees make it look different. Winter's on its way. Better get used to the cold. There'll be no shelter from that sea breeze.'

Sea breeze. What an understatement. Also, he doesn't need to warn me about it. I grew up with the lash of wind-shoved rain, I remember how it stings the skin. My parents' house was postcard-pretty; a thatched bungalow with whitewashed walls. Garage stuffed with Dad's diving gear, the kayaks, our little boat called *Water Pixie*.

The house Vinnie and I have bought is nothing like that. It's a blank cold box, built in the sixties. But it does have a killer view, or so Vinnie likes to remind me. That's why we took the plunge, did all of this so quickly. That uninterrupted sweep of the ragged cliffs surrounding the little cove, the endless expanse of sea; it'll ensure the house sells itself once we've fixed it up and put it back on the market. Or that's the plan. It'd better work, for the sake of our dwindling bank balance.

Shared bank account. Shared mortgage. All in just a few months. We really are tethered together now. Strange to think that we only met at the start of the year. What a whirlwind romance. Or whirlpool. We've been sucked into this.

No-one else would call it a romance either. No-one else would be that kind. All the whispering after we made our relationship public, it made it sound so seedy. It drove us out. To here. Literally the end of the country.

I live by the sea again, I think silently, letting it wash through me. Living in a house that no-one else wanted to buy, which has stood empty for several years. I can't help feeling it's a backwards move, and I don't do backwards, only forwards. No regrets, only focus on the future.

I regret nothing. It's important to remind myself of that.

He reaches for my hand, squeezes it hard. 'What's up?'

'Nothing.'

'This will be good for us. We agreed, remember?'

'What if we hate it?'

'We won't. Don't worry, there's a local pub. You can still go out and socialise.' His fingers squeeze harder. The car feels cramped, though that's probably because so many of our belongings are stuffed into the back seat behind us.

One pub. *Great.* I think of bars, endless bars. In Clapham, at the other end of Tube journeys, dressed to kill, giggling with Miranda. She'll get to carry on with all of that without me. My best friend. More like my only friend. I'd happily rip off all my false nails – and my real ones too – if it meant I could make her live in the middle of nowhere instead of me.

'You need to be positive, because there's no other choice,' Vinnie says eventually. 'We had to leave. People asking difficult questions, you know how it was. This will be better. No-one knows us here.'

But I like being known. A little bit of attention never hurt anyone.

'We could've gone somewhere with more of a social scene,' I say.

'And lived in a tiny flat with no profit potential. This is an investment opportunity. It's only temporary.'

'What if we can't sell this place?'

'I'm sure we will.'

'You can't be sure.'

'Not this again. Not now. Let's be positive, please. You're the one who kept saying we had to get away.'

'You're the one who chose here.'

His jaw tenses. There's more he wants to say, none of it nice.

I pat his arm quickly. 'We'll make it look beautiful.'

'That's the spirit,' he replies, with the hint of a smile. 'So there's no need to plan your exit strategy just yet.'

Exit strategy. I imagine being out at sea. Nothing to grab hold of, no way of getting back to shore. I imagine sinking under the slapping waves, breath erupting in bubbles. I imagine silence and the sight of the moon above, twisted by the water. Strange, how the mind travels to places it shouldn't.

The little dig at me didn't go unnoticed either. They're commonplace these days. It's just the stress of the last few months. We'll make this work. We've come too far for it not to.

'Hey, look,' he says, in a lighter voice. 'I recognise that massive oak tree there. Not long now, it's just a few minutes longer.'

'We've been on this road for ages.'

'There's the stream that leads out to the sea, look.'

'It's a raging river.'

'That's the Cornish coastline for you. Isn't it stunning?'

'This road is so narrow. You couldn't turn around in it.'

'Luckily we won't need to.' He points ahead. 'There it is, look.'

I follow his pointing finger through the windscreen. The house is straight ahead and looks worse than when we came to view it. The painted pebbledash is grubby with age and streaked with moss. The windows are blank and wide, the paint on the front door's peeling. Slate roof with tiles missing. Front garden overgrown, a sea of gravel acting as driveway beside it. *An absolute steal*, the estate agent told us, when we looked around. That'd been back in late summer. White clouds, blue skies, warm amber light softening the cracks. Vinnie and I held hands then, I remember.

A steal. What a joke. I feel like I'm the one who's been stolen.

We drive through the metal gate. It's hanging off its hinges. The mail box has fallen over and is lying in the long grass like a dead thing. The stone wall surrounding the house is crumbling and broken. It blocks nothing out, keeps nothing in. It must have been part of an older property that once stood here. I see the sea next, the cod-grey expanse to the other side of the house. I'll see a lot more of it from inside, and now I'm here, I'm not sure I want to. Vinnie slows the car. The gravel growls in protest as he parks, then silence.

'This is it,' he says. The richness of his voice rings fake.

What is this, exactly? I don't even think he knows anymore.

We climb out of the car and into the cold. I'd forgotten how exposing it feels, being surrounded by nothing but nature. I'd got used to tall buildings, not much green space.

He reaches in his jeans pocket and pulls out the keys. Jangles them, attempts a grin, then sighs.

The black paint on the door is a dirty grey up close. The key grates in the lock and the hinges complain as he pushes the door open. It's dark in the hallway. The murky blue wallpaper doesn't help, nor the navy carpet tiles underfoot. They give under each step I take, like there are bubbles of liquid beneath, searching for a gap to spill up through.

It's vast. Empty. Grim, and so much worse than I thought it would be.

Welcome home. I bite back a laugh, or it might be a groan. I'm not sure whether to go with hysteria or horror right now. Vinnie paces ahead, footsteps thumping hard.

'I'd forgotten how big this place is.' His words echo, then deaden into silence. 'You could fit our old office in here, couldn't you?'

I can imagine it now. The rows of desks, the big printer in the corner, the little kitchenette. Our busy little workplace. Me on project management, Vinnie the rising star, the marketing maverick. Miranda too, in accounts. The good old days. I miss it; things were a lot easier then. But we don't look back, only forward. I've got to let all that go.

I step into the lounge behind him, taking in the stained carpet and unevenly plastered walls. It's massive. Empty. Like a drained aquarium. There are two floor-to-ceiling windows facing out to the sea. A kitchen area in a badly lit corner, with windows looking out across the drive.

Vinnie gravitates immediately to the sea view, pressing his hand to the glass. 'Isn't it beautiful?' he says softly. 'C'mon, Heidi. You've got to admit this is special.'

'It looks bleak. Unsafe too. You couldn't swim in that sea.'

'Rubbish, you just wouldn't go too far out. Look at those cliffs. They're so sheer, as though someone carved them with a cleaver.'

'I don't like it.'

His jaw tightens. 'You said you'd be open-minded.'

'I only said—'

'We've both got to be open-minded. Otherwise this won't work. Remember what we said? We've got to be positive.'

'This place is ugly, Vinnie. Look at the mould round the window frame, that's been there for years, you can—'

'Stop. Right now. You don't get to spoil this. Not on top of everything else.'

I step to the side, give him distance. At the start, he'd been easy to love. Big character, big drinker, always up for a laugh. He'd moved from another marketing firm in Shoreditch to work with us, got treated as a big deal and navigated the office space like he was. I wanted him right from the start. I sacrificed a lot to make this life for us.

Admittedly, he had a life of his own beforehand. *Noelle*. I wonder if there'll ever be a time when things don't lead back to her.

'When will the removal company be here?' I ask, changing the subject.

He brightens. 'Soon,' he says. 'Then we can start making this place our home.'

It's a lie. I know it. I'm sure he does too. This will never feel like home. We've made a mistake.

I smile and nod, and he nods too. Partners in crime, for better or for worse.

The removals van arrives about twenty minutes after us. I leave them all to it as they unpack our belongings. The house is a stranger's place. I tap my way along walls, feel the spongy damp of the carpet on the stairs, peer out the small porthole window at the top of the landing and feel lost at sea. The upstairs is dank and airless.

I duck from room to room as grim-faced men in overalls haul boxes and furniture around me. Run my fingers along dusty window ledges, stroke the rough wallpaper. Each window holds a view and it's all empty and wild. The sea to the front of us, the cliffs around the cove full of cracks and caves. The huge cloudy sky, weighting it all in place. Then at the other side of the house, nothing but field after field, grass wave-rippling in the wind. We're surrounded by waves in every direction.

Dad would have liked this. Mum not so much. She was always nagging Dad to move. Dad was all about the water. Sinking beneath those waves out there, exploring the seabed, it would have filled him with glee. Not anymore though. Nothing could cheer him now. It's been five years since I heard he died. Lung cancer. Ironic, given how well those lungs worked. Shame about the heart, though. That was never very functional, cold bastard.

His grave's somewhere in Sydney. I wonder if they buried him in goggles and flippers. Whether he held his breath as he was dying, for as long as he could. He was a professional free-diver, after all. I was never as good as him, but I wasn't bad. Useful skill, being able to hold your breath for several minutes, even in the city. It always served as a good party trick after a few drinks.

Slowly, each of the bedrooms fill with our belongings. I hadn't realised we had so much stuff. None of our furniture looks right here, it's all too slick and shiny, too sharp-edged. I slip downstairs, through the living area into the utility room, a generous space the estate agent called a *boot room*. The keys to the back door lie on the window ledge beside it. I unlock, step outside and let the wind steal my breath away.

The garden is on a steeper slope than I remember. There's a stone wall at the bottom, then after that, only cliffs and the little path leading down to the cove. The grass comes up to my knees in places. It's tangled and knotted, sticks to my jeans as I stagger through it. There's an old wood shed to one side of the garden, a statue of a mermaid in the corner, lopsidedly leaning to the ground. I touch her hair, feel moist lichen clinging to the stone. Her face is nearly worn away, but her tail-fin is sharp, a hard flick pointing upwards. It reminds me of a scorpion's tail, ready for attack.

My throat tightens. My eyes sting and blur and I blink quickly. I want comfort. Fun. Glamour too, I guess. Everything I worked so hard to get. This is the opposite. It wasn't what I signed up for.

I wonder what Noelle would think. Whether she'd be pleased to know that Vinnie and I can't find a way to be happy, despite our best efforts. I don't think so, though. Too dumb, too naïve. I don't want to think of her again. Vinnie and I promised we'd stick together, that we wouldn't let her ruin our lives.

I remember the first time I said her name aloud. It's a strange thing to stick in the mind. She visited the office to see Vinnie, to deliver a handmade stack of sandwiches to him. Noelle, who had a *creative job* doing illustrations in children's books. Who didn't work much, and it showed. Vinnie introduced us. He was awkward then. Didn't want to do it. I liked that. It said a lot.

Noelle, I said. *That's a pretty name.*

I look back at the mermaid's features, which are all but gone. There's a hint of a smile there, or a snarl.

'Pretty,' I whisper.

The grass rustles behind me. A hand settles at my shoulder. I jump.

'It's all done.' Vinnie's words break the quiet.

'Yes,' I reply, then add, 'what is?'

'Our stuff, it's all in. The removals company have gone.'

'That's good.'

'Are you enjoying the views?'

I turn to face him. The lines around his eyes and at the corners of his mouth are harder than I remember. He looks stone-carved. Not strong and pliant, but hard and immovable.

'The views are dramatic,' I reply.

'People would love to wake up every day to a view like that.'

Not me. The words start and stop in my throat. I swallow hard. 'We should start unpacking,' I say.

He nods, then gestures back towards the house. 'Let's make this place feel like ours. Then we can settle down with that bottle of wine to celebrate. Oh, and Heidi?'

'What?' I say, following him.

'Try to smile. You've got a face that could curdle milk, as my mother used to say.'

It hits me hard. He's different now, completely different. He used to tell me he loved my smile, said it many times, in dimly lit bars near the office, in bed, whispered in my ear. *You've got the most beautiful smile I've ever seen.*

I force a grin, but it's too late. He's marching ahead, hands in pockets, head down. Leaving me behind. It's becoming a regular occurrence these days.

Our sofa is dwarfed by the large window in the living room. Sitting side by side, we're made miniature by the views outside. The water looks black now, with only the faintest shimmer of moonlight across its surface. If I listen, I can hear the restless shush of the waves dragging the pebbles to and fro, like a whisper.

Vinnie raises his glass, then nods at me to do the same. We clink. The noise doesn't fit here, it reminds me of cities, laughter and people. Not this place.

'We're so close to the cliff,' I say, leaning back against the cushions.

'The survey said it was fine. Everything's structurally sound, don't worry.'

'It makes you wonder,' I begin, curling my legs underneath me, 'why no-one else bought it. Don't you think it's weird?'

'Nope. It takes vision to buy a place like this.'

'And money.'

'We've got savings.'

'They're going fast. We're both out of a job, remember?'

'I can get more money. Don't panic so much. You never used to.'

He's secretive about his finances. I don't get why he's not looking for another job. He's ambitious, he gets bored easily.

Maybe that's it. Being a marketing manager was no longer exciting enough and this is his latest project. Until he moves onto the next thing.

'Besides,' he continues, 'you can achieve a lot without money. Mum managed it when she did up our old house. She used to find amazing bargains at car boot sales. Made the place look a million dollars, sold it for a fortune.'

His precious mother: not someone I want to hear about now. I'm just pleased I've never had to meet the woman. I wave in the direction of the back door.

'What are we going to do with the garden? It's a mess out there.'

'It's not too much work. You don't like getting your hands dirty, do you?'

'You'll never get a mower up and down that hill.'

'I'll get you to do it instead. Unless you're too worried about breaking a nail or ruining your hair.'

'Very funny.'

He grins. 'Anyway, I'll be too busy pulling that old woodshed down.'

'Why are you making that a priority? Because of what the estate agent said?'

He drains his glass, then reaches for the bottle to pour himself another. 'Come on, it sounds fun, doesn't it? Our very own smuggler's tunnel hidden away underneath the woodshed?'

'Anyone could pop up from it. Like one of those real-life horror stories you see on YouTube.'

'Who's going to pop up these days? This place is deserted. The estate agent said even the people in the village don't tend to come down here much.'

'The tunnel might just be an old wives' tale.'

'The estate agent sounded pretty certain. There was an old cottage on this ground, before this house was built. Owned by fishermen turned smugglers. Sounds fascinating, I love a bit of history.'

His enthusiasm is almost infectious. It's been a while since I saw him get enthusiastic about anything. I miss it. It beats sullenness, which is what I mostly get from him these days.

He did this for me, because he loves me. And then, I like him again. Just like that. I rest my head on his shoulder, feel the warmth of his skin radiating through his jumper.

'If you want your own secret tunnel,' I tell him softly, 'then go for it.'

'We all need our little secrets,' he replies.

We both sit in quiet agreement.

⁂

I lie down in bed. My temples ache. It shouldn't feel this uncomfortable, it's our mattress, our duvet, the same pillows. But everything's strange. The walls are too far away. The ceiling's too low. The curtainless windows don't help either. I know no-one's out there, but it's easy to imagine someone watching us out there in the dark, and neither of us knowing it.

Vinnie comes in, rubbing his hair with a towel. The shower was so weak it barely rinsed my conditioner out earlier, but I don't dare mention it. He sits on the bed beside me then lifts the duvet. Strokes my exposed thigh, frowns, then moves his fingers to my hip.

He hasn't touched me like this in ages. When we first started seeing each other he constantly found ways to feel my body. The accidental brush against my arm in the office kitchen. The casual press of his knee against mine in the pub. A squeeze of my shoulder. Then frenzy, pulling clothes off, grasping, tugging, rubbing. It was intense, all that touching. I loved it. Loved Miranda's jealousy when I confided in her too. They were all jealous, all the women at the office. Everyone wanted him, they all flirted with him just as much as I did. But I was the one he chose. Even though he was with someone else at the time.

His little bit on the side. I didn't mind at first. It was worth it, to feel the things he made me feel. Now, nothing. I'm a china doll. Hard, cold, numb.

He bends down and kisses me. Then leans in further, climbs on top of me and rolls my camisole top upwards. His hands are freezing, fingertips rough and dry.

'I'm tired,' I whisper.

His lips travel to my neck and trace a trail to my collarbone. 'We need to make this place feel like ours,' he says. 'Ours and no-one else's.'

He says it like a spell. Something to paint over the cracks and put us back together again. I stare and stare, searching for the man I'd known before and I can't see him anywhere. I stroke his hair. He has so much of it, that and his beard, which tickles at my skin. He pushes a hand between my legs and guides them apart.

My phone vibrates on the bedside table. I sit up.

'Leave it.' He rolls to one side.

'It might be important.'

'Really? I doubt it.'

I pick it up anyway. It's Miranda, probably checking to see how the move went. Wanting to make sure that her life is better than mine, which it is. That life that doesn't even seem real anymore. Wine bars. Dancing in Soho clubs. Eating breakfast in bijou cafés the morning after, swearing to never do this, that or something else ever again. Then doing it promptly the next evening. My ex-work colleague, my favourite drinking partner. She feels a world away now.

I show him. He squints, pulls a face.

'Why is she calling after ten at night?'

'She keeps funny hours. This is early for her.'

'Don't answer it.'

'It won't take long.'

'Don't.'

I let it ring out. He bites his lip. The phone falls silent and I place it carefully back on the bedside table.

Vinnie rests his hand on my stomach, then removes it. 'I guess we're both tired,' he says.

'It feels wrong too.'

'Why? Because of Miranda?'

I frown. 'No, the window. Anyone could see us.'

'Only owls and bats. I don't think they'd be interested. Look, forget about it. We'll go to sleep just like you wanted.'

It's difficult to read his expression. Irritation maybe, but something darker. He's tired, that's obvious. Tired of me? Maybe, but he has no right to be. I've brought more excitement to his life than he ever had before.

He clambers off the edge of the bed, removes his pyjama trousers, then slips under the duvet. I wait for him to say something else or to give me a final kiss, but he rolls to his side. His shoulders are a solid cliff-face. I know he won't turn back to me any time soon.

I lie on my back and stare at the ceiling. The moonlight makes its surface look almost bubbly, like being underwater. I imagine being at the bottom of the ocean. No mermaid tail to flick me up towards the air. No breath left in my body. Nothing but sodden skin and heavy bones to hold me down here forever.

I think of Dad grabbing my hand under the water. Tugging me along the seabed and pointing, always pointing. All those secret things down there, seen by only us. It was special. It meant something. I always thought he'd be there. I imagine Noelle too, her face gazing back at me. *Noelle.* All that hair, thick and curling in the water. Dark eyes, watchful. Blank.

My partner, Noelle. Vinnie's words, when he introduced her properly to me at the work Christmas party. The pause before the word *partner* revealed a lot. His hand rested lightly on her hip, barely touching her. Her satin slip-dress skimmed the light curves of her body. She looked me up and down then smiled slowly, like she knew me already. Vinnie told her my name.

'Heidi, like the storybook character,' she said.

'Noelle,' I replied. And couldn't think of anything else to add. Other than silently, in my head like a mantra, *that's a pretty name.*

Pretty. An understatement because she was beautiful. Easy to resent. I went back to drinking my cocktail and Vinnie gave me a wink. Let his gaze linger on my red dress, the low neckline. A month after that we were sleeping together. That was when he became mine, or as good as, anyway.

I want to reach for Vinnie now, to remind myself that he still is. We've been through too much for him to pull away now. I need him to need me. I don't want to be alone again. But he's nearly asleep, his breathing is steady, getting deeper. So, I keep my hands where they are.

I close my eyes and pull the duvet over my head. I don't want the empty window staring at me while I sleep. I don't want to see Vinnie's back, turned against me all night. And I don't want to stare at this ceiling and think of Noelle either. Nor about the power she still exerts over both of us.

CHAPTER THREE

Daylight wakes me far too early. I'm disorientated by the dimensions of the bedroom, the heaps of cardboard boxes by the wall, confused at the cold too. The heating hasn't kicked in, although Vinnie said he'd set it to switch on this morning. I hate being cold. I hate all of this already, after less than twenty-four hours. I hate Vinnie too, right now. He's left me here. Got on with things in the house and left me alone.

I swing my legs out of bed, feel the dampness of the carpet between my toes. The whole place feels wet. The sea must be seeping up through the cliffs, leaking moisture into every brick and floorboard. We're like a lighthouse, isolated, exposed to the elements. Only without the light.

Vinnie's in one of the spare rooms, screwing his desk together. He winces when he sees me at the doorway, grim-faced between the wooden legs, whirling a screwdriver around and around.

'You've made an early start,' I say.

'There's a lot to do. I called the internet company; they'll be over later to connect us. I could do with another coffee if you're brewing.'

I return to the bedroom, pull on some jogging bottoms and a jumper. It's even colder downstairs, I wrap my arms around myself for warmth, not that it helps. Vinnie's already set up his coffee-maker on the kitchen unit, and I slot another capsule in the top, rubbing my hands together as hot water starts rushing through. Coffee will help, though not with the headache. That's the result of too much wine and too much late-night thinking. My eyes are puffy and I'm nearly out of my dark-circle serum. At least I can order that online, though it'll probably take longer to get here.

The walls in the kitchen area are streaky and stained. I place my hand against them. Cold, clammy; my palm comes away sticky. This is why no-one wanted this place, it's a leaking vessel. Purchasing it was madness. We don't know where to start with replacing pipework and plastering walls, and no amount of fake positivity will change that.

I pick up the mug of coffee, set the machine to brew another for Vinnie, then look around. There are more wet streaks over by the sofa, and where the dining table will be once we've screwed the legs back on. I hadn't noticed that yesterday, nor when we'd looked around. They must have been there, though. The stained paintwork suggests the leaks are nothing new.

An unfamiliar trilling pierces the quiet. It's the doorbell. It can't be the postman; no-one knows our address. I peer down the hallway. The trilling stops, then starts a second time.

Someone from London. Asking questions. It's a silly thought. No-one knows where we've moved to. No-one knows anything. Including where Noelle is.

I take a breath. It's safe, it's fine. Nothing to worry about. I pad to the door, twist the key in the lock, then pull it open.

An unfamiliar face is smiling in front of me. Unfamiliar is good, and male is even better. Less complicated, easier to read. He's messy-looking. Not in a bad way. Dark longish hair flopping across the forehead. Black-rimmed glasses. At least five days' worth of stubble, and a checked cloth shirt with a smear of mud across the front. Rubber boots too, also covered in mud. His smile widens as I take him in.

'Good morning!' His greeting rolls, heavy with Cornish vowels and something else too. A hint of Spanish perhaps, or Italian.

'Hello?' I can't think of anything else to say.

'I've caught you unawares, sorry. I'm Rick Smith. We're neighbours.'

Rick Smith. The name doesn't suit him. He looks more interesting than that. 'We haven't got any neighbours,' I tell him.

'When I say neighbours, I mean I'm the nearest house to you. Ten minutes or so across the field, just over the brow of the hill.'

'Hello, Rick.'

'Can't believe someone's finally bought this place. It's been on the market for years.'

This is obviously the sort of place where everyone knows everyone else. Just like the place I grew up in, not many neighbours but all of them nosey. I hold tight to the edge of the door.

Rick takes a step back, studies me closely. It's not an uncomfortable feeling.

'What's your name, then?' he asks.

I can feel my cheeks getting hot. I've got no make-up on; I must look a state. 'It's Heidi.'

'Are you here on your own?'

'No, there's my partner, Vinnie.'

'How was the move?'

'Hectic.'

He grins. 'I bet. Have you got big plans for the house then? It needs a fair bit of work.'

'Vinnie has plans to find the smuggler's tunnel entrance in the garden.'

Rick laughs. 'Old Mr Trewain boarded it up decades ago. He owned the place previously. Actually, I don't know why I'm laughing, it was a sad story. His wife fell down the stairs leading down to the tunnel, or something like that. Ended up breaking her neck.'

'That's awful.'

'It is, isn't it. I'm sorry, that's a gloomy story for an otherwise pleasant day.'

He pauses. I don't know what to say or do. I used to be able to turn it on in a heartbeat in social situations, but now, even superficial conversation unbalances me. The silence stretches.

He coughs, then gestures behind him. 'I'd best get back. The barn won't clean itself.'

I raise an eyebrow. 'You're a farmer?'

'Not like my father was. It's all gone downhill in the last few years, supermarkets squeezing us for lower prices all the time, wanting too much in return.' He waves a hand dismissively. 'You don't want to hear about my woes though. Nice to have met you, Heidi. I'll let you get back to unpacking. If you need anything, just come over.'

He smiles again. *An attractive smile*, I think. It lights him up. I notice his forearms. Strong, good muscular definition, slightly tanned. Overall, compact but well-built. A man who can hold his own.

'It was nice to meet you, Rick,' I tell him. 'Maybe next time you can come in for a cup of tea. I don't want to invite you now, everything's in chaos and–'

'I wouldn't expect it. I've never moved house in my life but I imagine it's stressful. Hopefully we'll speak again soon.'

Hopefully. I nod as he turns and makes his way back down the driveway, boots crunching on the gravel. Shutting the door feels rude after his friendliness. It's been a while since I've had any kindness from strangers. Or anyone for that matter.

Don't think about our ex-colleagues, not now, I tell myself. Not Noelle's friends either, or the judging neighbours. Not all the questions, the suspicion. Screw them all.

'Who was that?' Vinnie's voice trails from up the stairs, just as I lock the door behind me.

I pause. 'Someone from the village.'

A few moments later, his head appears over the banister, above where I stand. 'Who?' he asks again.

'A farmer from over the other side of the hill. He wanted to say hello.'

'How did he know we'd moved in?'

'I don't know. I guess news travels fast in small places like this.'

The stairs creak as he makes his way down, screwdriver still held tight in his right hand. I lean against the wall and wait.

'I thought we agreed to keep ourselves to ourselves?' he says. 'The fewer people we talk to, the less they're likely to pry.'

I nod. 'He told me the old smuggler's tunnel was boarded up by the previous owner. Mr Tremain, Trewain, something like that. His wife fell down and broke her neck in there.'

He winces. 'Why would someone tell you something like that? The guy sounds like a creep.'

He wasn't, but it's not worth me saying anything. I feel a little flare of pleasure at his jealousy. I used to love it when he raged about one man or another looking at me on the Tube, or glancing my way in the pub. Vinnie likes to keep his prizes for himself.

'I'm going to walk to the village,' I tell him. 'I could do with some fresh air. I'll buy us something nice for lunch.'

'I don't think that's a good idea.'

'Why not?'

'You don't know the way.'

'The estate agent said there was a public footpath across the fields, just up the road.'

'Why not wait for me? I'll finish the desk, get the table put together, then come with you.'

'It's not a big deal, is it?'

He crosses his arms 'It is, actually. It's the first time. We should do these things together.'

He never used to be like this. The memories of when we were first together are punctuated by the forceful moments, all led by me. The first time we kissed, in the dark by the beech tree in the office car park. I leaned in first. The time I booked myself onto his work trip to Prague, said I was a necessary part of the team, though I spent the entire two days exploring, or else in bed with him. When we went late-night swimming in the outdoor pool, on the team-building trip to Kent. Semi-naked, clutching each other with cold, feeling each other in the dark. My ideas, all of them.

He made me do the running back then and I liked it, taking on the role of the huntress. This clingy, controlling version of Vinnie doesn't sit well with me.

I need to stop thinking so much. Instead, I nod and head back toward the kitchen, to my mug, and his too, still positioned under the machine. His dwarfs my smaller one. A beast of solid ceramic next to elegant purple-blue china.

'Your coffee's here,' I call, but no answer. I lean by the wall and feel dampness at my back. *Maybe we should convert the place into an aquarium, because that's what it looks and feels like*, I think. Then force out a laugh that doesn't sound like me at all.

'It's an odd house,' Vinnie says, after he finishes attaching the final leg of the dining table, then flips it the right way up. 'I keep thinking I hear water.'

I rinse the last of the lunch plates and turn to him. 'That was me running this tap.'

'Very funny. It's not like that, it's more a steady noise. Like water sloshing from side to side.'

'The waves in the cove below? When it's quiet you can hear them.'

He shakes his head. 'No, not waves either. It's probably my ears playing up again. You know what my hearing's like these days.'

I put the sponge down beside the sink and move over to join him. 'Maybe it's the leaky pipes that you can hear.'

'What leaky pipes?'

'All of them.' I gesture around the room. 'Look at the state of the walls.'

He wipes his hands down his sweater then squints around the living area. 'What do you mean?' he asks eventually.

'All the water marks everywhere.' I wave again at the walls, before looking more closely. I can't see them now. I scan again, but there's nothing there, apart from uneven plastering and the dated wall-lights.

Vinnie frowns. 'I don't know what you're talking about.'

'That's weird.' I step closer. Maybe the water damage only shows in certain lights. I peer at the walls in the kitchen area, but there's nothing to be seen there either, only the faint tinge of grime against the paintwork. I press my palm to the lounge wall to test it. It's dry along the whole length.

'Have you gone funny in the head, Heidi?' He comes up behind me. 'We need to get you out of this house for a while.'

'I think you're right.'

He pauses, then pulls me against his body. I lean back

against him. Try not to focus on the vague musty scent of his clothes.

'Let's walk down to the beach,' he suggests, breath tickling my ear. 'Have a quick dip in the sea while we're there.'

'The sea? I thought we said we'd take a stroll into the village.'

'We don't need anything, do we? We've got food in for the next few days.'

I turn to look up at him. 'It's cold. We'll freeze.'

He grins. 'We've bought wetsuits especially for this. Let's put them to good use.'

He bought them, not me, off the internet a fortnight or so ago. When they arrived and he held them up for me to see, I stared for ages, not sure if it was some sort of sick joke or a test to gauge my reaction.

'It's in your blood, little miss free-diver,' he said. Mocking. A challenge. I didn't reply.

'The waves look big out there,' I say weakly.

'We won't go in too far.' His eyes crinkle in thought. 'We both know how dangerous the sea can be.'

There are so many things I could say now. Hurtful, hard things. I could take him back to that day in a matter of seconds. I could remind him how much he has to lose, and how lucky he is that I'm on his side, not against him.

He leans down and kisses the tip of my nose. 'This will be good for us,' he says. 'Cathartic. Sometimes it's good to face your fears.'

'I don't see how this can help.'

His finger presses to my lips. He shushes the words away. 'Mum used to say it was best to face up to things, tackle them head on. We have to live our lives. Start small and build up. This is a good place to start.'

I blink against the fabric of his sweater. He's so big. Right now, I feel small by comparison. A harmless little thing. Powerless if this beast decided to turn. That's never how it used to be.

'You trust me, don't you?' he asks.

I nod. But only slightly.

'Then let's do this together, try something new. That's what this is all about, remember? Building something fresh, freeing ourselves from everything?'

I nod again. It's easier this time. I'm in control here, I can handle this.

He pulls me away, placing both hands on my shoulders. 'Let's be bold, then. Let's dive into that water and say *sod it* to everything and everyone.'

Just don't go under those waves, I think, as he heads out of the room.

CHAPTER FOUR

The cove-path is steeper than it looks from the top. I'm mummy-wrapped and stiff in my wetsuit. God knows how I used to wear these things all the time as a girl and not hate it. They're so unflattering too, they bulk the waist, make my curves flat and unfeminine.

Tall nettles and gorse sprout from the stones underfoot, and parts of the path have crumbled completely, creating dangerous gaps with a sheer drop the other side. I press as close to the cliffside as possible, cursing how slow I am compared to Vinnie. He's striding ahead as though this was nothing more than a stroll along a London pavement.

We finally reach the bottom. He dumps the bag with our towels inside next to a large boulder, then rests against it. The wind lifts his hair, blowing it backwards. He's receding, and he doesn't even bother hiding it anymore. Standards have slipped since summer, and since Noelle.

'Would you listen to that roar?' His voice rises above the noise. 'Impressive, isn't it?'

He could be Dad, in that moment. Hands on hips, surveying

his sea, his kingdom, ready for the next dive. I don't want to think of him like that. Him, this landscape, it reminds me of endless sessions down on the beach, training to hold my breath for as long as Dad could. I reached the one-minute milestone on my seventh birthday. I was at three minutes by my ninth. He never reached the time of his hero, some guy who set the record back in 1916, but both of us used to stay under for seven or eight minutes at a stretch. Those minutes felt like a lifetime sometimes.

I feel I could stay under longer. He used to say that a lot, when he emerged. Mum used to say he must have been a whale in a past life, only surfacing when necessary. A creature of water. Single-minded too, determined when he put his mind to something.

What that makes me, I don't know.

I watch the waves thumping against the edge of the beach. They're more forbidding than the settled sea by my childhood home in Dorset. These are slate-grey, frothy with dirty water-suds. I remember other seas. Kentish coasts. Bluer waters and a scorching sun, in the middle of a heatwave. A little hidden cove, only reachable by boat. No-one else but Vinnie, Noelle and me. No-one at all.

What do you think lives down there? Noelle's voice chants in my mind. *Do you think there are sharks, waiting to grab us?*

She wasn't stupid, she knew there weren't. Maybe it'd been a joke. Whatever it was, she made a note of it in that silly little notebook of hers. Doodled a picture of a shark across one page, then showed me. A slender shark lurking in the weeds, watching a pair of paddling feet above, eyes slitted, mouth wide and full of jagged teeth. It was good, considering it'd taken her just a few minutes. She had talent.

Vinnie reaches for me and his touch makes me jump. I'm here, not there. Out in the cold, not on a sun-soaked shore. Not back in my childhood either. This is now and Noelle isn't a part of this. Or Dad. I have to remember that.

'You're dwelling on things,' he says. 'Stop it, please.'

'I'm not. Stop accusing me of that, it's you who broods over it.'

He stiffens. 'Don't presume you know what I'm thinking.'

He's angling for an argument. I won't give it to him.

'Are you sure you want to go in?' I ask instead. 'It'll be freezing, even with the wetsuits on.'

'Yeah. Come on, let's stop stalling and get on with it.'

I could just say no. The old me would have done, then sashayed back to the house with an alluring backward glance. Instead, I nod, follow him towards the sea and try not to think of the last time we were in the sea together. And what we did.

Our long weekend away in Kent. A terrible idea. The worst. But he did look good, back then. Especially on that first night. Open shirt. Tight shorts. Sun-kissed skin, muscles like a modern-day Hercules. I remember staring at him. Catching him staring at me. Feeling like it was all worth it.

The difference between then and now is unnerving. Vinnie's wetsuit makes him eel-like, stocky of body. He turns and grabs my hand, but it's a parent guiding a child, not a hero holding his lover. There's a yank to every step. I let myself be pulled along. Maybe it'll be what we need, maybe he's right.

The pebbles underfoot give way to grit, then rough sand. My toes sink in, leaving puddles as they rise. The sea-breeze makes me breathless. Vinnie turns again, determined. This means something to him. This is more than just a quick swim; this is a statement.

My feet reach water. It's ice-cold. My muscles clench with pain which I know from experience will turn to cramp. Still, I keep moving forwards as the water reaches my shins, my knees, my thighs. I feel slimy rocks beneath me, seaweed clinging to my wetsuit. I hate the weeds. I don't like to think what might be lurking in them, waiting to be found.

Down we go, Dad would have said. *Let's see how long today, shall we?*

I don't want to go swimming, Noelle told Vinnie, back then. *Do you think there are sharks?*

'Heidi?' Vinnie looks at me. 'You need to dive in, it's better to get it over with.'

I look out to the horizon, see what looks like a half-submerged head, bobbing in the distance. It wrenches me to a halt. No-one would swim so far out on a day like this, not with the rocks to either side of us, and with the tug of the tide being so strong. I squint to make out details. I think I see hair, dark and matted. The prow of nose, the furrow of eyebrows lowered in concentration.

A woman. The rising waves keep obscuring the head from view, and when it reappears, it's not in the place I would have guessed.

I open my mouth to tell Vinnie, then stop. It's too close to home. A woman out at sea. A woman alone with no-one to help her. No-one to see what happens next, apart from us.

I look again. She's gone. I scan the sea but find nothing. I don't know what to do. The water pulls and drags around me.

Vinnie looks at me in confusion. 'What's going on?'

There's no-one there. Nobody would be mad enough to go swimming in this. I wish I hadn't seen it. I can't get it out of my head.

'Can we go back now?' I ask instead. 'My legs are cramping.'

He grimaces. 'We need to have a quick swim, now we're in.'

I look back at the horizon. Still nothing. There never was anything. My head's going places I don't want it to go.

'Just a quick swim?' I repeat.

'As we're here.' He pouts. 'You go back if you want, but it seems silly now we've got this far. Embrace it, Heidi.'

I take a deep breath then give a thumbs up. He grins. I glance to the horizon again. I feel watched. I feel someone's waiting to see what we'll do.

He ducks down into the water, then breaks the surface gasping and laughing. I do the same, an act of blind obedience. The freeze of the sea constricts every part of me. My palms tighten, pulling my fingers into fists. My face stings with it. This isn't what I remember from my childhood.

'Swim, then!' he shouts. A wave hits the back of his head, sending a halo of spray around him and he laughs again. It has a wild note to it. No longer a Hercules, now more a monster, deranged and damaged. I move my arms and legs, but can't get coordinated. Another wave comes in and covers my head. I can't hear anything but the rush of bubbles around me, before I emerge again. I could start swimming properly; I know how to get myself warm. But I don't want to. I rejected all of this many years ago. This isn't me anymore.

'Isn't that good?' Vinnie says, swimming closer.

I shake my head. 'It's horrible.'

'Rubbish. The sea's in your blood. Besides, you look like a pretty mermaid.'

Noelle. That's a pretty name.

He swims around me in a circle. I start to move too, it's either that or freeze. All the while, I look to the water beneath me. My toes no longer touch the ground, I'm out of my depth. I watch for shadows.

Vinnie swims away. I try to keep up with him, then change my mind. Better to swim back to shore. I've done what he wanted me to, though I know it'll annoy him. In his mind, this isn't done yet.

If a woman was out there, she's dead now, I think. The

thought is numbing. Plenty of people have lost their lives to the sea.

Dad left us. The echo of Mum, three days after my fourteenth birthday. *You know why. Why did you do it, Heidi? That was the worst thing you could do.*

Cramp is setting in, turning my feet to lead. My calves will follow soon after. *Massage the muscle,* Dad would have said. *Get the blood flowing. Breathe through it.*

I don't want to do any of those things. Or think about him either. The pain's getting worse. I could put a stop to it, start a fast front crawl. Dive under the waves and glide through the water. A pretty mermaid, though I feel more like a fish in this suit. I look down at my fake nails, hard blue and shining. That's me now, who I want to be. Polished. Prized. Protected.

He's up ahead, arms cutting cleanly through the tossing water.

'Vinnie!' I call. The rise and fall of his name rings out. He turns, then looks away again. I try a second time and he raises a hand. I don't know what that means. A wave hits me in the face and I'm submerged. A moment later, above again, gasping, helpless.

The cramp's unbearable, and the water's murky, a sludge-green landscape of drifting bubbles. I have to get back to the shore, plant my feet on dry land again.

Something moves in the darkness, just out of sight. Something large.

Do you think there are sharks? Noelle's dumb question, still ringing in my brain.

It's not a shark. Not a shark. I repeat the mantra, but still imagine something gliding in the depths. I think of the swimming woman who wasn't there, but who might have been. Someone adept at silently gliding underwater. I look down and see weeds, so many weeds, long tendrils drifting towards the surface. It'd be easy to get tangled in them.

My legs are too heavy. I should have got them moving when I had the chance.

Cramp can feel like someone pulling you down, Dad once explained. Like something's grabbing at you.

Something brushes at my leg. I look down and see only weeds, curling a lazy spiral below. Things could be down there. Things that want to get hold of me and never let go.

I feel something wrap around my calf. A tight grip. I kick hard. It's tugging me beneath the waves. I go under, crane my neck and see light above, blurry, distant. I lose my bearings, the world's turned to water and darkness. I'm sinking.

Fight, then. I start kicking again. My muscles scream. Then, release. I drive my arms forward, follow the light, then burst through to the surface in a spray of ice. I gasp, splutter. Feel a hand at my neck.

'Don't!' I cry out above the waves.

'Heidi? What the hell are you doing? Are you all right?'

I struggle in the clutch of the arm around my waist.

'Stop fighting, I'm trying to help you.'

Vinnie's face, up close. Beard dripping, hair in his eyes. He frowns, tugs me into his chest and starts swimming back to shore. Powerful strokes, while I lie limp like a broken puppet. Water soaks my face again and again, but I scarcely feel it. My thoughts are full of hands. Bringing me down to the seabed. Holding me under.

I watch Vinnie's hands slice through the water. They're strong, big palms and long fingers. Strong enough to pull someone underwater. In fact, anyone could do it, providing they knew where to grip and when to tug.

He wouldn't, not to me. In the past, he's told me he loved me, over and over. But then, I think *Noelle.* He must have told her he loved her too, once. He was with her for far longer than he's been with me.

My feet touch sand. I place them down gingerly. The water only comes to my waist, we were hardly out any distance at all. The sea here gets deep quickly.

Vinnie takes a deep breath. 'Bracing, eh?'

There's no acknowledgement of what just happened. No questions, no checks to see if I'm all right. Only *bracing*. Did it even happen at all? It felt like I was under for a minute at least, though maybe it was just a second or two.

'It was more than bracing,' I say. The words are shaky and weak. I start walking back up the beach, reach our bag then pull out a towel. I snag a nail on a loose thread, swear loudly. It helps, somehow. Beautiful nails are part of the old life, the old me. This reminds me of that, and what matters.

I look out to the sea again. Think I see a head, bobbing above the waves, a great distance away. When I look again, it's gone.

Vinnie spends the afternoon pulling down the roof of the woodshed. As the sun starts to set, I stand at the back door and watch him work, his cheeks ruddy with exertion and cold, body wrapped in a thick fisherman's jumper and gloves. He's made progress. The roof and one wall are down, reduced to a splintered pile of wood beside him.

It's an avoidance tactic. He does this every time when he doesn't want to think about something, or wants to slip past my questions. Gives himself an activity, throws himself into it, false cheeriness in place. Anything to prevent his mind from wandering to where he doesn't want it to.

'Vinnie likes his world to be happy,' Noelle told me once, when we were eating lunch together on the park bench outside my office. 'He likes to fill his life with things that give him pleasure. It's my job to make sure he gets what he wants.'

We laughed, hers genuine, mine not. The irony made me want to get up and walk away. I was doing a much better job of keeping him happy than she was. She kept that toothy smile pasted in place, even as she bit into her baguette. Never lost eye contact with me, not once.

Why did she want to be friends with me? It never made any sense. Stupid, naïve Noelle.

I raise my head to watch Vinnie again. He catches my eye and flashes a grin. Then rips another bit of plank from the timber frame, throws it casually on the pile. *Big hands*, I think again. They could have held me down earlier. That's just paranoia, though. Panic, hiding beneath the surface, fighting to break free.

A good diver never panics. Dad's advice. I should have kept it in mind earlier in the water. I always did back then, hung on to his pearls of wisdom like a hoarder, repeating them to myself when I couldn't sleep. What had Mum's advice been? I can't remember anything of any value she ever said to me, apart from the importance of presentation. *Make yourself appealing and you'll go far.* It didn't work out too well for her in the long run. After Dad left, she rotted alone in the cottage she'd always wanted to escape from until cancer finished her off.

I haven't thought about these things in years. I hate looking back. It's a waste of time.

Vinnie's muscles flex underneath his jumper. He's bear-like. Capable of hurting someone easily, without even giving it much thought. And it's just me and him now, all alone. No-one to keep an eye on either of us.

I head back inside and close the door. Pick up my phone and dial Miranda's number, then settle on the sofa. She doesn't answer, but calls me back a few seconds later. It's her way; she likes to check her schedule first before committing to a chat.

'You took your time getting in touch,' she barks, without any greeting.

I can feel myself relaxing already. It's good to hear her voice again. More of a comfort than I predicted.

'I've been busy,' I say lamely. 'Moving house is hectic.'

'I know *that*. But aren't you gagging to tell me all about your adventures into the back-end of nowhere?'

'No adventures so far.'

'Don't be boring. Give me the scoop.'

'There is no scoop.'

'How are things with you and Vinnie?'

'They're fine,' I lie.

'Don't give me that. Last time we spoke you were in tears. Totally unlike you. You're the toughest little cookie I know.'

'I'm sorry.' I feel like crying again. She's taking me back to the *before*, when I could walk ten minutes down the road to hers, sit on her velvet sofa and drink until things felt better. 'Honestly, we're okay. Tired but busy.'

Miranda sighs. 'I can't believe you both went through with this move. A new house won't make everything all right, you know.'

'I don't know what you mean.'

'Yeah, you do. And you said the place is a wreck.'

'It's got sea views to die for.'

'Since when did you give a shit about views? Thought you hated growing up in a place like–'

'What's with all the questions?'

'Nothing.' She pauses. 'How's Vinnie been?'

It's a casual, throwaway question, but doesn't ring quite right. The two of them were odd with each other before we left. Awkward, like they'd had a fight but didn't want to talk about it.

She'd been even pricklier than when she found out that Vinnie and I were together. Jealousy's a bitch.

'Vinnie's okay,' I say slowly. 'He's a bit moody, but getting stuck into DIY. New start and everything.'

'If you need a new start, it usually means there's a bad ending on the horizon.'

'Thanks for the optimism.'

'Hey, you know me. I shoot from the hip.'

'Don't you ever feel like a change?'

'Hell no. I like my life the way it is.'

We both laugh, which helps. I can't imagine her ever changing. The late nights, the excessive drinking, the lack of kids or partner to prevent her doing what she wants; she's always made it clear that she loves the life she leads, that she'll take what she wants to stay happy That was me too, once. We were two of a kind. Sirens out on the prowl, always up for a laugh. Now look at me.

'So, are you going to invite me to visit?' she asks.

'It's hard to get here.'

'You've gone to Cornwall, not Mars. It'll take me six hours max.'

'The house is a tip. We need time to get it sorted.'

'Something tells me I'm not wanted.'

It's always difficult to know whether she's angry or teasing. But the fact is, I don't want to make small talk at the table with her and Vinnie. Once, the three of us comfortably spent entire evenings drinking together after work. Now, things are different. Have been since Vinnie and I got together.

'I miss London,' I tell her, easing into the cushions of the sofa, staring at the darkening sky outside. 'It's too quiet here. Our nearest neighbour lives quarter of an hour away. And he's a farmer.'

'A hot one?'

'He's not bad.'

She cackles. 'That's my girl. You should get to know him better, ask him to show you his prize bullocks. What does Vinnie think about him?'

'He hasn't met him.'

'You minx.'

'It's not like that.'

'The old Heidi wouldn't have wasted an opportunity to get yet another man dangling off her every word.'

'I can't be the old Heidi anymore. Not down here. There isn't even a hair salon in the village, let alone a bar or a spa.'

'Where are you going to get your bikini line waxed?'

I laugh harder. 'I have no idea.'

'Vinnie likes his women well groomed, doesn't he? Are you really okay with all of this?'

'Why wouldn't I be?'

'The tears before you left. You've been acting weird for months. About the same time you got together with Vinnie, actually. Or officially got together with him publicly, rather than sneaking around together behind a certain someone's back.'

'Miranda, stop it.'

'Just saying. It's weird that no-one's heard from Noelle for so long. Like she's dropped off the face of the earth.'

'I told you, she's probably gone abroad. Her rich parents paid for her to swan off to the South of France.'

'You remember Josie in Finance? She tried popping over to Noelle's apartment a couple of times. Both times no-one answered the door. The letter box was stuffed with mail too.'

I sit up. Inhale slowly. 'There you go, then. She's definitely abroad.'

'Yeah, maybe. You know, you can come back to London if you hate it in Cornwall,' she continues. 'You and Vinnie can stay at mine for as long as you need to.'

Me and Vinnie? The idea of a cosy threesome in Miranda's tiny flat doesn't appeal. 'I don't need to do that,' I tell her. 'Maybe I can come and stay on my own some time? We could have a girly weekend.'

'Well, sure. I guess.'

'Or a week? Get drunk every night like we used to?'

'Yeah. Maybe.'

It hits me then, like a punch in the gut, how much I miss London. Fun nights with a bottle of chardonnay in the wine bar down the road. Running through the rain to catch a bus, holding my work bag over my head to keep dry. Laughter. Lots of laughter before everything went wrong.

I hear the back door creak open, then footsteps on the tiled floor. Vinnie's unmistakable cough.

'I need to go,' I tell her. 'I've got a million things to do before bedtime.'

She sighs. 'Go, then. I presume that's Vinnie I can hear stomping around in the background?'

'He's just come in from pulling down a shed.'

'Impressive. He's quite the macho man. Well, ciao, bella.'

I hang up, just as Vinnie enters the room. He rubs at his face, stares at me with suspicion. 'Who were you talking to?'

'No-one. Just Miranda. She called yesterday and I–'

'Yeah, I know she called. You don't have to justify calling her back. Is she all right?'

'Why are you being strange about her?'

He frowns. 'I'm not. What makes you say that?'

'I don't know. I've noticed recently, when you and her–'

'You're being paranoid. As usual.'

I bite my lip. 'I'm not. The last time we were all together, you two hardly said a word to each other.'

'Let's leave it alone, eh? It's not worth talking about.'

That's it. Conversation over. Vinnie stalks across the living room and out of the door. A moment later, I hear his feet pounding up the stairs, then in the hallway above. Every sound in this house is amplified. I feel small by contrast, miniaturised by the huge window beside me. That's what I've become. A child again, dependent on him to keep me safe.

I could always leave, as Miranda said. But I'd be leaving my investment in this house, thousands of pounds. My furniture, all the pieces I've collected over the years from designer shops, things that can't be bought anywhere else. My other belongings, any hope of a stable future too. I can't give that up, not while there's still hope that things will work out okay.

Is there hope? A smaller, quieter voice deep in my head. A question I'd rather not answer.

There's wine in the fridge, that's all that matters. The rest of it can wait for now.

CHAPTER FIVE

Sleep finds me in the end, after a couple of hours of trying. I slip into dreaming quickly, to images of things I don't want to see. Visions of skin, corpse-blue and moist. Sharp fingers running down my bare legs, bone-hard, too many knuckles. Dark bubbles bursting around me, full of a sticky liquid that makes the water thick and stinking. Those fingers, I feel them climb around my legs. They envelop me, take root through my skin and muscle, and I can hear laughing, high and shrill. *You drowned, you drowned,* someone screams. I think it's me.

My eyes open. My heart's pounding against my ribcage. It's too dark to see anything, it must be late. It was a dream. I'm in our bedroom, Vinnie is asleep beside me. There are no fingers scraping into my flesh.

I'm safe, I tell myself, but it doesn't feel true. I move my legs tentatively, feel the duvet shift against them. My breathing's still uneven, I can't shake the feeling that someone's here in the dark with me. Standing in the corner, watching, hidden among the piles of unpacked cardboard boxes.

The air is clogged with moisture, I can taste it when I inhale.

The sheets are tacky with it, like a sheen of dew has rested on the fabric.

'Vinnie?' I hiss, reaching for him.

His breathing hitches, then steadies again. I place a hand on his shoulder and shake, first softly, then more firmly.

'What?' he murmurs, still full of sleep. 'What do you want, Noelle?'

The name hits me in my stomach like a wrecking ball. *Noelle.* He was dreaming of her. A tumble of emotions wash through me; anger because he told me she meant nothing, that he was just waiting for the right time to tell her; jealousy, biting and hard and wanting to hurt him for making me feel like this. But most of all fear. Fear that she's infecting us both, even now. Even after we left her behind.

I wait as he groans and rolls over. All I can make out of him is the dim line of his nose, the bush of beard resting against his shoulder.

'What's up?' he mutters.

'You said her name.'

'What? Whose name?'

'You know whose.'

He sits up. A moment later, his bedside lamp lights up the room. I glance instinctively to the corner. Empty, of course. Only my imagination running riot again.

'You're talking rubbish,' he says, glaring.

'I'm only telling you what I heard.'

'Because you can't stop bringing it up.'

I retreat into myself, shocked by the bite in his voice. 'I only did because you said her name, Vinnie. Why did you say it? Were you dreaming about her?'

'What does it matter if I was? I can't control my dreams.'

'We agreed never to mention her again.'

'But you can't leave it alone, can you?'

'Why are you dreaming about her?'

'For God's sake, drop it, Heidi!' His fist, smashing into the mattress, is enough to make me jump.

'I want to,' I whisper, holding the duvet tightly against my body. 'But it's impossible. You–'

'It's not impossible, you just don't make any effort. Everything I've done since then, I've done for you. I've taken on all the guilt you've laden on me. But you still can't let it lie.'

I don't understand how he can say that, when I've tried so hard to say nothing, to *keep moving forwards*. I've swallowed down all those words of wisdom he force-feeds me, most of them parroted from his precious mother. A whole buffet of meaningless platitudes and fake-positive phrases, until I feel sick with it all.

I turn to him, just as he climbs out of bed, flinging his legs out of the covers, throwing the duvet back in my direction.

'Where are you going?' I ask.

'You've made me angry. I'm going downstairs. Go back to sleep.'

'I don't want to. We should talk about it. I don't want to fight, I only–'

'I said go back to sleep. I don't want to talk to you right now.'

I can only watch in silence as he stalks out the room. The air feels thick with damp now, clogging up my throat, making it hard to breathe. How can a name have so much power? Two rounded syllables, the exhaled negative of *No*, the fading curve of *elle*. So small a name, but it feels so big. A swollen, bloated thing between Vinnie and me, squeezing both of us aside.

A tear slips down my cheek, to the corner of my mouth. It tastes of salt. Gently, I lean across to Vinnie's side of the bed, then switch the lamp off.

I wake to sunlight. Vinnie's asleep beside me. I don't know what time he came back to bed. I won't wake him, not even to offer him coffee. I don't want to give him the chance to shout at me again.

Or to pull me underwater. To try to drown me.

That didn't happen. I need to let that one go. I grab a hoodie and my jeans, then head downstairs.

The air tastes of cold. Last night's plates and cutlery are still piled up in the sink. I know I should wash them up, but can't. I don't want to feel any more water against my skin. I rifle through the cupboards, then the fridge. We've run out of bread. Milk too. Hardly any wine left either, and that worries me most.

Vinnie won't notice I'm gone. He likes to sleep late, sometimes. I pull on my coat, rummage in the nearest packing box for my lace-up boots. He told me not to go to the village, that he wanted to go with me, but this is different. We need food. He'll want breakfast when he gets up, something comforting to make up for his bad night's sleep. I know what keeps him happy.

My job to make him happy. Noelle's words still jar. Vinnie should be making me happy. He always liked spoiling me in the past. Miranda would agree, tell me that we're there to be worshipped, to be given nice things. Not to scuttle around like a downtrodden drudge.

I'm going to the village for me, not for him. I want to see what it's like. See if there's any sort of civilisation out there, or whether it really is the village that time forgot. I want to get out of here too. I'm starting to suspect it's warmer outside than it is in this house.

The door groans as I open it. I slip outside, close it quietly behind me, flinch at the brightness after the gloom of the hallway. A fine mist hangs in the air, heavier over the stream beside our house. I stand for a moment, watching it drift over the bubbling water.

The path to the village is just a short distance up the road. I pull my zip up to my chin and start walking. It's downhill, which helps, though the icy temperatures force me into a sharp pant. Soon enough, I spot a narrow wooden stile, leading to an overgrown route along the edge of a field. This must be it.

I underestimated the mud. Within a few minutes, my boots are caked in it, muck sucking at me with every step. I slide, recover my balance, swear under my breath. For someone who grew up in a rural location, I'm doing a convincing job of acting like a born-and-bred city girl.

The next field is easier to navigate, as I start climbing the incline and leave the waterlogged soil behind me. It's freeing to be out here alone. To be away from Vinnie, his sullen glares and barbed comments.

It hurts to admit it, but this has all been a mistake.

A large metal gate blocks the path, held shut by a rope looped over a wooden post. I unhook it, then follow the track to a herd of sheep, all bleating loudly. Somewhere among their round, swaying bodies, there's a trough full of food-pellets. That explains it.

I watch with confusion, then spot someone approaching from the other side, woolly hat pulled down over their head, body decked in a thick puffer jacket. He holds a hand up in greeting. It takes me a moment to make the connection. Rick, the neighbour. The farmer. The guy who seemed friendly enough, from the brief chat we'd had the day before.

'Good morning!' he greets, pushing one sheep to one side then another, wading through the mass of woollen bodies.

I smile. 'Are these your sheep?'

'No, I haven't kept sheep for years. These belong to the farm across there.' He points, just as he reaches my side. 'Are you settling into your new house?'

'I'm not sure yet.' I point at my boots. 'I'm not really equipped for this level of mud.'

He laughs. 'You need a good pair of wellies. Where are you headed?'

'Into Nairbourne.'

'The village? It's down that way.'

I cringe. 'You mean I'm going the wrong way?'

'Just a little bit. I'm going that way too, I need to pick up my morning paper. Let's walk together.'

We fall into step. It's comfortable, strolling along with him. Non-threatening. Vinnie wouldn't like it, especially not after last night, while he's still angry. Serves him right.

I glance across, take in Rick's profile. Good cheekbones balanced out by a strong jaw, a sprinkling of stubble. A lock of hair has escaped from his hat, curling over his forehead. Cute. He catches my eye and grins. One of us needs to say something; this pause in conversation shouldn't drift into an awkward silence. I don't want him thinking I'm drab, colourless, boring.

It shouldn't matter what he thinks of me. It shouldn't be important at all.

Yeah right, Miranda would say. I bite back a smile.

'What brought you here, then?' Rick asks, standing to one side as I climb over another stile. 'I presume it can't be work, because there are no jobs here. Are you one of those canny property developers? In a few months' time, will the house be turned into a luxury millionaire's pad?'

I can't help but laugh. 'That's the idea. But I've got no DIY skills whatsoever. I'm useless at practical things.'

'I don't believe that; you've got a clever look about you. Let me guess, university educated?'

'Aren't most people?'

He raises an eyebrow. 'Not me. My dad thought it was pointless for a farmer's lad. He was probably right; a good education would have been wasted on me. I can't sit still for more than a few minutes, let alone sit through long academic lectures. I get bored too easily.'

'I know what you mean,' I say, falling into pace with him. 'Life's too short to not live the way you want to.'

'Variety's the spice of life. Have you been down to the cove yet?'

I pause. The cove is something I could do without talking about, after yesterday. I nod, realising he's waiting for a response.

'Awe-inspiring, isn't it?' he says. 'Not that many people bother going down there. When the tide comes in, there's no beach left. Makes it bloody treacherous.'

I think of the woman I saw out at sea, bobbing through those waves. The woman who'd only been in my imagination, but who I couldn't help believing in anyway. Moving fast. Disappearing without warning. It was like watching myself, from a distance. Watching, wondering what I would do next.

'Do people go swimming down there?' I ask.

'The sea's too rough most of the time. As a lad, I'd sometimes go down to the lowest rocks when the tide was in and go crabbing. But that was paddling, not much else. The best swimming's at Rylane cove, it's a fifteen-minute drive from here.'

'People wouldn't go too far out then? Because it'd be too dangerous?'

He gives me a look. 'I've never seen anyone go far out. The pull of the tide, the rocks by the cliffs; it's a lethal combination.'

The woman was just conjured up by my subconscious, tricking me. I have to let it go.

'Why do you ask?' he says. 'Are you a swimmer?'

'Not these days.'

'You need to be careful of the nixie,' he adds with a grin. 'Every cove around here has a legend, and that one's ours. The nixie of Nairbourne, that's what she's called.'

'What's a nixie?'

'A water sprite. We've even got our Nixie Day in January, just after Christmas to perk everyone up. Legend has it she lives beneath the waves and roams in the old smugglers' tunnels. She lures unwary sailors into the water and drags them to a watery death. Cheery stuff, isn't it?'

I shiver, in spite of myself. *Hands, wrapped around me, pulling me down.* 'Sounds like a dumb fairy tale.'

'Too right. But the tourists in the summer, they lap it up. You should see the rubbish that Clarrie has in her gift shop in town. She always sells it all, though.'

We emerge onto a paved path, then out onto a road lined with bungalows. Another minute later, a steep little high street comes into view, with shops flanking the road to either side. It's quainter than I thought it would be, lines of whitewashed stone facades, low slate roofs, wrought-iron lamp posts and trees along the edges of the pavement. I want to laugh at my own preconceptions. The harsh boxiness of our new house had me thinking every building in this place was ugly and unwelcoming.

'Welcome to Nairbourne,' Rick says. 'A scenic little spot, as you can see. You'll find the baker's over the road, the butcher's next to it, the grocer's just ahead, and the most important place, the local pub, at the end there. The Fisherman's Rest. Does a good draft ale, if that's what you're into.'

'Thanks. I would have ended up in the middle of nowhere if it hadn't been for you.'

'You would have found your way in the end. You look like a lady who's cool-headed in a crisis.'

Cool-headed. It's a fair appraisal. I can certainly act decisively under pressure.

'By the way,' he adds, 'if you and your partner want to meet people, there's a great live music evening every Thursday at The Fisherman's. I'll be there, I always go.'

His eyes are green. I hadn't noticed before. Leaf-bright, flecked with gold. They twinkle in the light; I've never noticed anyone's eyes doing that before. I look away quickly.

'I'm not sure,' I reply. 'I've still got a lot to do. Unpacking. Deep-cleaning. DIY. You know how it is.'

'Ha, and you had me believing you weren't a DIY person.' He holds up a hand. 'It's no problem. Just come along if you fancy it. There's always room for another person or two. I have been known to take to the stage with my guitar, but I'll spare everyone this time around.'

I want to ask more, but it's starting to feel too comfortable. I should be getting on with the shopping, ideally before Vinnie wakes up, so he doesn't worry about me not being there.

'Thanks again,' I say, turning to leave.

'Any time. Hopefully see you soon.'

Rick crosses the road, just as a tractor appears around the corner, rolling noisily along. It hides him from sight as it passes, then when I look again he's gone. He must have entered one of the shops. I feel a mild tug of absence. He'd been good to talk to. It's the first time I've had a normal conversation in a long time.

I find the grocer's easily enough; wide bench against the window laden with pallets of carrots, potatoes, something that looks like kale, piles of apples. I push the door, hear the tinkle of the bell above my head. The shop's small, stacked with shelves which are piled high with cans and cartons. It smells of herbs and something older, staler, but it's blissfully warm.

A woman stands behind the tiny counter at the back. A knitted jumper slides over one bare shoulder, and her mass of hair is slung up in a messy bun. Effortless, that's the word that comes to mind. Someone who's attractive without even thinking about it. I stiffen, turn my attention deliberately to the shelves beside me.

'Hello there,' she says neutrally.

'Morning.'

'We've got a holiday-maker's pack if you're interested. Bread, milk, range of cheeses, teabags...'

'I'm not a holiday-maker, thanks.'

She pauses, then leans over the counter. 'That must make you the person who bought the Trewain's house then.'

'How did you know?'

'If you're not here on holiday, that's the only person you can be.'

I wait for her to go on, but she doesn't, only continues to survey me with cool interest. This shop is her domain and I'm the untested stranger. I deliberately shift a few cans out of place, put one carton back in the wrong place completely. That'll teach her to make me feel uncomfortable.

'It's been stood empty for years, you know,' she says, as I place the items on the counter.

'The estate agent told us.'

'All the local kids call it the *death house*. Kids are funny.'

I scan her face for signs of humour, but see none. 'Because of Mrs Trewain falling down in the tunnel?'

'You knew the story and still wanted the house?'

'We didn't know until after we moved in. But it was a good price so it doesn't matter.'

Her lips press together. 'It's got a bad reputation. The original cottage was owned by smugglers. There are all sorts of nasty stories about it. Folk being left to rot in secret parts of the tunnels, or else being shoved onto the rocks in the cove. Some old hermit woman lived down there too, hundreds of years ago.

Everyone called her a witch. A friend of mine went to look around it when it came on the market the first time around. She said it felt horrible inside. Nasty atmosphere.'

I don't know why she's telling me this. Maybe the goal is to make a stranger feel even more unwanted. She won't succeed. I've come up against worse women before.

'I haven't noticed a bad atmosphere,' I tell her. 'Do you have any eggs?'

'I didn't mean anything by it. Just thought you'd like to know. My name's Bea, by the way. Welcome to Nairbourne.'

Bea. Bee. A stinging thing. I give a tight smile.

'I like a good story,' she carries on, reaching beneath the counter and pulling out an eggbox. 'Don't you?'

'I don't read much.'

'Ah. Okay.' She fiddles with the till, then flips the digital display at the top, showing me the total. 'Six pound forty-five.'

I pull off my gloves, then fumble with the coins inside my purse. Every movement is clumsy. It makes me angrier. I never had this problem before. I was always poised. Alluring. Ready to take action.

'Fantastic nails, by the way,' she says. 'The colour, it's... bright, isn't it?'

'Thanks.'

'Mine are bitten down to the cuticle. Not much point trying to look nice around here.'

I won't engage, keep my eyes to my purse instead, then check my watch to show I'm in a hurry.

'The house is fine,' she says, handing me the change. 'I'm sure you got it for a song, and you'll make loads of profit out of it.'

'That's not the only reason we bought it.'

'Fair enough.'

She dislikes me, I think, as she puts the items in a paper bag.

I've only been in this village for a few minutes and already I've made an enemy.

Why did you do it, Heidi? Why are you like this? Mum's voice again, creeping into my thoughts. I shake my head clear, then leave. I don't need to listen to anyone questioning me, dead or alive.

CHAPTER SIX

W*hy am I here?* The question runs around my head while I walk back, traipsing through mud and puddles. It bothers me that I don't know, and don't know what to do next. It's not the way I am. I usually make good decisions. I take action, I get things done and life gets better as a result. This is the opposite. This feels like I'm unravelling.

The house was an impulse buy. We didn't have enough savings for the deposit, though somehow Vinnie found several thousand pounds more to make this happen. He didn't tell me where it came from, and I didn't ask. Just one more secret to keep from each other, on top of the others. We might drown in them in the end.

Now we're stuck here. With each other. And nothing feels right anymore.

When I arrive at the house, I pause. Reach down for the mailbox and pull it up from the grass. It hasn't fallen over, it's been laid down deliberately, presumably to let any passing postmen know the house is empty. There's a hole in the ground beside it, which I slot the pole back into. It leans slightly, in a drunken slant. It should make the place look more homely, but it doesn't. Nothing will improve this house, no matter how hard we try.

I open the door. Find Vinnie in the kitchen area standing on a chair, hanging curtains in the window above the sink. They're too short by an inch or two, but I know better than to mention it, or that I'd prefer he started on the living-room windows, which feel so much more exposing, especially at night.

'You're up,' I say, dumping the bag of groceries on the countertop.

'There's work to be done,' he grunts in response, as he loops the last curtain-peg up. 'Where have you been?'

'Buying our breakfast. We were out of nearly everything.'

'I was going to drive us to the proper supermarket later.'

'I didn't know that.'

Again, another grunt. He gives the curtains a testing tug, then climbs down from the chair. 'Internet connection's been done while you were out,' he says. 'What did you do in the village? Where did you go?'

'Just to the one shop. It has everything you could possibly need, stuffed into one tiny space.'

'Did you speak to anyone?'

I choose my words carefully. 'In the shop? Only the woman behind the counter. She was pretty hostile, actually.'

'Places like this don't like newcomers.'

Why did we come here, then? I want to ask. But I know the answer he'll give. We weren't wanted in Clapham anymore. Not in our old jobs, not where we used to live, because people were talking. And what they were saying was getting worse.

'What time did you come back to bed?' I ask instead, keeping my tone light.

'I don't know. I had a couple of whiskeys, slept on the sofa for a bit.'

'You didn't need to do that.'

'I did.'

I start removing the shopping from the bag. The rustle of paper helps. It's something to anchor myself to.

'What should we do today?' I ask, placing the loaf of bread beside the hob.

'I've got plenty to get on with. I need to drive to Tannistock later today, get a jig-saw and some wood. Some floorboards need replacing, over there by the dining table.'

'They're not that bad. It could wait.'

'I don't think so.'

He never used to be like this; surly, always holding a grudge. He's like a spoilt child, sulking at not getting his own way.

'I'll do something on my own, then,' I say, crumpling the empty bag and throwing it in the bin.

He slams his palm on the countertop. The ring of it echoes through the space and I take a step backwards.

'Why are you being like this?' he snaps.

'Like what?'

'You're on my case all the time. You always want more and more. Don't you think I've got enough of a burden to carry?'

I hold my hands up in surrender. 'I'm not doing anything wrong.'

'You weren't like this before. You sold me a lie.'

'What's that supposed to mean?'

'You know what it means.'

The force of his anger leaves me speechless. I run his words through my head, try to unpick them piece by piece. He's talking rubbish. I sold him nothing he wasn't desperate to buy.

'You don't know what you're saying,' I murmur, more to myself than him.

He shakes his head. 'You're making this place feel like a nightmare. We've only been here two days. *Two days*, Heidi.'

'What do you mean, a nightmare? Coming here was your choice.'

'Only because we had to get away. This place gives us options.'

'What options? We can't go out, we can't have fun. This isn't living.'

'If you hadn't turned up in Kent, we'd still have a life. Back in London.'

The comment leaves me speechless. I want to get out. We've fought before, plenty of times, but nothing like this. He's never looked at me like this before, with open dislike.

'What do you mean by that?'

'You weren't invited. It was meant to be a weekend away with *her*, not you.'

'Which you moaned about for weeks before. I didn't hear you complaining that Saturday evening. On the beach.'

He grunts. 'If you hadn't been there, then–'

'We both know you can't pin it on me,' I say quietly. 'Should we start talking about whose fault it really was?'

His face darkens. 'Stop it.'

'You started it.'

'Do you want to finish it, then?'

A challenge. Finish the conversation, or finish us? I'm not sure how deep it goes. I swallow my anger. *Retreat, like the tide.* That's the best thing for now. Until I have a chance to think things through properly.

'We're both tired,' I say eventually. 'This is getting out of hand.'

He takes a deep breath, wipes a hand down his face. 'We need to get this out in the open. Things are bad between us. You're punishing me, making yourself less attractive to turn me off you.'

'We've been unpacking a house. Sorry I haven't had time to doll myself up for you.'

'I didn't mean it like that. When we got together, we were all over each other. It was spontaneous, we had fun. This isn't fun.'

'Relationships aren't always fun, Vinnie.'

'I know that. Don't talk to me like I'm an idiot.'

We glare at each other. He needs to trim his beard, it's trailing down his neck like a plant. His eyes are bloodshot, lips cracked from the cold. Not a Hercules anymore. Someone petulant and dishevelled. A foot-stamper, a tantrumming toddler.

'Did we do the right thing?' he asks quietly.

'What, moving house?'

'And the rest. Perhaps we should have gone to the police.'

I freeze. Press a hand against the countertop to ground myself. 'What makes you say that?' I ask.

'Because it was the right thing to do. We should have done it. Right away.'

'It wouldn't have changed anything. You can't undo what's done.'

'We wouldn't have this hanging over us though. It'd be out in the open.'

'You wouldn't have it hanging over yourself, you mean.'

He hardens again. 'Trust you to put it like that. You say you love me. That's not love.'

'Neither is pulling someone under the water.'

He freezes. For a moment, I think he's going to hit me. I brace myself.

'I'm talking about yesterday,' I clarify.

'You're talking nonsense.'

'It felt like someone was pulling me under.'

He meets my eye then looks away. I know what he's thinking. I wish he'd have the courage to speak it aloud.

'This conversation is ridiculous,' he says finally. 'Our whole situation is. I spoke to Mum earlier. She said I needed to stick this out, brave the storm. She's right of course.'

Of course, I think. His hallowed mother. I'm only glad I haven't met her yet, and I'm not likely to unless she fancies a long trek from East Anglia to here.

He moves toward me. I flinch as he raises his arm, then he pulls me in, tightly to his chest. It's restrictive. I used to love being held like this by him. Now, I'm restless in his arms. A worm on a hook. Mindful of the seconds ticking past. He kisses my forehead, an awkward practised gesture. Then kisses me on the mouth. Forces my lips open with his tongue. His breath tastes of coffee.

'Why don't we have some fun?' His beard tickles my ear. 'Remind ourselves what fun is. Do it like we used to.'

I don't want to. But he's insistent, lips trailing down my neck and across my collarbone. It's easier to give in. Perhaps I want to, I'm not sure. There's a chance it'll take me back to how it was when things were better.

Sex, the ultimate weapon, Miranda used to say. Whatever you want, you've got it. As long as you put out after. We used it as a lure. Something to pull men under.

'Heidi?'

The question of my name makes me blink, nod without thinking. He reaches for my hand then guides me towards the hallway. I don't resist.

CHAPTER SEVEN

It's over quickly, this act of sex. It never used to feel like an act, but now, we're performers in a second-rate film. Moaning, muttering, groping blindly at each other under the covers. He feels too heavy, a brick wall of body thrusting against me. I smother in the coldness of the pillow and wait for it to be over.

Afterwards, he's cheerful, or outwardly so at least. We sit in bed for a while, discussing plans for the house, plans that I know will never happen without money. This is all a fantasy, one that's decaying fast, though neither of us want to admit it.

Our relationship is close to breaking. Even while we're here together, naked, talking about the future. We don't have a future. It's so obvious.

After a while, we get dressed. Head out to the car and take the narrow road towards Tannistock. It's close to an hour on the narrow road until it finally widens and we see streetlights, the first signs of town. It starts to rain just as we get out of the car, building to a relentless thrash as we run to the DIY store. We laugh, but it's forced. Neither of us like being cold and wet.

It rains the whole time we're in the town. We return to the car as drowned things, and sit in silence the whole way home.

When we finally get back, the clouds have gone, leaving bleached-grey sky overhead. The air is thick with moisture, signalling another rainstorm to come. Vinnie makes his way out to the garden to carry on breaking the woodshed apart. I start unpacking upstairs, sorting through clothes, hanging them in the inbuilt wardrobes which have seen better days. I move from bedroom to bedroom, marvelling at all the space, wondering why we chose somewhere so big, when it's just the two of us.

I hate it. Even my parents' pokey little cottage, with its moss-coated thatch and black-mould corners would have been better. But I've got to snap out of this. I can't keep walking around with a *face that'd curdle milk.*

Make yourself appealing and you'll go far. Mum's voice, echoing back to me. But no amount of lipstick or hairspray would have brought Dad back to her, or me. Neither of us could ever compete with the bottom of that sea. I loathed the sea, after he left. And now look at me; living right beside it again. The world really is twisted at times.

I feel like crying. I grab another cardboard box, yank the packing tape apart and pull out the knife rack, our expensive knives encased separately in bubble wrap. Kitchen stuff, then, not bedroom. I carry it down with me.

Eventually, after dumping the empty boxes outside by the wheelie bins, I join Vinnie in the garden. He's pulled most of the shed down, the pile of broken wood beside him is almost as tall as me. He spots me then points to the ground in front of him.

'Look what I found,' he says.

I move to join him, peering downwards. There's not much to see. Only a thick slab of stone, wedged deep in the dark soil.

'Was that under the shed floor?' I ask.

He nods. 'I reckon it's the blocked-up entrance to the tunnel.'

'Or just a big stone?'

'No, listen.' He stamps a foot on it. 'Did you hear that? There's empty space beneath it, I'd put money on it.'

'It could just be a little hollow in the ground.'

He rolls his eyes. 'Have some imagination, Heidi. I've got myself a genuine smuggler's tunnel right here. Who knows, there could be treasure chests down there. Anything really.'

'Treasure chests belong to pirates, not smugglers.'

'Whatever. Shall I pull it up?'

'Do you want to?' I glance at the bottom of the garden. To the forbidding sea the other side, the sheer crags of the cliffs. Why he'd want to connect this house even more to that is anyone's guess.

'Of course I want to.'

'You'd be creating a tunnel for anyone to use. They could get into our garden.'

'If anyone was interested in trespassing in our garden, they could just wander through the gate, or jump over that broken wall.'

He has a point. But I don't like the thought of a gaping hole in the ground, leading to who knows what. A place that was boarded up and for good reason, because someone broke their neck and died down there.

Folks being left to rot in secret parts of the tunnels. That's what the woman in the shop, Bea, said. Felt horrible inside. Nasty atmosphere. Hostile. Strange. Haunted, even.

I think of watery marks on the wall that vanish the day after. The damp in the air that lifts without warning after a few minutes. Wetness underfoot that can't be explained. The feeling of a hand at my leg, dragging me down to the seabed.

'You all right?' Vinnie asks. 'You've gone quiet.'

'I'm fine. Pull it up, then. You're going to anyway, I can tell.'

'If we find something valuable down there, it's ours,' he says. 'That'd solve a few problems, wouldn't it? I'll admit, I like the idea of discovering some shiny treasure.'

Was I a shiny treasure once? I think, as I head back into the house. *Noelle too?*

I don't have an answer for that, and it's probably for the best.

He triumphantly prises the stone up half an hour later, revealing a heavy wooden trapdoor, swollen with age, wedged in its warped frame. His frustration grows with each futile attempt to lift it, especially when the best of the light disappears and twilight sets in.

Conversation over dinner is limited. He eats his omelette like an attack, hunched over, fork stabbing like a bird diving for fish. I consider reminding him that there's always tomorrow and the day after that. It's not as though either of us are working at the moment. But I keep quiet instead. For him, this isn't a laughing matter, though it's making him look idiotic enough.

He goes to bed early, muttering about his aching back. The pooch of his lower lip, the furrow of brow, it's childish, embarrassingly so. I watch as he leaves the living room. Struggle to see the man I fought so hard to get. He's always had an element of the little boy about him. His impulsive energy was what drew me to him. I didn't realise back then there was a flip side to that too. The accompanying entitled brat.

This is where whirlwind romances lead. Disappointment. As Miranda said, a bad ending.

I stay at the dining table for a while, cradling my glass of wine. Better here than on the sofa by the large window, without curtains to hide me from view. I don't like the thought of the sea out there, hidden in the darkness, lapping at the coast. It makes me uncomfortable to be *seen* by it. It remembers me. Remembers what happened with Dad. With Noelle.

The wine eases me into half-dazed relaxation, makes me care less about things. I pace the room, eventually sink into the sofa. Rest my head against the cushions and ease my legs across the length of it. The window is a dense wall of black beside me, with only a few vague outlines visible beyond. I can see the rough line of the garden wall, a hint of the cliff-top beyond. I realise in a disconnected, drifting way that I want to escape. This place is hostile. Not just the sea or the village, but the house itself too. It wants us out.

Maybe just me, actually. I'm always being rejected, sooner or later.

I could leave, before Vinnie has a chance to reject me too. Pack some belongings, head back to London. I wouldn't even need to tell him. Not sure he'd even care much anyway.

My eyes burn. I can't believe it's come to this. I was so sure that Vinnie and I were stuck fast to each other, for better or worse. But it's the terrible things that have happened that bind us together now, not any great love for each other. I'm a fool. I never should have gone to Kent. I should have walked away. Stuck with wild nights out with friends, a career, moving forward, going places. Stopped trying to win a prize what wasn't mine.

I think of him upstairs, probably fast asleep now, oblivious to my thoughts. I could take the car and drive through the night until I reached London. I'd force Miranda to let me stay, at least for a few weeks until I found my feet, got another job. Got my old life back again.

But I'm half-drunk and in no state to drive. Shame. The irony doesn't escape me either. I chased Vinnie so hard, and now all I want to do is run away.

I remember Noelle telling me how they got together. How he'd chased her down Upper Thames Street, late at night after they'd eaten in a noisy Chinese restaurant in the West End. It was in a lunch break that she told me; another of those tedious meet-ups I had with her in the café down the road. I sensed she didn't have anything better to do. That she spent her days sitting in her Victorian apartment with all its period features and natural charm, just waiting for Vinnie to finish work so she could spend time with him. Sad. She had no life at all, not really.

A pursuit. She gave more details too, how he'd finally caught up with her. Scooped her up, threw her over his shoulder, made her laugh until she cried. How the double decker bus going past had tooted its horn and the passengers had grinned at them both. The image burned in my head. A handsome prince rescuing his damsel, a happy movie moment. Enough to make anyone vomit.

I'm so glad we're friends, Heidi. Her hand pressing mine, quickly, but lingering enough for me to feel the smoothness of her palm, and notice the porcelain perfection of the back of her hand too. *I did a drawing of you in my book. Do you want to see?*

The sketch was dark, the pencil lines pressed hard into the paper. I looked like I was underwater, hair around my face, eyes shining wetly. Teeth showing, bared in a smiling snarl. Something sexual about it, predatory too. There were words beside it, but she didn't give me time to read them.

That drawing made me ache with something. I didn't know what. It was too tangled to be jealousy. Too deep to be just anger. She was too beautiful, too sweet. He'd pursued her because she was perfect. Whereas I'd had to chase.

She was sketching when we were in the boat too, on the little mini-break in Kent. A merry little trio we made, bobbing in the waves, basking in the sun. Rucksack full of food, bottle of wine resting against her smooth, bare leg. Vinnie rowing, biceps bulging with exertion. I sat in the other end of the boat, studying the coastline for the perfect hidden cove, empty of other people. The ideal place to eat, drink and enjoy the water.

It's too risky, you being here, Vinnie told me the evening before. *You shouldn't have come.* That didn't stop him screwing me on Margate beach, after she'd gone back to the hotel. Nor from letting me come with them on the boat trip. What a stupid thing for me to do.

We need to get shot of her, I said.

And he nodded. *Yeah. It'll happen. Leave it with me.*

His words, not mine. Dispose of the treasure that had lost its shine. I never imagined it'd turn out the way it did.

I shiver, blink and come back to the present. Everything's darker, the window feels larger than it did before, as though the house itself is feeding off my memories. It's welcome to them, I don't want to think about it anymore. Not her, not Dad, not that damned sea. Nothing.

Something slaps at the window. I startle, nearly drop my wine glass.

Fingers.

I strain to see detail, before it fades back into the darkness. It looked like a hand. A wet hand, colliding with the glass. Not just wet but soaked through like a sponge. Peeling. Pallid. Something dead.

I stand slowly. The room swims. I move away from the window. Watchful, holding my breath, just as I was taught to. Let the heartbeat slow. Sink into it. Don't let panic take over, because panic undoes everything.

It can't have been a hand. It's the wine, I've drunk too much, too quickly. The wind's up outside, it could have been a wet leaf, a piece of rubbish blown across from the village.

It was a hand, a darker voice in my head insists. *Drowned, left underwater for far too long.*

I look around me. The living space extends too far in all directions, an empty expanse, which the light from the lamp barely touches. The corners are dark, the shadows impenetrable.

My hands are shaking. I stroke the nails on my index fingers with my thumbs, focus on the smooth feel of varnish. Breathe again, then walk to the kitchen area, place my wine glass down softly. In times of stress, it's important to regain control of the body. Another lesson Dad taught me.

It *was* just a leaf. The more I think of it, the more it becomes truth. The wetness of the slap against glass. The way it'd peeled away and faded, like something carried in the wind.

But it had fingertips. Bony knuckles. Lines on the palm.

No, it didn't.

I switch the main light on. Look up and at the window again. Nothing to see. Just the dark outside, the low shush-shush of the sea below.

But for a moment, I see it. A shape, narrow and twisted, blending with the night. It sits perfectly within my own reflection, its head slotting into the shape of my own. I strain to see more and see nothing at all.

'Stop doing this to yourself,' I whisper, and back away. A moment later, I step into the hallway and close the door behind me. It should feel safer. But nothing about this house feels safe at all.

CHAPTER EIGHT

I wake. It must be late morning because it's bright in here, light bouncing off the mirrors of the inbuilt wardrobe doors. The bed's empty beside me. Vinnie's up already, keen to get on with yet more tasks probably. Anything to give his new existence purpose.

I feel wrung out. Hungover too. I go downstairs, search for him, then look in the garden. There's no sign of him anywhere. Peering out the kitchen window, I notice the car's missing. He must have gone to the village to get something, or back to the DIY store. It wouldn't have hurt him to leave a note. But then, I'm getting used to expecting no better from him.

When I have a mug of coffee cupped between my hands, I feel better. I go outside, avoid concentrating too hard on the trapdoor in the ground, and the pile of wood that'll need getting rid of. Although the sun's out, it's colder than before. Hints of a frost sparkle at the tips of the grass, and they crunch gently underfoot.

Last night feels hazy already. I walk around to the back of the house, scan for signs of something from last night, though I don't know what I'm searching for. A smear on the window, maybe, or a wet outline. But there's nothing to see, only our sofa through the salt-streaked glass. A reminder of how small and vulnerable I must look in there when it's dark outside.

I look down. The grass is trampled by the edge of the window, I notice. Crushed down by something heavy.

Footprints. Someone stood there, looking in.

I used to fantasise about finding Dad outside my house, after he left. That I'd leave for school and find him by the rickety old gate waiting for me so I could explain. I'd only done it to keep him with us, to stop him leaving. Didn't do much good. He couldn't have gone much further away than Australia.

There are sharks in the water there, plenty of them. All sorts of things waiting to hold a person down, for way longer than even they could hold their breath for.

I shiver in the cold, just as the sound of tyre on gravel cuts across the quiet. Vinnie must be back. I pause, unsure whether to go inside to see him or stay out here, out of the way. So I linger, despite the goose pimples over my bare arms. A minute later, Vinnie appears in the doorway. He's frowning. I wonder what he's angry about now.

'Where have you been?' I ask, as he wades through the overgrown lawn.

'Buying a crowbar to get that trapdoor open, and a few other things. Why are you out here? I looked all over the house for you.'

'I was taking in the view. That's why we moved here, after all.'

He doesn't smile. 'It's freezing out here. You haven't got a coat on. You haven't even got out of your pyjamas yet.'

'Does it matter?'

'It's slovenly, isn't it? Not like you, you usually take more pride in yourself.'

Slovenly. I doubt he ever used that word to Noelle. It hurts.

He said he loved me whatever, thought I was perfect as I was. I know now that he only loves shiny, flawless things.

'I'll get dressed.' I start walking past him.

He nods. 'Have a shower too. You could do with a wash.'

There are things I want to say to him. Things I want to do, too; none of them nice. I feel his hand at my shoulder as I try to pass, sliding down to my arm, holding me tight.

'What's that look for?' he hisses.

My arm feels twig-like under his grasp, about to snap. 'There was no look.'

'There was. I only made a suggestion.'

'And that's what I'm going to do. Have a shower. Get dressed. Stop looking *slovenly*.'

His eyes narrow. 'You don't need to take it personally.'

'I haven't.'

'It's impossible to make you happy, isn't it? Nothing ever pleases you.'

'Are you trying to make me happy?'

'Everything you ever wanted, I've given you. All your over-the-top demands. Fancy meals in expensive restaurants, new clothes and the rest. I've done things for you that I'd never have done for anyone else.'

I flinch at every word. I didn't know he'd been keeping a tally of all the things he thinks I owe him for. I thought he just wanted to make me feel special.

'I've done plenty for you too.' I stand straighter, aware of how much he towers over me. 'I kept quiet when I could have spoken out. Remember that.'

He releases my arm, runs a hand through his hair. 'There you go again. Bringing up the past.'

'Stop making me, then. Stop pushing me in that direction.'

'Pushing you? Don't tempt me.'

'Is that what you said to her, in the sea that day?'

'Stop it.'

'Say her name, then.'

'I said stop it.'

'Why can't you say her name? I'll help you. Noelle. Noelle. Poor Noelle. What a mistake she made, getting mixed up with you.'

'Say one more word and you'll regret it. Go and have your shower.'

I open my mouth then close it. I've pushed too far already. But I can't deny it feels good. He needs to remember that day, and how much he has to lose.

'Go on.' He shoves my shoulder, not hard but enough to catch me off-balance. 'Get on with it.'

'Don't push me.'

'What, are you going to claim that's physical abuse, are you? You're good at spinning stories, playing the victim. But you're a lot tougher than you pretend to be.'

I look at him. *Really* look at him. His head, squarer than I'd realised before. The bullish line of his brow. A jaw concealed by beard but underneath, already going soft. This is the man I gave up so much to be with. Now I look at him and can't see anything I like at all.

'Just leave me alone,' I tell him. 'I've had enough. I'm exhausted with all of this.'

He sneers. 'This was meant to be a fresh start, but it doesn't feel fresh to me.'

'Yeah? What does it feel like?'

'It feels like hell, Heidi. Being with you. This is the pits.'

I stalk away. I need to get away from him, away from his expectations for this *new life,* the golden future his mother always told him he deserved. He's so far removed from the man I want him to be.

Upstairs, I grab my towel from the radiator. Lock myself in

the bathroom, rest my head for a second or two against the cool surface of the door, then start running a bath. I haven't relaxed in days, weeks, months perhaps. This won't miraculously remove the whirlpool of rage inside me, but it'll help me to ignore it for a while.

Outside the bathroom, I can hear him stamping around. Pacing from one room to another. Muttering occasionally, though I can't make out what he's saying. I wait until the tub is nearly full, then peel off my pyjamas and climb in. It's lukewarm, far from the soothing heat I was hoping for. But I don't want to get out again, not with Vinnie so close and so angry. He needs to cool off first.

I stare up at the ceiling, then the spartan white walls, the stainless-steel taps. It could be a bathroom in a sanatorium or prison. Some place where they lock people up, anyway. The tap drips a slow rhythm into the water. I move my toe across to break the impact, feel coldness trickle along its length to the water, still aware of Vinnie clattering around outside. He might knock in a moment, to find out what I'm doing in here. Or skulk back to the garden to prise up his precious trapdoor, then descend into the tunnel below.

He'd better remember what happened to the previous owner. *Ended up breaking her neck.* I can imagine it now. An elderly lady, decked out in corduroy skirt and woollen jumper, slipping on a steep step, pitching forwards into the dark. The sickening crack of bone snapping. Her husband's wail at her discovery.

Dark thoughts again. Even darker still; *it'd serve him right.* He said I was making this place a nightmare. He needs to take a long look in the mirror.

I hear the distinctive noise of a zip being fastened. Once, twice, then a third time. I can't match the sound to anything, I've no idea what he's up to out there. Next, his feet marching across the landing, descending the stairs. Silence, at last. Maybe he's making himself a drink. Or on the phone to his precious mother, giving her the sob-story. Poor little Vinnie. His pretty prize wasn't quite what he expected. Shame the old prize won't be returning to him anytime soon, and he's only got himself to blame for that.

His fault. All his fault. It was his idea to make Noelle go swimming. Without that, it never would have happened.

The front door slams. I lift my head upwards, hear nothing more. Then, tyres on gravel. One extended crunch, a pause, and another. A car reversing then driving out of the gate.

I sit up in a rush, water slopping over the side of the bath. He's stormed off again. Unsurprising. I climb out of the bath. The water's too cold anyway, I feel like a dead thing lying there, muscles slowly hardening to ice. The draining water sounds like a death-rattle, it sets me on edge. This feels significant, his sudden departure. A statement, rather than an impulse decision.

It feels like hell, Heidi. Being with you.

When I emerge from the bathroom, the house is too still; a held breath, waiting for something to happen. I steady myself against the wall and cringe at its dampness. Of course it's damp; everything in this place always is, when it's just me and there's no-one else to feel it or see it. This house rejects me, but it does it slyly when Vinnie's not around. It doesn't want me here. I'm never wanted, not really.

I want to shake myself. I left all that negative talk behind when I was younger. Swore to focus on the future and never look back. When he returns, we'll talk. Like adults. We'll work out how to sell this place as soon as possible, recoup our investments, then move to somewhere in London, or anywhere that's not this place. Then we'll probably go our separate ways and the world will start making sense again.

I go downstairs, wondering how long he'll be gone for. If he's driven to Tannistock, it'll be at least an hour and a half. I pour myself a glass of water and settle at the dining room table. There's not much else to do.

Lunchtime comes then goes. I try to eat but I've got no appetite, the bread's too hard, the cheese cheap and rubbery. The hours pass. Mid-afternoon, sky already darkening. I try calling his mobile, once, then again, then at ten-minute intervals until I run out of energy to do so. No answer, just the same infuriating answerphone message.

I'd love to talk to you, I really would, but I'm a busy kind of guy. So leave a message or give me a call later. Ciao.

I used to find it funny. Now, the faux drawl, the pretentious *ciao*, turns my stomach. I think about leaving a message, then change my mind and hang up. He can see I've called, that's enough. Maybe he's sitting in a café in Tannistock, spending money that was meant to be saved for the house. Or perhaps he's driven further away, is still driving now, jaw set, righteous rage keeping his foot on the accelerator.

He'll be back later. He's just punishing me. It's pathetic.

The gloomy clouds over the sea are making it much darker. I go upstairs, marvelling at the strangeness of being here for so long all alone, then pull out a thick jumper from the wardrobe. Something's wrong with the scene in front of me. It takes a moment to realise what. Then another moment or two to let the truth sink in. Most of his clothes are gone.

My mind races while I make sense of it. All that pacing to and fro along the landing, from bedroom to bedroom. He was gathering things to pack, to take with him. Those three separate zipping sounds were a suitcase being closed. The car leaving at speed, all sounds of a man who wanted to get away as fast as possible. To stay away for a while. Without telling me.

I reach for my phone and try calling him again. The answerphone message kicks in again. Words fight to fly out of my mouth; *pathetic, cruel, coward,* but I hold them in. It'll only make him less likely to call back.

Get your thoughts straight, I tell myself. Anger mustn't take over. So, he's gone for a while. To cool off, maybe away for just a night or two to calm down. *I can survive this. I've got through worse.*

He took so many of his clothes from the wardrobe, though. He must be planning to be away for more than a night. A week, perhaps. He has to call me soon to let me know. He can't just leave me here, stranded without a car. He wouldn't be so callous.

A hand, pulling me underwater. Revenge, for not being the perfect woman he thought he'd invested in. No. Think clearly. He wouldn't. He didn't. Those are my own dark memories bubbling to the surface. He'll call me back eventually.

I reach for my phone again and dial Miranda's number. She answers after a few rings. It catches me by surprise. She nearly always lets it ring out the first time, then calls back.

'Heidi?' It's a question more than a greeting. She sounds breathless.

'Everything all right?' I'm caught off guard, this isn't usually how our conversations start.

She pauses. 'Yeah, everything's fine. What about you?'

'Not good. I'm sat here alone. I don't know what to do.'

'That's rough,' she says.

'Rough?'

'Sorry. Yeah, you know. That sounds lonely. Go on, I'm listening.'

'Really? You sound distracted.'

'You caught me at a bad moment, that's all. What's up?'

'Seriously, Miranda, it doesn't matter if you haven't got the time.'

'Ha, I never have time. Too much to do, right?' She sounds odd, like she's been drinking, though it's not even four in the afternoon yet. Rushed, almost. Not her usual self.

'I've got a problem,' I say slowly. 'Vinnie's gone. As in he packed his bag and left earlier today. Took the car, didn't tell me where he was going. I don't know what to do.'

A pause. Her attention's not with me, I can tell. I wish I hadn't called.

'That's bad,' she says finally. 'Why?'

'We had a fight.'

'That sucks.' She doesn't care. The truth hits hard, not that I'm surprised. Miranda doesn't do *negative vibes*.

'I can tell you're busy,' I say. 'I'll let you get back to whatever it is you've got going on.'

'You sure? I've got a few minutes?'

'Don't worry about it. I should go. Call me back when you're free, okay?'

'Yeah. That's easier. I'll give you a call later. Don't worry, you'll be all right. You're a tough chick.'

I don't feel tough at the moment, but force a laugh anyway. 'I'll speak to you soon,' I tell her.

She grunts then says goodbye. I keep my ear to the phone after she's hung up, aware again of the quiet that surrounds me. So much stillness and silence. I haven't felt this alone since I was a teenager.

My gaze shifts to the windows, to the sky that's already dimmed to a bruised purple-grey. Give it another hour or so and it'll be completely black. No stars. No moonlight. Just me and all those leaves, slapping at the window.

And Vinnie, it's anyone's guess where he'll be. In a hotel

somewhere or at his mother's house, or with a friend. Down the pub, laughing with a pint, clearing me from his thoughts with ease. He likes new places, new things. I've become old. A has-been thing. I hate him for making me feel this way.

He's so joyous, Noelle said once. *I love how excited he gets, how he sees things he wants and goes for it.* She forgot to mention how easily he gets bored afterwards. And how easy he finds it to get rid of things he no longer wants.

If he's in a bar now, I hate him even more. If he's laughing with old work colleagues, mutual friends of ours, and not giving me a second thought, I hate him twice as much. I need wine, something to make me care less. I don't let people put me aside, not anymore. I'm the one who chooses when to move on. Not him.

I think of wine. Bars. Pubs.

I pause, hand hovering over the fridge door. Rick invited me to a live music evening in the pub in the village, The Fisherman's Rest or whatever it was called. He invited Vinnie along too, but that's beside the point. Live music night every Thursday, he said. That's today.

A cosy little country pub, the laughter and chatter of others, just like the pubs back in London. Noise and bustle. The chance to get to know Rick better too. It's a nice idea. Better than sitting around here filled with fury, anyway.

I glance again at the window, still curtainless, and at the thrashing sea beyond. It's just about light enough for me to slip across the fields safely and make my way into Nairbourne. As for getting back; I'll figure that out later. I'm not staying here though. Not a chance. When I have to return, I plan on being drunk enough to not worry about any of this anymore.

CHAPTER NINE

The path to the village is as muddy as before and the darkening sky doesn't help. Every step I take sinks into the giving muck, every time I lift a foot, the mud releases it with a greedy slurp. My winter coat's keeping me warm at least, and the dry, crisp air feels like a blessing after the damp inside my house. This was a good idea. I already feel more like myself. Vinnie can do what he likes. I don't care right now, and I'm not sure if I'll care ever again.

After a time, houses come into view, then the high street itself. It's even quainter in the twilight, with rows of strung-up lights dangling from lamppost to lamppost, and several of the windows lit by the cosy glow of candles or table lamps. It's sheltered here too. The wind has lost its bite and the stinging scent of the sea is less noticeable. It's not London but it has its own charm, which is more charm than I've experienced in a while.

I make my way to the pub; its wooden painted sign swaying to and fro in the breeze. The picture's of a man with a fishing pole standing in a river, a pile of silver fish at his feet. Already, I can hear the thrum of noise from within, and see people at their tables through the window. It looks busy.

Only a few short months ago, I would have marched into a crowded pub on my own without a second thought. I hate that I've become this nervy and this uncertain. I should have done my hair, applied more lipstick. At least my fake nails are still gleaming. A hint of my trademark look; stylish, sharp. *Appealing*, as Mum might say.

I set my shoulders then push the door, which swings open. The volume of the chatter hits me like a slap in the face.

Rick is by the bar, elbow propped on the edge, pint glass in hand. It's the first time I've seen him without his coat on. His hair looks darker in this light, slightly curly too. Roll-neck jumper hitched up to the elbows, dark jeans and black boots. Handsome without trying. He'd do well in any one of the bars in Clapham. The girls would eat him alive with pleasure.

He spies me, wrinkles his eyes, then grins and waves me over. 'You decided to join us!' he says as I reach him.

'You sold it to me the other day.' I unzip my coat. 'How could I resist?'

'You made the right choice. Where's your boyfriend?'

I pull a face. 'Don't ask.'

'Fair enough, I won't. Would you like a drink?'

'Now you're talking. A white wine would be good.'

The man he'd been talking to, older, balder, decked in checked shirt and slacks, nods a greeting to me then turns to chat to someone else. Good. I'd rather not face too many questions from the locals.

Rick passes me a glass of wine, which I sip straight away.

'Are you playing tonight?' I ask, shrugging out of my coat and looping it over my arm.

'Nah, I'll give others the chance to show off their talents. What about you?'

I shake my head. 'I'm not musical, I wouldn't want to torture anyone.'

'Anything goes, you know. Sometimes bands come along to perform, at other times it's just us lot entertaining each other. It's not just music, some people read poetry or tell stories.'

'Sounds fun.'

'You city slickers probably think this all looks very rustic.'

'No, I like it. Besides, I'm not really a city slicker. I grew up in a place a bit like this.' I meet his gaze, notice how green his eyes are again, almost feline in the intensity of the colour. *He's attractive*, I think, with a thrill of excitement. Easy-going and fun to be around. Not surly and aggressive. Not the sort of man who'd walk out without giving any clue where they'd gone to.

'You're a country girl at heart?' he says. 'You could have fooled me. You've got the polished look of someone who has a high-profile job in media or something like that.'

I laugh. 'I used to work in marketing, so you're not far off.'

'Me too. Well, a side-line in website design. There's not enough money in farming these days. I only keep it going because Dad always wanted me to.'

We clink glasses. I smile, surprised at how genuine it feels. Rick's easy to talk to, open, friendly, interested without asking too many uncomfortable questions. An older woman steps onto the little stage area in the corner. She is greeted by a roar of applause from the people crammed into the space, then starts to strum her guitar.

Rick gestures to the other side of the pub, near the stone fireplace. 'Let's go and sit over there,' he shouts over the noise. 'We can talk, then.'

We settle into a pair of small armchairs, the only free table in the pub. The fire's warm, too warm almost. I can feel my cheeks turning pink.

'You sure I'm not keeping you from the music?' I ask. 'I don't want to put a dampener on your night.'

'It's only Nigella from up the road, I've heard her play a million times. Whereas you're new and interesting, Heidi.'

I can't help but smile. It's flattering, this undivided attention. 'Why don't you tell me about yourself?' I say, relaxing back into the chair. 'I've never met a farmer-cum-website designer before.'

He laughs. 'We farmers have got a reputation. People imagine we're all ruddy-faced whiskery yokels.'

'Do you keep livestock?'

'Not much these days. It's mainly the website design that pays the bills.'

Now it's my turn to laugh. 'That's a classic city slicker job.'

'I'm a traitor to my people. To be fair, my cousin got me into it. He's one of the top website designers in Malaga, or so he likes to tell me.'

'Malaga? As in Spain?'

He grins. 'My mother was Spanish. My full name's Ricardo.'

Ricardo. *Hot*. I quickly drain the rest of my glass. 'What about your dad?' I ask.

'British. Both of them are no longer with me, though, sadly. Mum died when I was young.'

'My mum's dead too. Dad too. He left for Australia when I was a teenager; died out there. Wanted a life doing what he loved best.'

'What was that?'

'Free-diving. He was a UK champion in his prime, could hold his breath for almost ten minutes.'

'That's insane. Can you do the same?'

I shake my head. 'I reached about eight minutes when I was

thirteen or so. These days I could probably get to five or six, if I prepared myself carefully beforehand.'

'Wow. You really are interesting. There's far more to you than meets the eye.'

He's flirting, I'm sure of it. A fast mover, not that I'm complaining. I feel young again, wanted; opening up under the warmth of his attention. It's harmless, nothing to be ashamed of. Besides, this is all Vinnie's fault. He's the one who left.

Suddenly, I'm aware of someone standing over us. The abundance of hair is the first thing I notice, a mass of unruly curls, a suspicious face in the midst of it all. Navy pinafore dress, loose fitting. Multicoloured knitted top underneath. Arms folded.

'I didn't know you were here, Rick,' she says, through tight lips. 'Why didn't you come over and say hello?'

I make the connection. It's Bea, the woman who runs the general store. Who told me my house had a *nasty atmosphere*. She looks different with her hair down. Wilder, sexier too though it pains me to admit it. Above all else, more unpredictable.

Rick raises his glass. 'Evening, Bea. I've found a newcomer to Nairbourne. Meet Heidi.'

'We already met,' she says without smiling. 'She bought the *death house*.'

Rick groans, gives me an apologetic look. 'I'm sure once you've done the place up nicely, people will stop calling it that.'

Bea sniffs. 'Rick, are you coming to the meeting on Saturday?'

'Don't know, why?'

'It's about the community library. Agnes is hoping for a good turnout.'

'Don't know. I've got a lot to do this weekend.'

She shifts from foot to foot. 'We're planning on going to

Marciano's for dinner afterwards. You're coming to that, aren't you?'

He groans. 'Damn it, I'd forgotten. I'll see how it goes.'

She shouldn't pull that expression, I think, watching her. She's pretty, but when she scowls she looks hard and old. Actually, maybe she should. Maybe I should keep giving her reason to pull it. Maybe she should just take the hint and leave.

'Did you want to join us?' I offer with false eagerness. It's a gamble, but one that'll pay off. She's too nettled by my presence to want to make small talk. Plus, there are no free chairs; she'll have to stand.

She shakes her head. 'I'm not planning on sticking around for long. Do you want a drink later, Rick? I could do with us having a talk.'

Rick attempts a grin. 'Not sure I'll be here too late. Another time perhaps?'

Triumph flares in my chest as her face falls. Asserting her ownership of him hasn't worked too well; it serves her right. She mutters something, then slopes off to the other side of the pub to join the crowd. Rick shifts in his seat, flashes me a rueful smile.

'Bea can be intense,' he explains. 'She's good-hearted though, she's done a lot for the community. She's one of our local storytellers too, she loves a good folkloric yarn.'

I try to look interested, then gesture to the bar. 'Shall I get the next ones in?'

'I never say no to a drink.'

I think of Vinnie. He used to insist on paying for every drink, meal, ticket to the theatre, every taxi fare. I thought he liked all of that, being the gallant hero. But instead, he spent the whole time holding it against me. Totting up the totals, working out how much I was in his debt. The gallant hero, what a joke. A coward instead, hiding behind secrets, running away from difficult questions. I could ruin everything for him, if I chose to.

As I move to the bar, I feel stronger than I have in a while. More like myself, more in control.

Without Vinnie here, I can do whatever I want again. There's a power in knowing that.

The live music dwindles towards the end of the evening as an old bearded man takes to the stage, singing sea shanties with a battered old ukelele in hand. About half the people have left, which makes the place feel comfier, more like home. I've had too many wines but I'm past caring; I feel flushed, slightly feverish even. The heat of the fire makes this all feel unreal. A dream. Something without consequences, with no fear of what comes after.

Bea must have left earlier because she's not here now. I spotted her glaring at me earlier. It can't be comfortable, knowing that you're beaten. I suppose I should feel sorry for her. Maybe I would if she hadn't been such a bitch to me first.

The bar-man rings a brass bell at the back of the bar. Its clanging pulls me to the moment. The lights suddenly brighten, all the illusion of cosiness stripped away in an instant. He calls, 'Closing time, folks,' with genuine remorse. I glance at my watch and realise it's gone midnight.

'Is there a taxi service around here?' I ask Rick, noting in a disconnected way how hard it is to get the words out properly, in the right order. My thoughts are scattered and mulchy.

'There is. Shall we share, as we live close to each other?'

I agree and he pulls out his phone and dials for a cab. His fingers are long. Elegant, more a piano-player's digits than a farmer's. I can imagine what other things those fingers are good at, though I probably shouldn't.

'Ten minutes,' he says, hanging up. 'We'll have to wait outside. Don't forget your coat.'

The ice-chill of the night air sobers me up. I remember countless other nights similar to this one. Staggering from seedy bars with Miranda, tugging down our mini-skirts, giggling about some bloke or other. I feel light, in spite of the cold. Free.

'Bit brisk, isn't it?' Rick says, leaning against the wall.

'It's not so bad.'

'Did you enjoy the evening?'

I lean next to him, tug my zip up to my chin. 'I did. Thanks for inviting me.'

'So, you want to tell me why your boyfriend isn't here? You've been alluding to it all night.'

Here it is, the moment. His interest extends beyond just friendly, I can see it, barely hidden beneath a casual expression. I feel bold. The alcohol has loosened me, made Vinnie seem like a bad actor in a soap opera. Something to be laughed away then dismissed.

The man you love, a voice corrects. *Or were in love with, anyway.*

'We had a fight,' I tell him flatly. 'He pushed me over, hard. I had a bath and by the time I got out, he'd packed a suitcase and left.'

Rick's eyes widen. 'I had no idea. If he's that sort of man, you should call the police.'

That sort of man. Using the word *hard* to describe the shove was unfair, but it doesn't matter. Vinnie shouldn't have laid a hand on me and that's the truth of it.

'There's no point calling the police,' I say. 'He's gone now, anyway. It's probably for the best.'

'But you've only just moved in and the house is a state. How are you going to manage?'

'I'll find a way. It'll be tricky without a car, though. And we share a bank account too; he insisted. I worry he might do something to prevent me accessing the money.'

As the words slip from my lips I realise I am worried about that. I don't know how easy it'd be for him to limit access to the account, but it might be something he can do. Then I'd be really screwed.

'Do you know when he's coming back?'

'I've no idea. He won't be back tonight, anyway.'

There's meaning in those words. I hadn't meant for them to sound so suggestive. Rick meets my gaze evenly and the silence stretches, though without any discomfort. He wants to say more, but doesn't know what words to say. I'm not sure I do either. My head's tangled, my vision soft and fuzzy at the edges.

A car pulls up beside us. It takes me a while to realise it's our taxi, that the driver is leaning across, looking at us both with a mixture of irritation and resignation. Rick opens the door and I do my best to clamber in without falling off the seat. The blast of the car's heating is enough to make nausea rise in my stomach.

'I'm tired,' I murmur. 'I need to get some sleep.'

Rick shuts the car door then pats my arm. 'I think we both do. But it's been fun, Heidi. It really has.'

It really has, I think, wrapping my arms around my belly. In spite of the dizziness, the sickness, the confusion of it all, it has been. Tomorrow, I'll try to make sense of it all. For now, I just need to get to bed and pass out with no disturbance from anyone. Or anything, for that matter.

CHAPTER TEN

I wake, still half-tangled in a dream. It was a mess of being restrained, someone screaming, my own hands working against me, dragging my own body somewhere dark and unforgiving. Claws at my skin, digging deep, refusing to let go.

It takes me a while to ground myself. Drizzle distorts the view outside my window, twisting the clouds into wrung-out dirty rags. I need curtains and quickly. I can't keep sleeping with a potential audience, even if it's only the owls in the surrounding trees.

I remember all the details of my evening at the pub, which means I wasn't embarrassingly drunk. Nothing happened, not even a goodnight kiss. I've got nothing to feel bad about. I'm not sure whether to feel proud of myself or a little regretful. Rick's a good antidote for ridding my mind of Vinnie.

Idly, I reach across and grab my phone. Rick gave me his number in the taxi last night. As a friend, a neighbour, nothing more. There's a text message waiting for me from him. A short, chatty message to see how I'm feeling, to say he had good fun. Light-hearted, non-committal, but I grin nonetheless. He's testing the waters. I should know. I've danced this dance several times before.

I text back quickly. *I've only just woken up. I had fun too, thanks for inviting me along.* I put the phone down; there's no need to wait for a reply. I know he'll get back to me.

I tug on pyjama bottoms and a sweater and make my way downstairs. The house feels better, despite the gloomy weather outside. No water streaks on the wall. Dry, almost a bit homely. More importantly, I don't feel an urge to run away from it all anymore.

Maybe Vinnie got it right, and wrong at the same time. It was the place for a new start, but for me, not him. Regret and sadness are what I should be feeling, but I don't. I don't feel much of anything other than relief. God, what a pair we made. Four months into our official relationship, as a legitimate couple rather than secret lovers, and we're already at breaking point.

The rumours and whispers didn't help. At first, it wasn't much. Sniffy, judging comments. *They broke her heart. Destroyed her. Poor Noelle.* Then later, a more worrying tone. *Where is she? Why has no-one heard from her? What do they know?*

The police are looking into it, I overheard in a bar one night. Three men staring at us, one an ex-colleague, someone I used to get along with. None of them looked away when I met their eyes. One muttered loudly enough for me to hear, *She's got a nerve. After what she did.*

The police. Nothing to worry about; they would have got in touch with us before then if there was. There's no proof those men were even telling the truth. They were just spouting hearsay like everyone else. But still. That level of pressure's a death-blow for any blossoming relationship.

I notice the plastic bag on the side, still full of Vinnie's DIY tools. There's nothing very interesting inside. A pack of sandpaper, a tube of grout, and the crowbar for prising the trapdoor open. The marks of his precious project, gaining access to his own private smuggler's tunnel. I pull the crowbar out and cradle it in both hands. It's slim, with a satisfying weight.

If I wanted to go to the DIY store, even to the nearest supermarket or train station, I'd need a taxi, or resign myself to a walk that'd take hours each way. He's hobbled me, left me helpless; an act of deliberate sabotage. But it hasn't worked. I feel better than I have done in ages. I even feel I could do something with this place. Some paint, some smoothing out of rough edges, a bit of colour, and it could start to feel like home.

Somewhere I could invite Rick over for dinner, I add silently. Or anyone else I choose to.

My phone vibrates in my pyjama pocket, over and over. I pull it out and study the screen. Unknown number. It could be Vinnie. Or a sales call, or someone misdialling. My thumb hovers over the answer button, then presses down.

'Hello?'

I wait, anticipating Vinnie's gruff tones, or perhaps a disinterested person from a call centre far away. Nothing. I listen harder. There's vague breathing at the other end. An echo of a mutter too, like someone speaking from inside a distant cave.

'Hello?' I repeat.

The same silence in response, another muffled mumble, then the dead tone. They've hung up, whoever it is. My arms break out in goose pimples and I shiver. It feels cold again.

Noelle, I think. The idea lingers and won't go away. She's found me. In a moment, I'll see her hand at the window, pressing against the glass, looking for a way to get in.

She won't haunt me today. Not after such a good night out, not after I feel like I've found myself again. She's stolen too much from me already, both her and Vinnie. But I can't block the images that race through my head. Her in that boat, one leg crossed over the other, hair pulled back in an effortless ponytail. Running her hand through the water while Vinnie rowed. A creature of beauty, drawing and writing beautiful things in that damned book of hers. So talented, so much potential to do amazing things with her life.

I thought after what happened, she'd stay hidden forever. So why is she still *here* all the time, in my thoughts? I don't understand why I can't get rid of her. Vinnie should be carrying this burden, not me. It's all on him.

I woke up feeling positive. I need to regain that and not let any of this drag me down. The phone rings again. It's the same unknown number. I let it ring out, wait to see if someone leaves a message, which they don't.

Someone might be watching the house. Watching me through one of our curtainless windows. I turn towards the view of the sea, and for a second, see something out there in the distance. A shadow of something flitting past. A shark, gliding through water. A swimmer, doomed to go under a few seconds later.

There are no sharks, no shadows. No nothing. I need to grow up and take back control. I turn away from the window, then eye the crowbar sitting on the countertop.

Vinnie's little project. The thing that brought him excitement, the idea of uncovering a precious new toy to play with. Hidden treasure. If I opened it up instead, that'd make it my discovery not his. He'd hate that.

Childish, I know. But I pick up the crowbar anyway, make my way to the back door. There's no time like the present.

It's hard work, far harder than I thought it'd be. The wood of the trapdoor is so swollen with moisture, it feels glued in place. Every time it lifts under the pressure, it subsides back into the frame a moment later. I try different angles, first one side then the other. Break a nail, swear loudly. Throw the crowbar into the grass and curse Vinnie to hell, even though I know it was my choice to start this in the first place. It needs brute strength. Or else a bit of cunning.

The stone slab that covered it previously is lying nearby. I pause a while, calculate, then push my fingers under each side and test its weight. It's heavy, too heavy for me to carry far, but I should be able to move it just enough to work.

I pick up the crowbar again and wedge it between the trapdoor and the frame, as far as it'll go. Its handle sticks upwards, erect, proud. Then I lift the stone slab again.

This'll be an open hole in the garden. Something anyone could fall down. The thought of a network of pitch-black tunnels underfoot isn't a comfortable one either. I think of Mrs Trewain and her tumble to the bottom. A sickening crack of neckbone snapping. A final sigh as her vision faded to nothing.

I hope they brought her body back up. Someone must have done, I'm not going to find a mouldering old skeleton down there. Nor a ghost lurking about in the shadows, keen to return to the house she once lived in.

'The nixie of Nairbourne perhaps,' I mutter, forcing a laugh. 'Maybe this is where she likes to hide.'

I lift the stone higher, then thrust it down hard against the side of the crowbar. The trapdoor lifts with a groan, rises further than it has done before, but slams back down before I can wedge my foot into the gap. I curse, drop the stone with a dull thud and brace myself for a second attempt. Lift, calculate the trajectory, then throw it downwards. Perseverance is the key. Never give up when you want something badly enough.

This time, the trapdoor flies upwards, creating a big enough gap for me to thrust my foot underneath and kick hard, flinging it completely open.

I whoop, startling a crow resting on the stone wall. The bird soars off in a clatter of wings. Victory. I'll take any small wins I can at the moment.

Then I peer down the tunnel. It goes down a long way and it's darker, more suffocating than expected. There's a smell rising out of the hole too. Rotting seaweed and other decaying matter. The stink of a place that's been shut away for far too long.

The top few steps are roughly carved from stone, their surfaces smooth with decades of use. No wonder the old woman fell. I tentatively place a foot on the first one, then retreat. It doesn't feel safe.

Down we go, Dad used to say. *Let's see how long today.*

'Too long, you moron,' I mumble. 'Everyone has their limits.'

I don't want to go down there. Suddenly, this doesn't feel like a good idea. It's a petty act that'll start a chain of events, starting with making Vinnie very angry. Grabbing one of the broken planks from the pile nearby, I place it across the entrance, then lower the trapdoor so it can't close itself fully. Exploration will have to wait for another time.

I go back inside and lock the door carefully behind me. Take a moment to breathe. Then focus on putting it out of my mind. It's done. No regrets, there's no point.

My broken nail looks a state. I do a rushed job of removing it, then smoothing down the nail underneath. It happens, I'm always breaking them. But I'd hoped this set would last a little longer. It's not as though I can get them replaced anytime soon, not without a beauty salon within walking distance. I catch sight of myself in the mirror in the bedroom. Messy hair, hollow eyes.

Pale. I need to sort myself out. I don't want to let my standards slip.

There are another couple of missed call notifications on my phone. Miranda this time, not the unknown number. I weigh up not returning her call. See how she likes it, feeling that I haven't got time for her. But in the end, curiosity gets the better of me. I want to see what she has to say this time.

She answers on the third ring. Unlike her, again. Something's going on.

'Hello there, stranger,' I say, before she can speak.

'Hey. Hang on, just a minute.'

I hear a door being closed, then a rustling sound, perhaps her sitting down.

'Did you have a nice time last night?' I ask.

'What?'

'You sounded rushed, like you were going out somewhere.'

There's a pause, an uncomfortable one.

'Did I touch a nerve?' I say, after a time.

'No. Nothing like that. I just heard something awful. That's why I called. Are you sitting down?'

'What? No. What did you hear?'

'It's really *holy shit* stuff, Heidi. Like seriously, you need to brace yourself. Josh called me this morning. You remember Josh? From the design department?'

'With the Clark Kent specs? And the tight shirts?'

She tuts. 'Does it matter? Anyway, he phoned, and–'

'Why are you still in touch with him?'

'Jesus, stop interrupting, would you? We dated for a while, that's all.'

'You never told me.'

'It wasn't a big deal. We don't tell each other everything, do we? In fact, you're very good at keeping secrets.'

She's referring to Vinnie, to our affair. Always a prickly subject. Jealousy's a bitch, and she can be too, sometimes.

'What did Josh tell you?' I ask.

She pauses. 'I don't know how to say this. It's horrible, a real nightmare story. They found Noelle, Heidi. The police, I mean. As in, *they found her body.*'

The world freezes at the sound of her name. My chest tightens. It's hard to inhale.

'Heidi? You still there?'

I grunt. Can't do anything else, not right now.

'Noelle's dead,' Miranda continues. 'Can you believe it? We all wondered where she'd gone, but nobody ever imagined this.'

My knees give. I move towards the dining table and quickly sit down. My ears are ringing, though with words, not sound. *They found her. They found her. Nightmare.* Then the memory of Vinnie's voice. *You're making this place a nightmare.* So many nightmares. Too many to process.

'Where?' I say, eventually.

'That's where the story gets weird. Her body was in the water, somewhere off the coast of Kent. Why the hell she was there is anyone's guess.'

No-one knows I was there too. Not even Miranda. I kept that story to myself. I don't need to panic. But this is bad, really bad. How like Noelle this is. Always showing up and making waves. Even after death.

'Heidi?'

'I'm still here.'

'Do you think she killed herself? She was pretty smitten with Vinnie. You getting together with him could have finished her off.'

Savage. But typical Miranda, speaking without thinking.

'How the hell should I know?' I rub my face, try to stop my mind from racing. I don't know how to react. Because all I can think of is that day at the beach, Noelle saying *I can't swim very well.* Asking about the sharks. Vinnie insisted she swam. Vinnie, not me.

'Her body was tangled up in some weeds,' Miranda goes on. 'So messed up. She was such a babe. What a waste of a beautiful face.'

What a waste. She's right, it's all been a waste, everything that's happened since then. I wonder how many people Vinnie told about their little *mini-break in Kent.* How soon it'll be before people start asking him dangerous questions. And how soon before he drags me down with him.

Miranda coughs. 'Josh said the office was buzzing with it. I feel for Vinnie, it's awful for him.'

'What, Vinnie knows about this already? He only left here yesterday.'

Again, a pause. A calculating one this time. 'Josh said he'd told Vinnie too,' she says finally.

'Vinnie didn't ever talk to Josh when he worked there, did he? They weren't friends.'

'Josh told everyone.'

'So Josh knows where Vinnie is right now? Even though I don't?'

'Oh, Heidi, I don't know. I didn't question it.'

'You should. He walked out on me. After physically assaulting me.'

'Really?'

'Yes, really. I wouldn't say it otherwise.'

'Hey, chick, don't get cross. It's just that... I don't know, it doesn't matter.'

'What?' I'm losing my temper, despite my best efforts not to. Miranda's meant to be on my side. Not implying that I'm lying about things.

'It's tragic, isn't it?' she continues.

'What? Noelle? Yes, of course it's sad.'

'Someone our age. With so much potential.'

'Yeah.' I rest my head in my hands, feeling the start of a headache coming on. 'Can you ask Josh how he got hold of Vinnie? I need to find out what's going on.'

'I don't think that's a good idea.'

'He's been an absolute shit and just abandoned me. You're meant to be my friend, do it for me.'

'It's between you two. I guess he'll call you when he's ready.'

I take a deep breath. It feels like a betrayal. It *is* a betrayal. As far as I was aware, she doesn't even like Vinnie. Why would she put his feelings above mine?

'I've got to go,' I tell her. 'I need some time to think.'

'Yeah, you sound upset.'

Of course I'm upset. Biting back a sarcastic comeback is a challenge, but I manage.

'I'll be fine,' I tell her. 'I'm processing the information, that's all.'

'I get it. It's horrible. Puts your troubles with Vinnie into perspective, doesn't it? I mean, what's the end of a relationship compared to that?'

'Thanks for that.'

'I didn't mean it nastily. I guess you won't go to the funeral, though. Probably wouldn't be appropriate.'

'I'm going now.'

'Heidi, come on. Don't be like that. I'm just being honest with you.'

'Are you? Because it feels like you're trying to make me feel worse.'

I hear a voice in the background. Muffled. Masculine. It takes me by surprise. She didn't let on there was anyone else there with her.

'I've got to dash,' she says quickly. 'Take care of yourself.'

I end the call without replying. My temples are throbbing now. The silence is all encompassing, suffocating. *Like I'm underwater*, I think, as my vision starts to swim.

My fingers fumble for the edge of the table to steady myself. I can't let myself pass out, I'll be okay in a moment or two. It's the shock, that's all. I knew Noelle wouldn't let us be. Wouldn't let *me* be.

Pretty Noelle, down there among the weeds. Hair curling upwards, skin white-blue and bloated. Lips pulled back in a post-death snarl. *A nixie*, I think, swallowing something in my throat. Hysterical laughter or a sob, it could be either.

Vinnie won't know what to do. He'll flounder this way and that, desperately searching for someone to make it better for him. It's all his fault, everything. I wish I'd never got tangled up with him.

My phone rings again. If this is Miranda, trying to undo what she said, she's wasting her time. But the screen says *unknown number*. I hit the button to cancel the call. A moment later, it starts again.

I can't deal with a crank caller, not on top of everything else. Before I can get up out of the seat, the phone vibrates again, a text message this time. Clearly whoever it is just won't take no for an answer. I glance at the screen. It's Rick, not an ominous stranger. I mutter a silent thanks.

It was a pleasure chatting to you. How are you feeling today? I won't lie, my head hurt this morning.

I read then reread the message again. So casual, so keen. But this is messy. Things are bad, far worse now than they were a few minutes ago. Her name rises and falls, slowly, a dying breath. Noelle. No. Elle. No. Hell. Hell. Hell.

This isn't hell. I can't let this beat me. As long as Vinnie remembers the facts. He made her go swimming. He was more than happy not to go to the police. He left her there.

Saying it that way, like a mantra, helps. I start texting back.

> My head hurts too. I spent the morning crowbarring a trapdoor to a smuggler's tunnel. What have you been doing?

I put the phone down and wait, though not for long. Rick's response comes through a minute later.

> You opened it up? What was it like down there?

> I didn't go down. Too dark. Probably not safe to go alone.

He replies a few moments later:

> Do you want help? I've got an industrial torch, it's ideal for spaces like that.

He's offering to come over. That might be good. Or not, I'm not sure, my head isn't anywhere near settled yet. There's a tsunami of panic wavering just below my surface. *They found her body. Noelle is back.*

'Stop it,' I mutter. No-one knew I was there. I wasn't staying at the same hotel as them. No-one paid attention when I *bumped into them* in their hotel reception. Vinnie's confusion, Noelle's shock, that was our private drama, ours alone. No-one noticed when we got drunk together that evening. It was busy, we blended with the crowd. No-one would remember us being on the boat the next day. We cruised along the coast with several other vessels; speedboats, water-skis, sailing boats, a few kayaks. No-one would have given us a passing glance. And then we were out of sight. Completely on our own.

It's okay. I'm going to be okay.

Inviting Rick over is no big deal. He's coming over to help me, and we'll focus on something that's in the here and now, rather than the past. If I sit here alone and dwell on Noelle, it'll grow and grow in my mind until I can't think of anything else.

I type quickly, before I can change my mind:

> If you're in the mood to be a smuggler-hunter, come along, I was planning on heading down there this afternoon.

I wait a few minutes.

> That's an offer I can't refuse. I need to feed the pigs first, then I'll be over.

I sit still, chew my lip. It's an impulsive thing to do, when I should be thinking ahead. Mum used to accuse me of not thinking things through. Screamed it in my face the evening Dad packed his bags and left. *Why did you do it, Heidi? You're impulsive, destructive. It was the final straw.*

I did it to keep him close. It was a weird way to go about it. But I was young, I didn't stop to weigh up my actions. She should have understood and recognised her part in it all too. It was Mum he was trying to get away from, not me. Well, at first, anyway.

I just made things worse when I tried to hang on to him for longer.

CHAPTER ELEVEN

An hour later, the doorbell rings. I'm better equipped now; I've had a shower, put some make-up on, tied my hair up in a bun. I look more presentable than I have done in a while. Sexy again, confident. A force to be reckoned with, not a nervy little girl afraid of her own shadow. I scurry down the hallway and unlock the door.

Rick is flushed with cold, torch in hand, with a bulb that looks big enough to light up a football field. He wasn't joking when he said it was for industrial use.

'Are the pigs fed?' I ask, standing aside to let him come in.

'They are. I'm happy you gave me something to distract myself with. I had an email from one of my buyers in Tannistock that I'd rather not think about right now.'

I lead him through to the living area. His gaze roams freely over every corner of the space, taking it all in.

'Sounds ominous,' I say.

'They want my produce for next to nothing. They don't understand I've got to earn a living, none of them do. It's always squeeze, squeeze, squeeze.'

'Do you want a cuppa?'

'How about after?' He pauses, shifting from one foot to the other. 'After we explore the tunnel, I mean. I bet it's freezing down there. We'll enjoy a hot drink afterwards to warm us up.'

'You don't waste time, do you?'

'Not with something as exciting as this. Is your boyfriend back yet?'

The question's too casual, which reveals a lot. I pat my hair and give him a wide smile. 'I haven't heard from him.' I lower my eyes to the floor. 'It's probably best not to talk about it.'

'I'm sorry. I feel for you, sounds like you're in a tough position.'

'I'm okay right now. We're going to explore a smuggler's tunnel and it's going to be fun. Live for the moment, right?'

He raises his fist in a mock salute. 'Very true. I've got my torch, so I'm ready when you are.'

I lead him to the back door then out into the garden. It looks more of a state than before, the grass gleaming with wetness, the woodpile dark and sodden.

He spies the trapdoor straight away and lets out a low whistle. 'Wow, you guys really haven't wasted time, have you? You only moved in a week ago and you're already uncovering all the house's secrets.'

'This one was down to me,' I say, pointing to the crowbar. 'I take full credit.'

'I'd have been the same. If there's a mystery I have to solve it, I hate not knowing the truth. Call me Scooby Doo, if you will.'

'Does that make me Velma?'

'More like Daphne.'

'The dumb one?'

He waves his hands in protest. 'The brains of Velma and beauty of Daphne?'

Smooth, I think, stifling a smile. Already, this feels good.

Being around him makes me feel like I'm back in Clapham, like life is easy again. Like all the problems are locked safely up in the past.

'If you've got the strength of Fred, perhaps you can lift the trapdoor up,' I suggest.

He chuckles, then steps forward and throws the trapdoor open. It falls to the ground with a violent thud, making us both jump. Rick peers down into the darkness, nose wrinkled, frowning. I wait, letting him take it all in.

'Bit grim, isn't it?' he says. The jovial note lands wrongly. We both know there's nothing funny about this place. It feels all kinds of wrong, and we haven't even ventured down there yet.

'Someone did die down there,' I remind him.

'Yeah, but it's more than that. Imagine centuries of smugglers coming up and down those stairs with their stolen goods. Who knows what went on down there, what crimes they committed?'

'That's true.'

He holds up his torch. 'On that note, shall we?'

'You still want to go down?'

'Hey, I'm Fred and you're Daphne and Velma rolled into one. We have to, don't we?'

'I hope your shoes have got good grip.'

'I work on a farm: of course they have.' He switches the torch on, sending a dazzling beam down the rough steps. I follow its line, then gasp. It goes down a lot further than I'd realised and the stairs are steep. Precarious in the extreme. No wonder Mrs Trewain slipped down them. They're a death-trap.

I move closer, then hesitate. It's not the fact that it looks like something out of a horror film, though that isn't helping. It's not that I can't see further than the bottom of the stairs and have no idea what lies around the bend of the tunnel. It's the sensation that something's down there. Shifting around restlessly in the black. Listening to us and waiting.

I can't help but think of Noelle, beneath the waves. Waiting all this time to be found again.

Blame Vinnie, I think, anger blooming in the pit of my stomach. It's his fault. If I'd never met him, I'd have never met her either.

'Heidi?' Rick's voice snaps me back to the moment. 'Everything okay?'

'It's fine.'

'You want me to go first? You look a little nervous.'

'I'm no coward, thanks very much.' I place one foot on the top step. The chill of the stone seeps through my shoe. I take another step. Then another. It gets easier, once I find a rhythm. Rick follows, the torch beam bobbing a path ahead of us both, occasionally blotted by my back.

'You'd think they'd have installed a rail,' Rick says. 'Even a bit of rope would have done. Honestly, some smugglers have no consideration for others, do they?'

His words are dull and flat, the stone walls absorbing the sound. We carry on until we reach the bottom. It's noticeably colder, damper too. I place my hand on the wall beside me. It's as rough as expected and dripping with wet. I don't understand how it could be so damp when we're still a distance from the sea.

Rick squeezes beside me then shines the torch down the tunnel ahead. It's narrow, uneven, extending only ten metres or so before curving around another corner.

'This is incredible,' he whispers. 'When I was a lad, we all used to be obsessed with this place. I can't believe I'm actually here.'

'Why were you all obsessed with it?'

'You know what kids are like. We'd heard our parents

talking about it when they thought we weren't listening. We were desperate to get down here, especially after Mr Trewain sealed it up.'

'What, because you thought there'd be smuggler's treasure down here?'

He laughs. 'I think it was more the thrill of being somewhere where criminals once operated. One of my old friends even tried to get in from the other side, the cave in the cliffside. Silly bastard lost his footing, nearly fell onto the rocks below. Luckily he managed to grab the edge of the old smuggler's path. He would have died if he hadn't. He gave up and walked back in the end, but he was the talk of the school for ages.'

We carry on along the tunnel. The air's stale, suffocating. I taste something on my tongue, the ancient salty tang of undisturbed dust, or worse. *Something's listening to us*, I think, straining to see ahead. *It's keeping a distance, waiting to see what we'll do next.* I'm a child again, scared of being judged. A teenager, buried in regret, telling Dad I didn't mean it and pleading with him not to go. Older too, stifled with rage at the heat of a day not so long ago, the quiet of the cove, the low scribble of pen in a notebook. This tunnel is taking me places I don't want to go.

Rick coughs. The sound echoes flatly for a moment or two before being smothered by the surrounding rock. 'There's an atmosphere down here, isn't there?' he whispers. 'It's uncomfortable. Makes you think of ghosts of smugglers past, all watching us.'

'That's ridiculous.'

'I know. But when you're in a place like this, it's harder not to believe, don't you think?'

'No,' I lie. 'The dead don't linger.' *Don't they?* I think of

Noelle's face, shining through the darkness in front of us. It's all too easy to imagine.

'Maybe it's the nixie,' Rick says. 'Legend says she prowls the cliff-caves at night, looking for victims.'

'I'm not sure I want to hear about that right now.'

'Sorry. I was trying to lighten the mood. This place just feels *bad*, doesn't it?'

I don't answer. He's right, it does feel bad and the feeling strengthens with every step I take. It's a rot, something festering away in my gut. Tears prickle the corners of my eyes but I don't understand why. Everything feels hopeless down here. My thoughts bloat with Noelle, with Vinnie, with everything in the past that went so wrong. With myself most of all.

What's wrong with me?

'We should turn back,' I say, voice choked with supressed emotion.

The torch beam suddenly spreads into a plane of light. 'Hold up,' Rick says. 'What's this?'

We both stop, take in the surroundings as Rick twists the beam this way and that.

'We've found a cave,' he says eventually. 'A big one too.'

He points his torch upwards. The roof is still low where we're standing. Tiny stalactites cling to it like skeletal worms, their surfaces gleaming in the light. Ahead, the roof is higher, the stalactites longer. One at the back has joined with the floor, forming a lumpen, soaking pillar. It's unholy, a candle from a satanic ritual. I want to get out.

'Let's go.' I press against his arm. 'I don't like this.'

He nods. 'I know what you mean.'

The torch beam drifts to something in the corner, near the pillar-stalactite. It's a messy pile of something. At first I can't interpret what I'm seeing; the shapes are confusing, a mishmash of off-white jagged mess, distorted by the long shadows cast by the light.

It takes me a few moments more to register what I'm looking at. *Bones.* I'm standing here, casually observing a heap of bones.

'What the hell?' Rick mutters.

'I don't want to know.'

'They're animal bones, not human.'

'Do you know that for sure?'

'Yeah.' He pauses, flicks the torchlight across them. 'Look, a sheep skull. That bone there's a cow femur, I'd put money on it. No human skulls, thank God.'

'Why are they down here?'

'That's the million-dollar question. It's weird, isn't it?'

'We should go.'

He takes a deep breath. 'Fair enough, I don't feel comfortable either. You lead the way.'

I'm grateful for the gesture. He knows I don't want to be the one bringing up the rear, the vulnerable one at risk of being picked off by unseen monsters. He trains the light back up the tunnel we'd emerged from, the light bouncing off the wet walls, turning them to oil. I start to walk, slowly at first, then at greater speed.

I need to slow down. But something's following us. I don't think it, I know it. It's her, Noelle. She's found me. She's here.

'Heidi, take it easy.' Rick's voice sounds far away. He needs to hurry. We both do.

Why did you do that? Dad chimes in my head, an echo of the past. *You could have killed me.* It's deadly in dark places where there's no air. It's a real killer. I can't get caught down here. My knees feel watery and insubstantial; the only way to keep my balance is to keep surging forward. Faster, faster, until I'm jogging.

My foot catches something in the darkness below. I stumble,

reach out to steady myself, then slam a hand into the surface of the tunnel beside me. Knife-sharp pain screams through my palm and I cry out, unable to stop myself. The noise warps and distorts, before being swallowed up in the silence.

'Are you okay?' Rick shines the torch at me. I blink then hold my hand out. It's starting to bleed; big beads of blood bubbling along a jagged line across my palm, blossoming even as we stand there. I stare, mute, as they form a single angry line of dark red.

'I caught it on something sharp. A stone in the wall or something.' I press my other hand to it. It's bleeding far more than it should be, already starting to trail down my wrist.

'We need to get it bandaged up,' Rick whispers. He casts the beam across the wall, then focuses its beam on something sticking out from the stone. The light throws a sharp shadow against it, a curving miniature scimitar, distorted by the unevenness of the rock surface.

I move aside as he peers closer. 'It's not a stone,' he says, looking back at me.

'Is it a nail?'

'No. Or at least, not one you'd use in DIY.'

'What do you mean?'

'I know what I *think* it looks like, but I don't want to think about it at all, to be honest.'

I come closer, ignoring the burning sensation in my injured hand. *Another bone*, I think initially, belonging to something tiny like a bird or mouse. Then I study the rough moon-crescent shape of it, its sickly yellow edges, the off-cream surface.

'A fingernail,' I whisper. 'That's a human fingernail.'

'It looks that way. Why would it be stuck in a stone wall?'

It's to snag something in the dark, I think, then wish I hadn't. To stop something in their tracks, then grab them.

'Let's go.' I nudge him hard. 'Now.'

He doesn't argue. We continue along the tunnel, scurrying like rats in a pipe. My palm is starting to throb now; the numb shock of the initial injury giving way to a deep, hot pain. The nail went deep. A fingernail. A claw.

I see the bottom of the steps up ahead. Relief soaks through me as my knees loosen again. They only need to hold me up for as long as it takes to get up to the surface again. It's not much to ask.

'I thought I heard something,' Rick says, as we start to climb. 'Did you hear it, Heidi? Coming from behind us.'

I shake my head. I don't want to know, not before we get out of here. The last few steps are the worst, my thighs are shaking with adrenalin. Finally, I clamber out through the trapdoor and into the garden. It's started to rain, a light misty drizzle settled on my hair and face. I've never been so grateful to be back in the open before.

Rick hurries out behind me. A deafening thump makes me jump. I turn then make the connection. He's thrown the trapdoor shut. It's fallen against its rough frame, but hasn't closed completely; the wood is too warped. It'll stay ajar until I can figure out a way to shut it properly.

'Ow,' I mutter, studying my palm in the light.

He's by my side in a flash, reaching for my hand and holding it up to inspect it.

'That's a nasty wound,' he says, tilting my palm one side then the other. 'Maybe we should go to hospital.'

I think of the questions the doctors might ask. Explaining this one might take some doing. *Well, we were down in an ancient tunnel where at least one person died and I snagged my hand on a fingernail that had been caught in the wall. Did I mention there was a pile of bones down there too?* No, I don't want people to start probing. I need to process this myself first.

'I'll be okay,' I tell him. 'I've got antiseptic cream upstairs.'

'It might need a stitch or two. Maybe antibiotics.'

'I've got some bandages somewhere. That'll do.'

He studies me hard, then exhales. 'If you're sure. That was an adventure, eh?'

I say nothing. It's not the right time to be glib. Instead, I look back at the trapdoor, at its blistered, parched surface, at the dark gap where it doesn't quite connect with the frame. All it would take is one hard shove from below to flip it open again. Then whoever's down there would be here, right outside my back door.

I hate you, Vinnie, I think, a flare of rage bursting from the shock. *You insisted this was the right place for us. This was your idea not mine.*

'What did you hear?' I ask, turning to Rick.

'What?'

'On the stairs, you said you'd heard something.'

He winces, then looks away. 'My nerves got the better of me.'

'What do you think you heard?'

'It was nothing.'

I touch his arm, encourage him to meet my gaze. 'Tell me.'

'I thought I heard footsteps, that's all.'

'Footsteps?'

'Yeah. I heard it when we were in the tunnel itself, like something was following a good distance away, then it stopped. But as I was coming up the stairs, I heard it again, only they were far quicker this time.'

'Quicker?'

'Like someone was running.'

I shiver. It's impossible not to. The pain in my hand grows to a burn, and I look down at it, see blood spilling from the side and onto the wet grass below.

'It wasn't that,' I say firmly.

'Of course not. Probably the acoustics down there, making our footsteps echo back to ourselves. You know what it's like when you're panicking. It's so easy to imagine things that aren't there.'

I think of the house. The wet walls. Leaves at the window that look like hands. Swimmers in the water who disappear without warning. Panic. Imagination. I hate not knowing what's real and what's not.

'I need to put something on this wound,' I tell him.

He blinks, then nods. 'God, yes. We need to get it washed. I'm worried it'll get infected.'

Someone running. As I open the back door, I can't help but glance back. I imagine, for a second, a pair of eyes watching us through the gap between trapdoor and ground. Waiting down there for the right moment. Just imagination, though. Nothing more.

A single drop of blood falls from my hand and onto the doorstep. It's an easy trail for anyone to follow and it leads directly to me.

CHAPTER TWELVE

'Do you feel safe here?' Rick asks, later on. He sips his tea, elbows pressed to the table, eyes on my bandaged hand.

I shrug. 'It's the only home I've got, so it'll have to do.'

'I don't just mean the smuggler's tunnel. I mean all of it. I can tell things are bad with your boyfriend. You said he was physically violent towards you. Tell me it's none of my business and I won't ask anything else. But I'm concerned.'

Vinnie the violent woman-beater. It's a new label. Fits him too, given his stature, the bear-like hulk of his body. He did shove me. Admittedly it hurt my ego more than anything, but it's still assault. I could have reported it to the police and they would have taken it seriously. Maybe I should have done. I'll keep it in mind.

'I'll be fine,' I tell Rick, reaching for my mug with my good hand. 'The situation's not ideal, but that's the way it is.'

'You've got a lot of emotional resilience.'

'Thanks. I always had to be resilient when I was growing up. I guess it just stuck.'

'Why was that?'

I remember our cottage, the wisteria around the porch. The

garden, extending to the neighbouring fields. Sea, sparkling sea; endless days out on it or else underneath the waves. Relaying it aloud would sound like the recipe for a perfect childhood. He wouldn't understand. The father with an obsession, and not much room for anything else in his life. The mother looking for someone to blame for it all. All those boring underwater lessons, learning how to *master my breath*. My whole childhood was a held breath. I only learned to exhale when I left home.

'You know how it is,' I say, pressing the warm mug gently to my injured palm. It burns in response and I quickly remove it. 'Difficult parents. Mum liked to hold me responsible for everything, including Dad leaving.'

'You said your mum was dead.'

'Yeah, cancer. Dad too. After he left, he shacked up with some free-diving champion in Australia. Lived a dream life in Sydney. Forgot all about me.'

'I feel for you,' he says. 'I was lucky, my parents were great. Well, what I can remember of Mum was great, anyway. She had a laugh like a spurting hosepipe. Very explosive.'

'That's sweet.'

'I don't like the thought of you being here on your own.'

'That's sweet too.'

'Seriously. Your hand looks nasty, you've got a violent partner who could return at any moment and let's not even talk about that tunnel out there. I can't just leave you to it.'

'What's the alternative?'

He shifts in his seat. 'You can come back to my house. I've got a spare room; you'd be welcome to stay there. Then, if your hand gets worse I can take you to hospital.'

'What if Vinnie comes back?'

'We can deal with that when it happens.'

Rick's genuinely worried, I can tell. But there's something else in the offer too. His cheeks have flushed slightly, he's reluctant to meet my eye. *He likes me*, I realise. I thought so last night. This confirms it.

'Maybe just for one night,' I agree. 'To get my head sorted.'

He brightens. 'I'll cook something nice. I'm a good chef. I need to get back soon; do you want to come with me?'

'I'll come over later. I've got to do a few things here first.'

He nods. 'I'll feel much better knowing that you're not here alone, in this place.' His hand finds its way to mine and rests there for a beat or two. It's a pat rather than a touch, meant to be reassuring. But it feels like more.

I feel the impact of Rick's absence as soon as I've closed the front door behind him. The house is smothering, the sky outside threatening to pour rain any second.

Noelle's dead. I knew that already but wasn't prepared for how I'd feel about everyone else knowing it too. The tunnel's dangerous and for some reason, it felt like *her*. She was all around me down there. In my head and outside it too, circling me in the darkness. Now I'm all alone. And this house is unsettlingly silent.

I pause near the front door and listen. Not silent after all, there's a vague hissing sound coming from somewhere upstairs. It's steady, monotonous, scarcely noticeable unless I strain to hear. I run through the possibilities. Distant roadworks. The central heating acting up. A tap running at full blast.

A tap. I look up instinctively. There's a dark patch on the ceiling close to where I'm standing. A single drip of moisture hangs from the centre, waiting for gravity to release it.

That's how stalactites are formed. Stalactites like the ones down there in that tunnel. That's not the issue now, though.

Something's leaking. Pouring. The ceiling above me is saturated with water.

It's enough to galvanise my muscles. I sprint up the stairs and into the bathroom. The tub has a shining surface of water right to the very top. A waterfall-sheet is tumbling over the side, to a sodden puddle on the carpet below. The stink of cold moisture is like a slap in the face. I stare for a moment or two, gaping like a hooked fish.

The tap's on. There's no reason why it should be. I haven't turned it on or off since Vinnie left.

They found her tangled up in some weeds under the sea. A body, bobbing in the depths. The tug of the tide all around her.

I lean across. The tap doesn't give. I twist harder until it turns. At once the flow stops, finishing with a single drip, which plumes into a series of circles in the water below. The silence after makes my ears ring. The carpet squelches under my feet. I reach in, flinching at the cold, then tug the plug out. Watch without seeing as it empties slowly. The gurgle sounds like laughter.

My injured hand screams. I'm leaning on it; I don't know how I didn't notice before. It's bleeding again. The red blends with the wet, sending watercolour streaks down the side of the bath.

I didn't leave the tap running earlier. I know I didn't. I feel watched. Something's out to get me. Something impulsive. Destructive.

Whatever's going on, I can't cope with it. I refuse to. I can just leave. Rick offered; I can be out of here in a few minutes. I have a place to escape to. Not much, given I have to return at some point, but it's something.

The thought's enough to make everything feel less hopeless. I rush to the spare room, find my travel-bag on top of a pile of suitcases that need putting in the attic. Head to the bedroom, pack a change of clothes, then get my toothbrush from the bathroom, though I don't want to go back in there. The tap is still off, the stainless-steel surface misted with moisture. The quiet feels mocking, as though it'll twist itself back on the moment I leave the house.

I don't care though. In a few minutes I'll be gone and it won't be my problem anymore.

Before I leave, I dab more antiseptic cream on my palm. The pain is intense, a living thing burrowing deep into my muscle and tissue. The edges of the wound look ragged, death-white against the darkening blood in the centre. Quickly, I wrap a bandage around it and hope the cream's enough to start the healing process. It has to be. There's no way something as small as a fingernail can hospitalise me.

Unless it's an ancient, infected fingernail, I add silently. Best to imagine that's not the case. Some things aren't worth dwelling on.

My phone goes off in my pocket. I pull it out with my other hand and study the screen. It's an unknown number again. I answer. I won't let them scare me, whoever they are.

'Yes?' I snap.

Nothing, just like before. I can hear vague noises again. A crackling, which might be the connection. Something moving around too, maybe a low mumble of a voice, though it sounds an impossible distance away.

'Who is this?' I say. 'You're pathetic. Have the courage to say something at least.'

I hear a muted whisper, or think I do. It sounds like someone speaking from the bottom of an echoing stairwell. All the while, my ear rings with the same maddening crackle.

I hang up. My eyes burn with tears. I've started crying without even realising it. I wish I hadn't acknowledged it; it's made things worse. I sit on the edge of the bed and sob.

Everything is broken. I've fallen into a dark, confusing dream and can't break loose from it.

I remember the time I ran out of breath when out diving with Dad. I cried then too, swam back to the beach and curled up in a ball by the cliffside, holding my knees tightly. He emerged a few minutes later, sat beside me, waited in silence until the tears dried up and I'd stopped coughing. Then told me the only way to recover from a set-back was to be fearless, to try again.

So I did. He wiped my cheeks when I started to cry a second time and told me to trust him. I dived deeper the second time then saw him drifting through the weeds, watching me, and lost my focus. I came to the surface choking and vomited in the water. So much for second time lucky. He always pushed me too far.

I call Miranda. I can't think of anyone else to call. It rings out. However, a minute later she calls back. Just like normal. Normal is good.

'Heidi?' She sounds guarded. 'I wasn't expecting you to call back so soon. It sounded like–'

'Things are horrible,' I interrupt. 'Please, hear me out. I wouldn't call if I wasn't desperate.'

She waits a while. I can hear her tapping her nails against the back of the phone. 'Is it about Noelle?' she says finally. 'Are you in shock?'

'It's everything. This house is all wrong, I can't stay here anymore. There's a tunnel out in the back garden. I damaged my hand and it hurts like hell, and–'

'Slow down. You were on the edge before you left, and now you sound like you've jumped right over it.'

'The other day, you said I'd be welcome to stay anytime.'

Another lengthy pause. 'Did I?'

'Can I come tomorrow? I won't stay for long. I need to get away from here.'

'You can't come right now.'

'Why not?'

'It's difficult at the moment.'

'What about the day after, then?'

She sighs. 'I've got someone else staying.'

'Who?'

'A friend. Someone who needs me.'

'But I'm a friend. I need you.'

'C'mon, we're not like that, never have been. We're strong, independent girls, right? I'm sorry. I can't help it if—'

'You said I could stay. Now you're going back on it.'

She doesn't reply. We're meant to be friends. Not just a pair of *strong girls*. Maybe she only cares when I'm happy-go-lucky Heidi, happy to share a bottle or two of prosecco and flirt with strangers in a dingy city bar. She can't cope with this new version of me. A vulnerable person who needs someone to lean on.

'Why don't you wait a few days?' she says, filling the uncomfortable silence. 'You'll feel different then. You know what you're like, you change your mind all the time.'

'What's that supposed to mean?'

'Earlier today, you hung up on me and made me feel terrible. Now you're saying you want to stay at my house. That's pretty sketchy by anyone's standards.'

'I was upset, Miranda. You upset me.'

'I challenged you on one little thing and you flew off the handle. Look, I don't want to fight, but I'm not going to be your whipping boy, sweetheart. Sometimes, life throws things at us and we have to cope. Not have a tantrum.'

I can't believe what I'm hearing. In the whole time we've known each other, she's never been like this. Did I not know her before or has something changed in the short time I've been away? It makes no sense.

'You'll be okay,' Miranda adds, after a time. 'You're a survivor.'

'What would you know?'

'I know you pretty well. You got through what happened with your dad, and that was pretty dark stuff.'

I freeze. 'You said you wouldn't bring it up again. I only told you because I was drunk.'

'Yeah, you tell me lots of things when you're drunk. But it's mainly all about the daddy troubles.'

'Who's staying with you?' I ask softly.

'It's not important.'

'Then why don't you tell me? You hate secrets.'

'I hate other people keeping secrets from me.'

'Same here, Miranda. So tell me. You haven't got any other friends apart from me, only acquaintances. Remember?'

She sighs. 'You need to cool off. Why don't you call me tomorrow?'

'I need someone to help me now. I've got a place I can stay tonight, but nothing after that. This place is bad. I'm seeing things. Things that shouldn't be there.'

'Do you realise how mental that sounds, hon? Look, I need to go. Call me in a bit, when you've thought things through.'

'You sound like a parent. Do you mean I need to *reflect on my bad behaviour?*'

'Don't be silly.'

'Better silly than secretive. What the hell's going on?'

'I'm going now, Heidi. Pour yourself a wine. It'll help, it always does.'

She hangs up. I stare at my phone, then drop it on the bed beside me. Her parting shot echoes inside me, over and over. *Pour yourself a wine. Pour yourself a wine. That's all you're good for, Heidi. A drinking buddy and no fun when you're needy.*

A drinking buddy. A good time girl, looking for the next bit of fun. That was the excuse I gave to Vinnie and Noelle, when I found them in the reception of their hotel in Kent. *Just here for a little getaway. Amazing that you're here too.* Vinnie's confusion and anger, until the prospect of sex on the beach brought him around. Noelle's? Shock then surprising acceptance. *So nice you're here, Heidi. Join us tonight. We're going out for drinks.*

That night, we got drunk in a bar by the seafront. It was called *Cockles* or some other stupid name. Hot pink sign, yellow neon letters. Crowds of people, all drunk on cheap cocktail jugs, sambuca shots. It was still so hot, even though the sun was setting. Noelle's bare legs were propped up on the low wall beside her chair, her white linen dress draped over her thighs, hair bundled in a Grecian goddess sweep.

I'm so glad you're here, she said and poured me another glass of rosé. *It's fun.*

The word *fun* crawled all over me. *Fun. Fun trio. Fungus.* A parasitic loathing through my body, under my skin, into my bones. Heidi, the bit of fun. The jester, entertaining her royal highness and the king. My short black dress felt cheap when she said that word. My straightened hair too shiny with serum, my lips too glossy, my foundation too thick. Too try-hard. At that moment, I wished I hadn't come. My impulsiveness lands me in all the wrong places.

But she was the one who was out of place, not me. She was unwanted. Vinnie and I had been sleeping together for months at that point. I kept it all inside me, smiled and smiled. Vinnie joined us a few minutes after, wrestling a path through the holidaymakers and loud locals. His jeans fit snugly; his shirt clung to his broad chest.

He was mine, not hers. She just didn't know it yet.

'What'll we do tomorrow?' she asked. 'The weather's meant to be hotter than today.'

'I thought we'd explore the coastline,' Vinnie said. 'Find ourselves a secret cove.'

'Want to come along, Heidi?'

So gullible. So keen to be friends. Noelle's eyes gleamed in the strung-up lights of the bar. It was all too easy.

She went to bed early that night with a headache, claimed the heat had got to her. Vinnie and I went for a walk along the beach, beside the glowing lamplights of the promenade. The sea shushed and dragged, the cool sand soothed our bare feet. We kissed, sank down and screwed each other in the darkness; frantic, urgent, excitable. The best sort of passion, the secretive kind, and he forgave me as he came, muffling his groan against my neck. The scent of salt surrounded us. Maybe it was the smell of winning, of everything coming together. Or had it been a fungus-rot after all? I think now it might have been, because nothing good has happened since then. Everything after she died has felt rotten, diseased, ruined.

Deep-diving into the past is doing me no good. I have to stop. Right now.

I wipe my face then check my reflection in the wardrobe mirror. It's time to go to Rick's house. I can escape this and be with someone who isn't rotten. Who makes me feel good about myself.

Forget about Miranda, forget about Vinnie, forget about Noelle. Move forwards, not backwards. That's what matters right now.

CHAPTER THIRTEEN

I take the route across the field, travel-bag over one shoulder, boots sucking into the mud. It feels more familiar now, which is something. The air is thick with wet, I can taste it with every breath. There'll be rain soon, and lots of it.

My hand throbs. I press it to my chest. The skin across my palm feels tight, a balloon-skin stretching to bursting point with every step. It won't get infected. I just need to stay positive. No point dwelling on things that are beyond my control.

I quicken my pace. This hill is steeper than I remember, the hedgerow beside me pricklier than it looks. Branches snag at my coat and catch at my injured hand a couple of times. I wonder if anything about this place isn't out to get me.

The group of buildings ahead must be part of Rick's farm, though I can only see the upper floors above the hedge in the distance. They're stone-made, squat, with the same slate-tiled roofs that every house seems to have in this area. I spot a chimney spouting smoke like a kettle. Good, that means a fire. I could do with comfort and warmth.

I pass through a little gate then walk across the yard, which is mostly mud. A barn beside me houses a few fat pigs, who eye me as I try to find a route to the main house that won't leave me knee-deep in muck. There's a horse too, head hanging over a stable door, nose coated in dried dirt. The house has a broken pane in the window closest to the door, and the window ledges are blistered and falling to pieces. This isn't a place that's been looked after, which surprises me. Rick seems so well put-together. Maybe DIY isn't his strong point.

I grab the door-knocker and rap firmly. A moment later, the door flies open and Rick fills the space, rubbing his hands, which are floury.

'I've been baking,' he explains, holding his palms up for me to see. 'Apple pie; Mum's recipe. Hint of cinnamon, a sprinkle of nutmeg, brown sugar not white, and a dobble of golden syrup. You'll love it.'

I enter, aware of the creak of old floorboards under my boots, the wallpaper with its bobbled surface and tiny floral detailing. Nothing's been done to this place for at least five decades. An air-freshener pot sits in the window alcove close by, which must be where the vague scent of stale vanilla comes from.

'Apple pie sounds great,' I tell him, untangling the muddy mess of my laces, slipping each boot off with relief. 'You didn't have to go to any trouble, though.'

'After the stress of this morning, I thought we both needed it.' He gestures down the hallway, pulling a face. 'Sorry about the mess. This is classic farmer living. Nice home inherited from parents, no money to do anything with it.'

'It looks all right to me,' I lie.

'Now you're just being polite. Come on through.'

The kitchen is less uncared-for, though every surface is cluttered, stacked pots and pans, a packed mug-tree, a wire basket brimming with eggs, a pile of newspapers, dangerously close to teetering off the countertop. I prop myself on the stool by the breakfast bar. The units are old-fashioned, honey-amber wood with heavy metal handles on the doors, but it works. Makes the space seem homely, well loved.

Rick fills the kettle with a jaunty whistle, then sets about making us both a cup of tea. 'How are you feeling?' he asks, above the noise of the water boiling.

I don't know how to answer. I'm exhausted. Emotionally drained. Tired of everything. But I don't want him to see me like that. 'I'm okay, I guess,' I reply eventually. 'What about you? Hope your nerves weren't too wrecked after the tunnel.'

'I got scared, I must admit. And there was me, trying to be the strong alpha male.'

I chuckle. 'I was spooked too. It's easy to imagine something lurking in the dark.'

'There's nothing down there, apart from that pile of bones. I shouldn't have said what I did about hearing footsteps. It was just the sound of water dripping or our own echoing feet. Something like that.'

'I'm not so sure.'

'There was no-one down there. Alive, dead or otherwise.'

'Sometimes I think someone's out to get me,' I mutter.

'What was that?'

'Nothing. I didn't mean to say it aloud.'

He gives me a look, opens his mouth, then closes it again. Finally, he points at my hand. 'How is it?'

'It aches. But that's not surprising.'

'Does it feel hot? Swollen? Do you feel all right in yourself?'

'It's fine,' I lie. *It'll be fine* feels more honest. I'll make sure I am, whatever it takes.

He sets a mug in front of me. Proper builder's tea, brewed a bit longer than I'd usually choose. We sit companionably for a moment or two, before he leans closer.

'Sorry to bring it up again,' he says slowly. 'Do you think we should call the police?'

Police. My breath hitches. 'Why would we do that?'

'Because of those bones, mainly.'

Bones. Bones is fine, it's safe territory. 'You said they were animal bones,' I remind him.

'They looked like animal bones. But still, it's strange isn't it? As for the fingernail in the wall, don't you think that needs more investigation?'

I shake my head. 'I think I should just close the tunnel up again. The stairs are lethal for starters.'

We both wince at the choice of words, though the previous owner's death had been years before.

'What about your boyfriend?'

'What about him?'

'If you're worried for your safety, that's worth reporting to the police too.'

'I'm not worried,' I tell him. 'I doubt Vinnie will come home any time soon. He's a coward when it comes down to it.'

When I look up again, Rick's still watching me, or reading me, trying to unpick some truth underneath my skin. The attention is flattering and unnerving. But I deserve attention. I want to find myself again. Return to being the Heidi that could walk into a pub and make heads turn. The Heidi that could hold the gaze of a crowd of people with just a suggestive laugh. Confident Heidi. Classy, self-assured, stylish.

The Heidi that caught Vinnie's eye, over and over. That pulled him to her and wouldn't take no for an answer.

I place my good hand over his. 'I appreciate you doing this.'

'It's nothing.' He clears his throat. 'It's nice to have the company. You're good company, Heidi. In spite of all the craziness, you make me laugh.'

'You make me laugh too.'

It's a moment. His head moves closer and mine does too. *It's going to happen* blends with *it can't, he shouldn't*. And, *I want to*. His lips are full, fuller than I realised. White, even teeth.

My phone vibrates. That's all it takes to break the spell. He retreats, straightening his expression, as I rove around in my pocket. I look down, then groan. Unknown number again. I throw it down on the breakfast bar between us.

'Sales call?' he asks, clearing his throat.

'Crank caller. I've had about five of these calls today.'

He reaches for the phone then answers it, before I can stop him. 'Hello? This is Rick, can I ask who this is?'

I shake my head, hold my hand out to take it back, but he brushes me aside. A few seconds later, he hangs up and passes it back to me.

'Sounded like an older lady, muttering to herself,' he tells me. 'Driving, perhaps? I couldn't make out much detail.'

'That's more than I ever got.'

'Do you know any older ladies?'

'None.'

'You need to get out more.'

I grin, in spite of myself. 'So,' I say, sitting up straighter. 'You've got me for the afternoon, what do you want to do with me?'

I'm sure he's blushing. He scratches his chin, then nods towards the window. 'I've got a pile of jobs that need doing out there,' he tells me, 'but they're all mucky. Think you're up for the challenge? Especially with a dodgy hand?'

It's a world away from what I'm used to. But it's also a world away from thinking about everything, which is just what I need. I drain my tea, then smack the empty mug back on the surface. 'Show me the way, boss. I'm ready for anything.'

His eyebrow bobs upwards. 'You might regret that statement.'

I'm sure I won't, I think, as we both stand in unison.

This farmhouse has some witchery to it, an enchantment that kicks in as the sun sets. The lumpy old sofa has changed, moulding around my body to make me feel more relaxed than I have done in a long time. The cheap wine tastes better with every mouthful. The shabby rugs and unevenly plastered walls look homely in the light of the floor-lamps and the heavy curtains envelop us in safety and warmth. It's working its magic on Rick too. The soft glow of light catches his cheekbones, softening out his complexion, turning him into a Hermes, a Cupid, a light, slight thing of beauty.

A few months ago, I thought Vinnie was my future. We clung together through the suspicion and the rumours. We reassured each other that everything would be fine, because we were invincible together. That we could cope with anything the world threw at us, as we'd already been through so much. Now I'm here, in another man's house.

But Vinnie left. His decision not mine. Then Rick invited me over. His decision not mine. All I'm guilty of is going with their flow and seeing where it takes me. Not impulsiveness. The opposite, in fact.

Rick stretches his arms across the back of the sofa. 'This is nice.'

'Do you mean having someone to help with the farm-work? Or the wine?'

He laughs. 'All of that. And spending time with you. I haven't had anyone round in a while.'

'What, you mean there's not a queue of women waiting to be invited over?'

'Not that I've noticed. There aren't many women around

here. Classic village population. Limited number of residents and most of them over sixty.'

'What about Bea from the grocery store?' I ask, leaning closer to him.

'Bea? Why do you ask?'

'She seemed angry that you were talking to me in the pub the other night.'

He shifts in his seat. 'Don't worry about that. She sometimes reads things wrongly. It's not a problem.'

I've met women like that before. Usually, they're the ones glaring at me all evening. The ones who think they're entitled to male attention and who can't stand it when someone else takes it from them.

Noelle wasn't like that. She was too sure of her own beauty to imagine Vinnie would ever pick me over her. I notice that Rick's watching me and straighten my expression. Noelle won't spoil this, or Vinnie. I feel balanced, content, on my way to happiness. I won't let either of them ruin it.

'People are always getting things wrong.' I raise my glass and clink it against his. 'They're more trouble than they're worth. Though God knows what you think of me. I've only just moved here and already I've dragged you into my drama.'

'It's a relief that someone interesting has turned up. Nairbourne can be so boring. Same people doing the same things, week in, week out. The place never changes, never evolves. I like variety.'

Someone interesting. It's impossible to play it cool with a comment like that. I grin and he smiles in response. I could get lost in those eyes. In this light they look dark, and hungry too. Even the ache from my wounded palm can't distract me from them.

'I should get that apple pie in the oven,' he murmurs, moving closer.

'It can probably wait.'

He touches my shoulder, letting his hand rest there a moment or two, testing me. His fingers trail a line across the base of my neck. My skin tingles in response. I feel seventeen again, a knotted bundle of conflicting emotions. It's exciting. Worrying. Arousing.

Kiss him, I tell myself. *It wouldn't be wrong. He's a better person than Vinnie ever could be.*

The first time Vinnie and I kissed was in a booth in a crowded pub. It couldn't have been more different to this. Noisy with chatter and music, the smell of ale and fried food in our noses. The pressure of his lips surprised me. Forceful, urgent, needy. I remember the warmth of knowing I timed it right, that not giving in earlier had only ramped up his desire.

That feels like so long ago. But the lesson is the same. *Don't give in too soon.*

I pull away, give Rick an apologetic smile.

He draws back too, resting his hand stiffly on his lap. 'Sorry,' he says, as I open my mouth to say the same. 'I overstepped the mark.'

I shake my head. 'You didn't. I just need some time to–'

'I understand. Of course. You've been through a lot.' He stands, fumbling to straighten his jumper. 'You relax and drink some more wine. I'll get that apple pie cooking.'

I remain quiet, watch as he leaves the room. It feels colder after he's left, the sofa suddenly too big with just me sitting on it. My hand throbs harder in response. I can almost hear the blood pounding under the skin, keen to force its way through the scab and make me bleed again. I massage my wrist, listen to Rick clattering around in the kitchen.

It could work, him and I. We'd have a laugh, spend evenings down the pub, ignoring Bea. He'd help me to get the house sorted out, sell it on, then maybe we could sell this place too.

We'd make good money, move somewhere else, live in the way we wanted to. I can see it all laid out. A future that's happy and light. Where we hold on to each other and never let go.

I obey his orders and sip at my wine, taking in his bookshelf opposite. It's mostly battered hardbacks which I guess belonged to his parents, not him. After a while he returns, oven gloves in hand.

'I've popped the pie in the oven and a pizza too, as we can't start with dessert,' he announces. 'Sweet things get saved til last. That's the rule.'

Sweet things. I strain to keep the wolfish grin from my face. 'You're sweet,' I tell him. 'I can't remember when I've been this well looked after.'

He takes a bow. 'I do my best.'

And your best is just right, I think, making space for him on the sofa again.

CHAPTER FOURTEEN

For the rest of the evening, Rick is the gentleman he swore he would be. At just after midnight, he leads me upstairs, shows me to the spare bedroom and says goodnight. I wait for a while, standing by the closed door, then unpack my pyjamas with a smile. His mother obviously raised him well. Too well, maybe.

The following morning, I wake late. Shockingly late; my phone tells me it's nearly eleven, but it's unsurprising given how badly I slept. I kept rolling on my hand in the night, waking myself up. The ache is worse, my arm leaden. It must be the healing process. I don't want to imagine the alternatives. The bandage is stained in the centre; a curdled-milk cream, mixed with the pinkish tinge of blood. Rick mustn't see it. It's not exactly appealing.

I tug on my clothes, clean my teeth in the bathroom, then head downstairs. The house is warm, the range cooker in the kitchen pumping out heat that warms the entire ground floor. I spy Rick through the lounge window, carrying some crates across the yard to the pig-shed. His sleeves are rolled, his jeans muddy up to the knee. He's a lithe ball of energy, so different to Vinnie. Slighter, darker, more compact, less sprawling.

And sweeter, definitely sweeter. I could do with sweet right now.

He turns, sees me and grins over the top of the crates. Then loses his balance and wobbles in the mud, starts laughing at himself. I do too. I wish I could stay here and never have to go back. Then I remember the bath overflowing. All those other taps in the house, just waiting for the right time to turn themselves on. The damage all that water could cause in my absence. In fact, there are numerous ways that house could work against me, the moment my back's turned.

It's hostile, threatening even. What a place to call home.

Rick comes in quarter of an hour later, wiping his boots loudly on the doormat, then sets to work with brunch; frying squat sausages in a heavy iron pan, an egg each, toast and tomatoes too. I don't normally go in for grease – brunches with Miranda were always eggs Benedict with prosecco in the café down the road – but Rick's spread fits perfectly with this place.

We sit close together at his breakfast bar, elbow to elbow. There's an intimacy to it, an unspoken filling of the gaps between our shoulders, hips, thighs. An electric tingle of something waiting to happen.

'You're welcome to stay as long as you like,' he tells me, mopping his plate with the last slice of toast. His eyes are fixed on the window, but he's desperate to check my reaction, I can tell.

'I'd better get back,' I say reluctantly. 'I need to make sure nothing else has gone wrong in the house. I could come back later though?'

'You want to?'

'If you'd like me to.'

'Of course I would.'

He leans closer. My skin prickles with anticipation. I don't want to make him wait. I want him now. I want to feel something positive, something that's all about bright things ahead and nothing to do with the past. He kisses me, softly and chastely on the lips. A maiden peck, but there's more there, restrained by uncertainty. A test, to see what I'll do.

So I kiss him back, harder.

His hand finds its way to my hip. I like it there. His tongue is touching mine, we're breathing in time. I feel younger. Back to being the enchantress in dingy bars, in crowded clubs, spreading magic, bringing men to me and holding them close. That's the real me, the me I fought so hard to be.

He's a better kisser than Vinnie. Vinnie was harder and rougher. I used to like that, the force, the sense that he had to have me, and that he'd accept no refusal. But then, Vinnie always had so much more to lose. A devoted girlfriend, waiting for him to call. The perfect couple, and he was willing to give it all up for *me*.

I wish I hadn't let him into my thoughts. This is too much, too soon. I'll lose Rick if I don't play it right. I pull away.

'Thanks for brunch,' I say, filling the quiet. 'And for letting me stay.'

His face falls. 'Did I do something wrong?'

'Of course not.'

'I hope you don't think I forced you.'

'I don't.' I take his hand and squeeze it. 'I'll be back later, remember?'

Now he's smiling again. That's good. I could get addicted to that smile. Open, warm, impish too. The promise of more to come.

'You'd better be back,' he says.

I've caught him, I think.

I leave him to his work and head back along the field-path, ignoring the mud and cold. I shouldn't feel this happy, not after what I found out yesterday, but the feeling's there regardless. I can see now just how badly I've lost myself and what a relief it is to feel found again.

It's short-lived, though. The approach to the house strips the good feelings away, step by step. I don't want to go inside. I hate the thought of what I'll find when I walk through the door. A hand at the window. Another ragged fingernail, ready to rip me open. A tap, pouring water from bath to floor, soaking everything in its path.

It's a house, bricks and mortar, nothing else. There's no evil energy in there, focused on attacking me. No hidden monsters in the smuggler's tunnel. No nixie waiting by the back door, ready to slip inside. This is just trauma from the last few months talking. It's making my world slippery and upside-down.

I push open the old gate and step onto the driveway. Something's off, doesn't feel right. I scan the surroundings. Study the front of the house, the door, the kitchen window. It takes me a while to notice. There are tyre-marks at my feet. Deep tracks into the gravel revealing black earth beneath. The sign of someone who's spun their steering wheel in a hurry and kicked up a shower of loose stones behind them.

Vinnie. He returned here to challenge me, found me gone, then headed out again in a rage. Or just a delivery van, the local postman, the estate agent doing a courtesy visit to see how everything is. Either way, I don't like how the tracks look. They're gash-like curves across the drive. Someone wasn't happy when they took off, that's for sure.

A gash, like the wound on my palm. Ugly.

There's no point standing out here and staring. I pull my

keys from my bag, shove them into the lock, and curse at the effort involved just to get into the house. Finally the door gives way under the force of my shoulder and I stumble inside. The airless chill hits me straight away. It's a different cold, one that seeps through to muscles and bone. No amount of extra layers would block it out.

There's a folded piece of notepaper lying on the doormat, just by my toe. Something torn out of a little book. Handwritten. I stoop and pick it up reluctantly, open it up and read.

> *I tried calling several times, bad signal, couldn't hear what you were saying. Drove down to visit, thought it was time we met one another and sorted this whole mess out. Vivienne.*

Vivienne. I roll the name around, test it in various different social situations and come up blank each time. I don't know anyone called Vivienne, especially not anyone who would have driven down here, and who needed to *sort this whole mess out* with me.

It explains the silent phone calls yesterday, but sheds no light on who this person is. Or why they were at my house, why they'd made the effort to travel to get here. It doesn't tell me if they're a threat and if I should be worried.

Vivienne. It's an elegant name, like Noelle's. Pretty in an icy way. I think quickly. Did Noelle have any friends called Vivienne? Sisters? None that she told me about, but then, I didn't pay much attention to the things she said to me. She never had anything interesting to say.

This could be someone who's come to ask awkward questions. Someone from before with suspicions that have swelled over time. It ties in too well with the police discovering Noelle tangled in those weeds.

That's paranoia. It's Vinnie who needs to be worried, not me. He's the one with his neck on the line.

I put the letter down on the hallway table. Press my hand against it, willing it to disappear through the wood. Pain flares from the pressure against my downturned palm. There's no way of knowing whether this Vivienne will return. I hope she's given up, turned around and gone back to wherever she came from.

The lounge feels watchful. I walk through to the kitchen area and reach for a glass from the cupboard. I feel like I've stepped between one reality and another, into a place that's nothing at all until something happens. A glass of water will help. I'm parched after the cooked breakfast.

The tap judders as I turn it on, the steel surface pulsing with every spurt of water. It makes me jump, back away instinctively. It's never done this before. The rhythm picks up, becomes more urgent, the tap flinging water out in a fury, splashing against the surface of the sink, splashing my coat.

The water has a pink tinge. I can't move, only watch as the water pumps harder and harder, now accompanied by a shrill whine. It's a dirty pink, it reminds me of bloody cuts washed pale, drainage from a slaughter house, all things I don't want to think about right now. The whining picks up, it's piercing; a scream.

I turn the tap off. It spurts a final time then subsides. Everything is quiet after, and every sensible word I had with myself before I entered the house flies out of my head. Bad things *do* exist in this place. Every nightmare I've ever had is plausible here. Something's out to get me.

My phone vibrates and I gasp, then cover my mouth. I have to get a hold of myself.

It's a text message from Rick.

> I liked having you to stay. You can come any
> time, you know. Especially if you kiss me like
> that again.

I force myself to breathe. Let my thoughts drift back to him, the cosiness of his farmhouse, the wonder of being able to relax and enjoy. I can go back there later today. I need to remember that. I can escape this place; I only have to check in occasionally. Vinnie can sort it out. He caused all these problems in the first place.

The tap jerks again, a single jettison of water. Darker this time. More like blood.

It's sediment, nothing else. I know this. But it's hard making myself believe it.

I head into the village at lunch. The only food I've got in is half a stale loaf, a can of baked beans, and some crisps that won't do as a meal. I have to buy more sooner or later, so it might as well be sooner. I'm getting used to trudging to and fro across the fields, though I can't help but hate Vinnie for leaving me without a car. It's getting easier and easier to hate him, actually. I only wish I'd known what he was like sooner. Then I'd still be in London. With a job and a life. If I hadn't come here with him though, I wouldn't have met Rick. Maybe that makes it worth all the stress and struggle. All the sacrifice. I think of his kiss and feel optimistic.

The village is quiet when I get there, which I'm starting to realise is its usual state for this time of year. The pavements are empty. There's no evidence of anyone in the shops either. The sky's a bleached off-white that hints at a frost later in the day, and a single gull wheels overhead, its high scream echoing from the surrounding buildings.

I peer through the window of Bea's shop. I can't see anyone in there either, though I guess she's inside somewhere. I wonder if she's still angry at me for talking to Rick in the pub the other night. If so, she'd hate to hear what we got up to this morning. The thought brings a grin to my face.

The little bell tinkles as I push the door open, a cheery chime that doesn't fit with the gloomy interior. A moment later, Bea's head appears around the door frame at the back of the shop. Her expression falters at the sight of me, then becomes something harder, more tight-lipped.

'Hello, Heidi.' She steps out behind the counter. 'How are you?'

'Very well, thanks for asking.' I pick up a can of soup, read the ingredients, then put it back again.

'How's the house coming along?'

'It's exactly the same as when we moved in.'

'And how's your boyfriend?'

It's a laden question. I pause mid-browse of the shelves, then turn to her. 'I don't know, because he walked out on me,' I reply lightly. 'But that's life, right?'

'Sorry to hear that.'

'I'll be fine. I've survived people leaving before. How are you?'

She ignores the question, fiddling with something below the counter. 'Did you have a nice evening in The Fisherman's Rest the other night?'

'Very nice. Rick's good company.'

The resulting flinch is unmistakable. Bea needs to learn how to hide her emotions better. She's as easy to read as a children's book.

'You looked like you were getting along,' she says, refusing to meet my eye. 'You looked cosy.'

'It's a cosy pub.'

'Did your boyfriend know you were there?'

I shrug then pick up another can of soup, some bread rolls, a few bottles of wine for later. I place them deliberately on the counter, each item in turn. Keep fixing her with a stare until she has no choice but to look back. Finally, she does. The look of disapproval catches me off guard.

'Got everything you need?' she asks, squaring her shoulders.

'Have you got any chocolate buttons?'

'Right next to you.'

I grab a packet, then add a pack of pasta from the pile on top of the nearest shelf. 'That's it.'

She punches the till, rings everything through, nods at the little digital screen at the top to indicate the amount owing. The air rings with the unsaid, the swell of mutual distaste. She's got no reason to disapprove of me. She's not Rick's girlfriend. She has no ownership of him.

'I heard you got the smuggler's tunnel open,' she says, as I press my credit card to the reader.

'Who told you that?'

'Rick.'

'When did you speak to him?'

'Why do you ask?'

Why would he tell her? I pause, then tuck my card back into my wallet. 'He explored the tunnel with me.' I stuff the goods into my shopping bag. 'I was glad to have him there.'

'He said you sliced your hand open on something sticking out from the wall.'

I glance down at my bandaged palm. Notice that she does the same, with a hint of a smirk at her lips.

'It's nothing much,' I tell her.

'The nixie's claw.' She chuckles. 'If the nixie of Nairbourne catches you with her claw, the poison runs deep.'

'It wasn't a claw.'

'Course not, it's just an old legend. It made me think of it, that's all. The nixie of Nairburn once lured a sailor's wife to the water's edge, singing sweet songs to her. But the wife didn't know that the nixie was in love with the sailor and wanted him for herself. So she sliced the wife open with nails full of poison, then dragged her out to sea.'

I shake my head. I haven't got time for this. Bea needs to accept she's lost.

'Thanks for the story,' I snap, turning to the door. 'Have a good day.'

'It's an old tale, nothing more.'

'I know.'

'I'll tell Rick I saw you.'

I pull open the door, roll my eyes. She can do what she likes, it won't make any difference. It's me he's kissing, not her.

'Do you know anyone called Vivienne, by any chance?' I ask, glancing back over my shoulder.

She stares blankly, then shakes her head. I shrug. It was worth a shot.

CHAPTER FIFTEEN

ack home, each room feels colder than ever. The first
raindrops fall mid-afternoon, running fresh tracks through
the sea-salt caked on the window by the previous storm. It
blocks the outside world out, trapping me in here. I play a word
game on my phone, lose concentration. I'm listening for drips, I
realise. The telltale sounds of another tap spontaneously
turning itself on, or firing water somewhere it shouldn't.

I text Rick but get no reply. Spend some time pacing
around. Feel like a stranger in my own home. Unpack a few
more of the smaller boxes sitting by the breakfast bar. Then
stare out of the utility window at the entrance to the smuggler's
tunnel, its trapdoor still down. I don't like the gap in between it
and the frame. There's room enough for a pair of hands to
squeeze through, for fingers to curl around the edge and push
upwards. There's room enough in my head to imagine someone
doing that too, late at night while I'm upstairs sleeping.

I can imagine a pair of eyes, glittering in the darkness of that
crack. Watching me, watching them. Waiting for the right
moment. But there's nothing there. Never has been. The longer
I'm here, the more I'll unravel and loosen. I need to wind myself

up tight again. Gain control. Start planning my exit from this place. I don't want to end up like I was when I was younger. *Damaged. Traumatised. Pathological fear of rejection.* What a diagnosis to receive at the age of fifteen. I can thank Dad for that one.

Rick's text comes through, finally. It's less flirty than I was hoping for. I reread it. It's the rushed words of someone who's got other things on their mind. I don't like that; he should be focusing solely on me. I type a response, then delete it and put my phone away. Let him wait for a while. There's no *pathological fear of rejection* here. I'm fine with letting the rope go slack and giving some space.

I go upstairs and into the bathroom. The tap's still off, everything is as it should be. I pull out the antiseptic cream from the cupboard, sit on the edge of the bath, then peel the old bandage off my hand. It's glued fast with pus and blood, each tiny rip brings tears to my eyes. Once the bandage is off, I can see that it's bad. Bubbles of blood line the heart of the wound, shining in the weak light from the window. There's darker blood around the curve of the cut. Worst of all is the reddened skin around the edge. It might be infected. No, there's no *might* about it, it is. There's no point lying to myself. I just hope the antiseptic cream does its work.

I squeeze the tube across the wound and rub the cream in. The pressure wakes the pain with a jolt, taking it from a low throb to a hot scream. I feel the scab crack even further, and pinpricks of fresh blood blossom along the centre.

Like red wine, I think, closing my eyes. Noelle's chosen drink, a rich, dark Argentinian Malbec. The bottle she brought with her on the boat that day. I remember how it rocked and bounced against her leg. She sipped it on the beach while writing in her book. I studied her while she worked. Flat stomach, not an inch of spare flesh to her. Flawless skin, dark hair. A model fresh from a magazine. Then Vinnie joined us both. She stroked his back over and over, until the movement became a ritual. She, the goddess. Him, her strong wilderness man.

Not your man anymore, I wanted to scream. Then smash the bottle and watch it drench her red.

I quickly grab some tissue and dab the wound. It's becoming a mess, it needs covering up with another bandage. I wind the material around my hand, grab the sticky tape and fix it as best I can, tearing through it with my teeth. It's a bad job but it'll do for now. It has to. There's no-one else to help me.

There's the bottle of wine downstairs. White, not red. My preferred drink and not hers. It's probably too early to drink but it'll help with the pain, and make the past seem further away too. It'll help cope with the silence. No sound to keep me company aside from the steady rattle of the rain against the windows.

As I reach the bottom stair, I stop. I can hear something. Sense movement too. The loud, relentless patter of disturbed gravel, a flash of red at the glass in the front door. It's a car, pulling into the driveway. Not Vinnie returning because our car is black. Rick's car was white, I saw it parked outside his house. I freeze, rabbit-like by the banister pole and wait.

A door slams and footsteps crunch closer. Then a body appears in the frosted glass and the doorbell chimes. I jump, even though I know they're there. It's too loud, abrasive. I don't want to answer. It's a woman, I can tell by the general shape. The mysterious Vivienne, it must be.

I glance at the scribbled note, still sitting on the console table. *Time we met one another and sorted this whole mess out.* But I don't want to meet or sort out any mess with her. She's a complication I can do without.

The doorbell chimes again. Whoever this woman is, she's

not going to quit. Reluctantly, I turn the key in the lock and open the door.

A female stands in front of me, older than I expected. Bossy, over-confident; that's my first impression. Her hair is a swept-up nest of brittle grey, her blusher too pink, lips too thickly painted, deep red bleeding along the cracks around her mouth. Flouncy felt jacket, an attempt at flamboyance, emphasising the wide waistline and shelf of bosom.

'We meet at last,' she says, stepping into the house without being asked.

'We do?' I stand aside, then regret it. It's my home, I'm the one who gets to say whether she comes in or not.

She shakes the moisture from herself then looks around, nose wrinkled, frowning. 'I heard it was a state,' she says. 'But I had no idea it was so soulless. Ugh. It's a hideous box, isn't it?'

I block the way before she can wander through to the lounge. 'Who are you?'

That brings a laugh, a loud one with a hard edge to it. 'Vivienne, darling. It's about time we met, especially with all the nonsense that's been going on. I got him to give me your number a while back, but–'

'Got who to give you my number?'

'Vinnie. Sweetheart, I'm Vinnie's mother, Vivienne. Surely you knew that?'

I shake my head. 'He never mentioned it.'

'I'm sure he did. You must have forgotten.'

This is all happening too fast. Somehow, I find myself moving aside and letting her through to the living area, trailing after her like a puppy. She glides through with an arrogance that suggests a lifetime of having crowds part to make way for her.

'Vinnie doesn't look like you,' I say, as she sits on the nearest stool by the breakfast bar.

'He's a handsome thing, isn't he? Just like his father. You

don't look as I expected either. I could murder a coffee. It's been a long, taxing few days. How about putting the kettle on?'

I pause. She's serious, she actually expects me to jump at her command. Worse, I can't think of a way to refuse her. 'Milk or sugar?' I ask finally. It pains me. I dislike her already.

'Do you have cream?'

'No.'

'You live in the deepest West Country and no cream?'

'I've not lived in the deepest West Country for very long.'

'That's true.' She observes while I load the coffee-maker with a capsule and flick the switch. 'I was so confused when Vinnie said he was moving down here. But then, he hasn't been himself for the last few months. Have you heard the dreadful news?'

'Dreadful news?'

'Noelle, dear. *Noelle.*'

I turn, smash my hip against the nearest kitchen unit. 'Noelle?'

'Her body, under the sea. Gosh, don't tell me you've heard it from me first.'

'That? No. I mean yes, I knew already. My friend told me.'

'Miranda?'

'Yes. Wait, how did you know it was her?'

Her expression turns shifty. 'I presumed, dear. The coffee's brewed, look.'

How did she know? What else does she know? I pull the fridge door open and yank the carton of milk from the bottom shelf.

'How is Vinnie?' I ask. I don't really care, but can't think what else to say.

'He's going through such a tough time. The news of Noelle's death has hit him hard, I'm very worried about him. That's why I'm here. To find out what's been going on.'

It's hard not to smirk. Noelle's death. He's known about it for far longer than she thinks. *Stupid woman.* 'Nothing's going on,' I tell her. 'As far as I know, anyway.'

'Come on. There's something odd about all of this. People don't suddenly move to the middle of nowhere on a whim. And you and he have only been together five minutes.'

She got to the point quicker than I expected. I hand her the coffee. 'Why don't you ask him, then?'

'He's depressed. I can't get a sensible answer from him these days. Besides, I'm curious to hear what you have to say.'

I can't read her. I don't like it. I can't answer either. So I shrug instead, drink my coffee and spill some down my top. She's staring at me. It's too intense, too searching. Her eyes are peeling away at my skin, studying what's underneath and judging every part of it.

She sips, pulls a face, then puts her mug down again. 'So, shall we start from the top?'

I sit on the stool next to her. This conversation is racing, it needs to slow down.

'Where have you driven from, Vivienne?' I ask.

'Norwich. Did Vinnie not tell you where I lived?'

'Never. That's a long way to come.'

'I know. You can imagine my horror when I found you weren't here yesterday. I kept calling and calling, but couldn't hear anything when you answered, only crackling. At one point I heard a man speaking. Rick, he said his name was, or something like that? It was all very confusing. Anyway, I had to drive all the way to Penzance in the end. Luckily, I found a hotel with a spare room for the night.'

'Where are you staying tonight?'

She narrows her eyes. 'I thought I'd stay here. I can't drive all the way back. I've brought my own bedding and pillows, don't worry.'

'You're staying here? Does Vinnie know you're here?'

'I won't get in your way.'

'You won't, because I won't be here tonight.'

'Where will you be?'

My heart's racing. 'I'm going out. With a friend.'

'Surely you haven't had time to make any friends down here yet.'

You'd be surprised. I meet her gaze, fight to hold it without blushing. 'I've made a few.'

'Vinnie said you were a social butterfly, that you liked going out a lot. I've never understood that. I like friendships to be meaningful. Anyway, I'm sure your friend will understand that you can't make it. This is more important, isn't it? We've got a lot to talk about.'

I feel myself fall inside, just a little. It's not a big deal, Rick won't mind. But I do. I want to see him, to take my mind off everything and enjoy myself, if only for a short while. Spending time with this woman, having her interrogate me, that's the opposite of what I want to do. It sounds like torture.

'I don't have any food in,' I tell her.

'We can order a takeaway. My treat.'

There's no arguing with her. I nod, drink my coffee even though it's scalding and too strong. She nods too, the gesture of someone who already knew they'd get their own way, right from the start.

So this is Vinnie's famous, precious mother, I think, taking her in, every detail. I loathe her already. It surprises me a lot less than it should do.

CHAPTER SIXTEEN

The darkening sky brings more rain, then a gale that roars around the building, making the lounge windows shudder in their frames. Vivienne has already made herself at home. She managed to make herself at home almost from the moment she arrived, striding around the house like it was her own, putting things away in drawers, tidying without checking first to see where they should go.

She accepts the glass of wine that I pass her without thanks, then sprawls on the sofa. Her feet are propped up on the armrest. No socks. She's even changed into pyjama trousers, a blue silken pair with a pink ribbon at the waist. I spied the contents of her suitcase earlier, spread out on the bed in one of the spare rooms upstairs. There were a lot of clothes, too many for an overnight visit. She's planning to extend this visit and I don't know why. It's worrying.

I sit down in the armchair and check my phone. Rick's response earlier was understanding, but cold too. He wanted an explanation, but I didn't want to get into it. It wouldn't look good, telling him my partner's mother has come to visit. It implies I'm close to her, that Vinnie and I are close too. I don't want to put that idea in his head, because it couldn't be further from the truth.

'You're always looking at that thing,' Vivienne says. Her tone is light, but the accusation is clear enough.

I put the phone down instinctively, then wish I hadn't. 'I'm texting a friend.'

'So many friends to text! Though I suppose you don't have much else to do, given you aren't working anymore.'

'I'll start looking for a job soon.'

'In Cornwall? Vinnie and you are both living in a fantasy world. You won't find any marketing jobs down here.'

'It's the South-West, not the middle of the wilderness. There are jobs. My friend's a website designer.'

She sniffs, watching me over the rim of her wine glass. 'Does Vinnie know you've got *friends*?'

I hate the way she says it. Also, it's obvious Vinnie's been talking about me. None of it complimentary either, it's written all over her face. Heidi the social butterfly. Heidi the woman who can't be trusted. I don't even want to think what else he's said.

I lean forward. 'Why didn't Vinnie come down with you?'

'You know why not, dear.'

'No, I don't. This is his house as much as mine. He's my boyfriend. He left without saying goodbye, and now he's sent his mother down to do his dirty work for him.'

She puts her glass down, holds her hands up in mock surrender. 'Goodness, I've touched a nerve, haven't I?'

'This is insane. Vivienne, you turned up here without telling me you were—'

'I tried calling. The signal is so bad here, you can't blame me for that. Who's Rick, by the way?'

I ignore her question. It's easier. 'You could have tried a payphone. You could have asked if it was okay to come down before you even left. Vinnie could have called me. You could have–'

'Vinnie didn't want me to come. There, I admit it. I probably shouldn't have gone against his wishes. But he's being so secretive. Something's wrong; I feel it instinctively as a mother. It's not just Noelle's death, though that's taken its toll on him. It's something else. And I think you must have some answers, Heidi.'

More questions. More suspicion. I knew Noelle's body turning up would bring this to my door. I just didn't expect my interrogator to be Vinnie's mother. I read her face carefully. She's good, I'll give her that. Well versed in the art of making her decisions sound reasonable, of making the other person feel uncertain in the process. I need to play this carefully.

'I don't have answers,' I tell her. 'I don't even feel like I know him anymore. He frightens me.'

'That's a peculiar thing to say.'

'He was violent with me.'

'I don't believe it. Vinnie wouldn't hurt a fly, he's a gentle soul.'

We glare at each other. My phone vibrates in my lap and Rick's name flashes up on the screen. I could be at his house now, relaxing on his sofa and sharing a bottle of wine. Kissing again. Instead, I'm here with this woman, with no way to escape and no idea when she'll be leaving again. She glances over and I quickly flip the phone screen-down.

'Vinnie's violent and a coward,' I say slowly.

'A coward?'

'If he had any sort of courage, he'd be here now, sorting things out.'

'I told him that. I said, even if the relationship is over, he needs to talk to you. But he just shakes his head, tells me it's too complicated. He looks scared, and that scares me.'

'So, he wants the relationship to be over? Did he say that?'

Her expression shifts. Shrewd, scheming. 'I'm not sure. Things are bad between the two of you, aren't they? Any fool could see that.'

She imagines I care, which is stupid of her. All I want to know is what'll happen with this place. It's about money and moving on now, nothing else. She smiles at me, a smug twist of the lips. I sit and take her in. The flawless, adored Vivienne, finally here in person. It's enough to turn anyone's stomach.

She sits up suddenly, flipping her feet down to the floor. 'Shall we order this takeaway, then? I presume it'll take ages to arrive, out here in the middle of nowhere.'

'There's a little Chinese restaurant in the village; that probably does takeaway.'

'That won't do. Chinese food doesn't agree with me, nor anything too heavy like pizza.'

'The Fisherman's Rest might do food we can pick up. I'll ask, shall I?'

'A pub? God, no. I want something a little more refined. My stomach can't cope with anything stodgy and pubs just serve everything with chips, don't they?'

I pick up my phone again, slide Rick's message to one side and open the internet browser.

Vivienne shakes her head. 'There you are, on your phone again.'

'I'm looking for other takeaway options.'

'Perhaps you could cook instead. Demonstrate your culinary skills.'

I detest her and can't hide it either. I want to haul her to her feet, shove her to the doorway, send her packing. I want to throw my wine over her, tell her what I really think of her, until she leaves of her own choice. Instead, I stand and trudge to the kitchen area. I haven't got any food in, apart from bread, cheese and a few other basics. She'll have to put up with it, though. It's her fault, all of this is.

***

The rest of the evening is a tennis-match of words. Barbed comments, veiled references, with Vivienne always pulling back just before being openly accusatory. My rough attempt at a cheese omelette doesn't impress her. Instead, she subjects me to a string of unwanted tips on how to get the eggs fluffy, the texture softer, the cheese more evenly spread. The rain carries on hammering against the windows. This is a war, an onslaught that I'm underprepared for. I keep looking at my watch, wondering when I can reasonably tell her I'm going to bed. It's still only quarter to nine.

My phone rings. It's Rick, again. I put it to one side, aware of her attempt to scan the screen again before I flip it over.

'I should call Vinnie, let him know what's going on,' she says, after a time. 'Though I think he's out tonight.'

'He's not that depressed, then.'

'Depressed people have social lives too, Heidi. Some sympathy wouldn't go amiss. It seems that you've just forgotten all about him.'

'I tried calling loads of times since he left, I told you that earlier. Who's he out with?'

There's that crafty look again. 'I shouldn't say, it's none of my business.'

'A woman, then.'

'Oh dear, I don't know how to respond to that question.'

'It wasn't a question. I can read it all over your face.'

'He's hurting, Heidi. Noelle meant the world to him. I was so shocked when they split up, and when she stopped returning my calls. She and I used to have the loveliest chats.' She pauses, pulls out a tissue from her sleeve and dabs at her eyes with it. The theatrics are unbearable.

'Noelle didn't return your calls because she was dead,' I snap. 'And if she meant so much to Vinnie, why did he dump her to be with me?'

'That's a callous tone to take.'

'Why are you here, Vivienne?' I push my plate away, fold my arms. 'I want an honest answer. It's not to get to know me better, because you haven't asked me anything about myself since you arrived. It's not to repair things between myself and Vinnie, because you know we're going to split up and you look pleased about it too. So, what is it? Why are you sitting in my house right now, eating my food and drinking my wine?'

She sits back, unable to hide her shock.

Good. It's about time she remembered herself. She doesn't own this place, I do. 'Well?' I press.

She reaches for the wine glass, thinks about it, then pulls her hand away again. 'Fine,' she says eventually. 'What do you know about Noelle's death?'

'What?'

'You told me to be honest. I want to know what really happened.'

'How should I know?'

'I don't know, Heidi. You tell me.'

'You're asking the wrong person.'

'Am I?' She licks her lips. 'Vinnie and Noelle were together for a long time. Then all of a sudden, she's gone. Out of the picture. Dead, though I didn't know it at the time. And there you are, like a magician's assistant, appearing out of nowhere and suddenly moving in with him. Now, do you want to tell me more about it?'

My muscles clench, up and down my body. Adrenalin. I can't believe she's asking me this.

'Vinnie seduced me,' I tell her, fighting to keep my voice even. 'In the office. Before he split up from Noelle. There you go. There's your grubby little truth.'

'Vinnie seducing you? Are you sure it wasn't the other way around?'

'I made him happy. Happier than Noelle did.'

'He hasn't sounded happy for the last few months. Not since he got together with you. Tortured, more like.'

'Excuse me?'

'Poor Noelle. She was such a lovely girl.'

'She was boring. There was nothing to her. I should know, she latched onto me like a limpet. She was desperate to spend time with someone who actually had a life.'

'The last message she sent me was very worrying. I've still got it, you know.'

'What message?' I don't like her expression. It's fox-like, conniving. This is a trap. Or is it? I've drunk too much. My thoughts are muddled.

Vivienne nods. 'She and Vinnie went away for the weekend to Kent, during that heatwave. Before that, she used to send me little messages all the time. But the message she sent me from Margate was different. It revealed a lot.'

My mouth's gone dry. I drink some wine, which doesn't help. 'Go on. Enlighten me.'

'You look angry, Heidi. That's a strange reaction to an innocent comment.'

'I don't feel very well. I'm tired. It's been a long, hard week.'

She studies me hard, reads something in my face and nods slightly. Whatever she thinks she knows, she doesn't. 'Let's leave it for now,' she says eventually. 'All I'll say is that sometimes, it's better to let the truth come out. Wouldn't you say?'

'I haven't told you any lies.'

'My son's frightened. That's enough to frighten me.'

'Vinnie isn't frightened.'

'With the greatest of respect,' she says, resting her elbows on the table, raising her chin, 'you don't know him like I do. I rather suspect you hardly know him at all, actually. And for the record, you're probably not the first girl at work that caught his eye.'

Bitch. He might be many things, but he's not like that. I was special to him, even if I'm not anymore. She can't handle the truth of it.

I stand, then shove the chair back under the table. 'I need to go to bed.'

'It's still early.'

'I've got a headache and—'

My words are sliced to silence by a loud crack from the other side of the room. Both of us startle, heads swinging in unison to the source of the noise.

'What on earth was that?' Vivienne asks, pushing her chair backwards across the floorboards. 'It sounded like something being thrown at the window.'

'It better not have broken the glass.' I turn, stare at the large windows. 'It's blowing a gale out there, maybe it was a branch.'

We move towards the patio windows, stepping in time until I take the lead. It's my house. Whatever this is, it'll be my problem, not hers. Together, we study the glass, then squint through to the darkness beyond. There's no sign that the window's damaged, though the noise was loud enough to suggest otherwise. I instinctively study the patch of ground below, where I'd noticed the trodden down grass before. I can't see much in this light.

'I can't see anything to worry about,' Vivienne says, close to my shoulder. 'You'd best check outside though. Better to be safe than sorry.'

I can't imagine what else it could be, but then, she might have a point. I think of the pile of broken wood by the tunnel trapdoor. The wind sounds strong enough to lift some of that up and send it flying into the house. With a sigh, I make my way to the utility room and pull on my jacket and boots.

'Be careful.' Vivienne leans by the side of the back door, smirk in place. 'It's wild out there, you don't want to be knocked unconscious by flying debris.'

So why did you suggest I went out there? I want to snap back. Instead, I pull the back door open, flinching at the force of the wind, the wet slap of rain against my face.

'Do shut the door,' she says. 'You're letting all the cold in.'

'Don't tell me what to do. Besides, I haven't got a torch to hand; I need the light from the house to see by.' Without waiting for an answer, I step out. My feet sink through sodden grass, to soil that sponges underneath every step. My hair flies around me, before whipping wetly against my forehead. I push it aside, turn my attention to the woodpile. It's undisturbed, none of the broken planks look like they're likely to shift any time soon.

The entrance to the tunnel looks different though. The wrong shape, not what I was expecting. The shadows pull the dimensions outward, make the hole look larger than it is. Then I realise. I'm looking at a hole, not a trapdoor. The trapdoor's open.

The trapdoor's open.

I let the fact of it sink in. It doesn't make sense. It can't be open. No amount of wind would be strong enough to lift that trapdoor. Or would it?

My hand flares with pain, the bandage sagging under the moisture. It *can't be open.* In a few steps, I'm beside it, skirting around the periphery, reluctant to get too close. I don't want to look down there, I'm afraid of what I'll see.

Eyes, staring back up at me. A hand with claws, waiting to grab.

Two more steps. I reach down, seize the trapdoor with both

hands and throw it shut again. The resulting bang dwarfs all sound for a moment, then gives way to the roar of the storm again. But it's shut now, that's the main thing. Not totally, there's still a gap. In fact, it looks bigger than before, large enough a space for an entire arm to squeeze through.

The water's warped the wood, that's all it is. This can be explained away.

'Well?' Vivienne's shout cuts through my distracted thoughts. 'What's going on?'

I hurry back to the house, step inside and slam the door behind me. She winces as I shake myself off, peeling my coat off and hanging it back up.

'Nothing to worry about,' I tell her.

'Sounded like you were throwing some wood around.'

'Just the wood from the shed that Vinnie pulled down. That's all.'

She doesn't look convinced, but nods nonetheless. 'It's horrendous here, isn't it?' she says, as we wander back through to the lounge.

'Yes.' The irony doesn't escape me, that this is the one thing we're able to agree on.

CHAPTER SEVENTEEN

I wake through the night, listening to the panes rattling, the vague roar of the sea somewhere out there in the darkness. The heat of the wound, burning deep in my palm, is almost unbearable. The infection's become a living thing, seeping slowly up my wrist, snaking through my arm and into my heart. I should go to hospital. But I can't get there. I can't ask Rick to take me. And there's no way I'm asking Vivienne for a lift.

What little sleep I have is marked by bad dreams. Hands reaching for me with nails sharp as talons. A gaping hole in the ground, widening by the second. Seaweed all over me, holding me down and I can't get Vinnie's attention because my tongue's been ripped out and the rising scream is lodged in my throat. At just after six o'clock, I give in and get up. I can't bear lying there anymore, and besides, my bandage needs changing again. The blood has wept through the material, leaving a sticky, brownish-green stain. Brownish-green isn't good. I don't want to think too hard about what it means.

Vivienne emerges from the spare room at just past ten, with too much noise and muttering. She waltzes into the kitchen, helps herself to coffee and toast without asking, then marches off to the shower.

'I'm not a morning person,' she states over her shoulder, before sweeping back up the stairs.

'Go back to bed then, or better still, do your morning somewhere else,' I murmur once she's left. It's petty, but it helps.

I call Rick, wait until it rings through to his answerphone, then hang up. *Hope you're okay*, I text quickly instead. *I'm having a nightmare here. I'll tell you about it as soon as I can.*

No reply, not even after ten minutes. He's probably busy, doing something around his farm or finishing off a website for a client. The floorboards creak overhead. It's enough to make me put my phone away. A lecture from Vivienne about being *unable to take my eyes off that thing* would just about finish me off.

She saunters into the living room just after eleven, decked out in knitted jumper and corduroy trousers, thin scarf trailed artfully around her neck. She's annoyingly fresh, well rested by the looks of it. I don't want her getting too comfortable, she won't be staying long.

'I've confessed to Vinnie that I'm here,' she announces, pulling out a chair at the dining table. 'He wasn't best pleased.'

'Lovely, thanks for the update.'

'Don't be rude, dear. He's worried at me being here, thinks you'll upset me. You and he really should talk. Then I wouldn't have to intervene.'

'No-one asked you to intervene.'

'You could call him, you know.'

'He's the one who left. It doesn't take much for the selfish sod to pick up the phone, does it?'

'Remember that's my son you're talking about. He's very vulnerable at the moment.'

'To be honest, I don't care.'

Her eyes widen. 'That's harsh.'

'Is it? He walked out without telling me where he was going. Left me here on my own without a car. He's going out with other women. Do you honestly think he deserves my kindness?'

That's got her. She fiddles with the edges of her scarf, winding them around and around her finger. 'I came down here with the best possible intentions,' she says eventually. 'To help my poor son and to honour poor Noelle's memory, to get to the truth and—'

'You came here to antagonise me.'

'I'm not antagonising you.'

'Yes you are.'

'No, I'm not. Vinnie said you and Noelle spent a lot of time together.'

'What's that got to do with anything? Besides, it's not true.'

'Miranda said so too.'

'Why are you even speaking to Miranda? She's nothing to do with you!'

'Miranda is a friend of Vinnie's.'

I frown. That's news to me. They only ever spent time together when I was there too. Or that's what I thought.

'I think you should leave.' I sit up straighter, meet her eye. 'You shouldn't have come down in the first place.'

She gapes. It should be more satisfying than it is. But I'm tired. Tired of her, of Vinnie, of everything with Noelle. I just want her gone.

'That's very hurtful,' she tells me. 'I don't know quite what to say.'

'You don't need to say anything. Just go, please.'

'I understand what Vinnie means now. About you being manipulative and cold.'

'He said that, did he?'

'He did. Honestly, I feel sorry for you.'

I stand. I can't stay seated anymore, not with my heart thumping like this. 'You should feel sorry for me,' I tell her. 'And you should ask your son what he's capable of, Vivienne. What he's done. You might get a nasty shock when you find out the truth.'

'My son is a good man. I know that for a fact. Look, I'll leave now if that's what you want.'

'Yes. You shouldn't be here in the first place. Vinnie and I are breaking up. And I need to be alone.'

'I suppose some people are better alone.' She stands too, pushes the chair quietly back in place. 'I'll go and pack my bags. Don't worry about making me anything for lunch, I'll get something at the services.'

I push back a snort. She's had enough from me as it is. Also, the words sting. *Some people are better alone.* Yesterday, she was telling me I was a social butterfly. Which is she accusing me of?

Her departure from the room brings me back to the moment. I feel a stab of anxiety. She'll report this back to Vinnie. He'll be angry. He adores his mother, won't take kindly to anyone hurting her precious feelings.

And she'll tell Miranda too, a quieter voice in my head adds. Miranda, who is good friends with Vinnie now. Miranda, who's been cold for the past few weeks. Who was too busy with someone else at her house the other day, when I desperately needed a friend.

Miranda and Vinnie? I stop, think about it. It's not so hard to imagine: she always liked him. Before I was seeing him, she flirted with him all the time. She's clever enough to wait until the right moment, when he's soft and dim-witted enough to let her sink her claws into him. He's fickle too, he proved it by being with me while he was still with Noelle.

And all those other women, apparently.

The pair of them together. I can't believe it. I don't want to believe it. I might be reading all of this wrong, but it feels right. In fact, it explains a lot.

I wait downstairs, unsure where to put myself until I finally hear the creak of the top stair, the noise of someone lugging something heavy down with them. Vivienne pokes her head around the door frame, spies me, then sighs.

'I'll be going, then,' she says.

'Have a safe journey back.'

'Not sure I will. The weather's still dreadful out there.'

'I'm sure you'll be all right once you reach the motorway.'

She pauses, then sighs again and retreats. I walk after her. At the very least, I suppose I can show her out properly.

'Vinnie seeing Miranda again tonight, then?' I ask casually, as I unlock the front door for her.

She turns, gives me the sharp look I already feel too familiar with, then shrugs. 'Who knows what's happening? He doesn't tell me anything anymore.'

'That makes two of us.'

'Well, I'll say goodbye, then.' She nods down at my hand. 'You might want to get that looked at. I don't know what you've done to yourself, but it looks nasty. Smells slightly too, if you don't mind my saying.'

With that, she sweeps out into the cold. I stand at the doorway, watching as she flings the boot open, throws her belongings inside, then slams it shut again. Another few seconds later and the car pulls out of the driveway, gravel spraying to either side, mirroring the clatter of the rain. Then she disappears around the corner up ahead. Gone, as though she'd never been here in the first place. Just another bad dream to contend with.

I sniff my hand. Nothing. What a parting shot. Pausing another moment or two, I make a decision. I won't stay here, not on my own, not with all of this mess to contend with. I'll get out. Go where I'm happy. Escape.

Miranda's been sleeping with Vinnie. Miranda's with Vinnie. Miranda. Vinnie. The names circle on rotation as I make my way to Rick's. It hurts, more her actions than his, because I expected no better from him. I feel angry, humiliated. But relieved too. This lets me off the hook. Whatever I do now with Rick, it's fair game. Vinnie thinks he's won, but this isn't over. Not by a long way.

I reach the farmhouse, half expecting to see Rick in the courtyard, hefting bags of feed or herding pigs. But all is quiet. Serene. It feels better already. Even my hand aches less.

The mud underfoot has become a swamp after last night's storm, coating my boots in yet more filth. Eventually I make it to the door and ring the doorbell. It takes a while, long enough for me to panic that he's gone out for the day. Then, a shadow appears through the frosted glass. He wrestles with the lock, pulls the door open with a judder, then smiles at the sight of me. A confused smile, but it's good enough to make the moment better.

'I wasn't expecting to see you,' he says, waving me inside. 'I thought you had drama at home to sort out?'

I wipe my boots on the doormat. 'You have no idea.'

'Want to tell me about it?'

'Haven't you got work to do?'

'Nothing that can't wait.' He leads me to the kitchen, pulls a stool out by the breakfast bar, pushes a packet of cookies in my direction. 'Here, eat those. It's good to have sustenance while having deep and meaningful chats.'

'Not sure it's that deep and meaningful. Just frustrating and irritating.' Quickly, I outline the details; the unexpected visit, the uncomfortable questions, the things I found out about Vinnie and Miranda. Rick raises an eyebrow at the last piece of information, shaking his head.

'What a shit,' he declares, pulling another cookie out of the packet.

'Which one of them?'

'Both, by the sounds of it. Your friend and your boyfriend. Wow.'

'I know. I'm done with the pair of them. And I'll hopefully never have to spend time with Vinnie's revolting mother ever again.'

He chuckles. 'Amen to that. I've never been in a relationship long enough to get around to meeting the potential mother-in-law. Stories like yours put me off even more.'

'No long-term relationship ever?'

'Not as yet.' He pauses, fiddling with the biscuit packet, then smiles. 'I'm glad you came over. I missed you last night.'

'Did you?'

'Yeah, weird isn't it? We've only known each other a short time, but I like having you around. You're different to other women around here. Much more fun, for starters.'

There's the electricity again, the crackle of something more between us. I stroke his hand, making sure to keep my damaged one as out of sight as possible. In response, he presses his palm against my face, then kisses me gently.

'Too much?' he asks.

I shake my head. 'Not enough.'

We kiss again, more urgently this time. The pressure and warmth of his lips on mine causes something to crumble inside me. A damn of reservation, worry, fear of the past; it all breaks inside me. My fingers delve into his hair, his do the same through mine. We've become a machine of stroking, kissing, panting. I love how much he likes me.

'Tell me if I'm moving too fast,' he whispers.

'You're not,' I reply. His hand slides down, against my hip then under my jumper. Upwards. Deft, firm, confident. Mouth on my neck, a path across to my collarbone. I lift his head and kiss him again.

He pulls away, licks his lips. 'Can I suggest we take this somewhere more comfortable?'

The bedroom. We both know where this is going, we've passed the point of being coy. I can't help but compare this to the first time I was with Vinnie. They're so different, but I prefer it this way. I only wish I'd figured out what a waste of time Vinnie was right from the start.

I stand, pulling him up with me. 'You've got cookie crumbs on your sweater,' I tell him, brushing him off.

'You must think I'm a pig.'

'I like a man with a good appetite. Besides, that jumper's coming off soon enough, isn't it?'

He wraps me in his arms, presses me against his chest. He's lean, hard, there's something of the whippet to him. I lean in further and feel him against me, feel the effect I'm having on him. It's a turn on. I need this.

Screw you, Vinnie, I think. *And you, Miranda. And Vivienne, and perfect Noelle. Screw you all.*

'Lead the way,' I say aloud, before kissing him again.

I don't feel bad at all. Not with my head tucked against Rick's collarbone, my hand on his chest. Not while he strips my clothes off with more enthusiasm than any other man I'd been with before, nor when he's kissing me all over, pushing me down on the bed, pushing my legs apart, pinning my arms above my head. Not once. Presumably Vinnie's already been cheating on me, several times over with my so-called friend. So we can call this breaking even.

Rick lasts a while. Long enough for us both to have fun. Afterwards, he rolls off, places an arm around my shoulder and brings me closer. It's affectionate, sweet. A good way to finish up.

'What are you thinking about?' he asks after a time, stroking my hair.

'I'm thinking that this was a nice way to spend the day.'

'It beats working.'

'I'm glad I'm a better alternative to work.'

'You are, though doing this doesn't pay the bills.'

'I hadn't realised it was that sort of arrangement, Rick.'

He laughs. 'If you wanted to pay me, I'd be very happy to offer my services every day, from nine to five. I can also do weekends if you need it.'

I hit him playfully. 'I think, judging by how much you enjoyed it, you should be giving me money.'

'Who said money? I'm talking kisses, sexual favours, you name it.'

'You're weird, you know that, don't you?'

He leans over and kisses me again. I like the feel of him on top of me; the taut narrowness of his waist, the sprinkling of dark hair on his chest, trailing to a line down his belly. I ease my legs around him, using them to manoeuvre him closer.

'I'm glad you moved here,' he whispers, nibbling at my ear. 'Welcome to our little boring village, Heidi.'

'Hey, it's not all boring. You've got a nixie.'

'And your haunted smuggler's tunnel, let's not forget that.'

'Don't you start. I've had enough of the tall tales from Bea.'

He pauses, pulls back. 'When were you speaking to her?'

'The other day, when I needed something from the shop.'

'What did she say?'

'Why does it matter? Is me speaking to her a problem?'

'No.' He places a hand gently at my throat, pulls my head upwards and kisses me deeply. 'It's not a problem at all. Forget I said anything.'

'She seems fond of you.'

He grunts, then grinds his pelvis against mine. It feels good, better than good. I don't want it to stop. After a while, I feel him harden against my thigh and I spread my legs wider.

'Don't talk about Bea now,' he says, voice muffled against my neck. 'We've got better things to focus on.'

I gasp as he enters me. 'Agreed,' I reply breathlessly, moving in time with him. It's so unlike Vinnie's pounding, animalistic, powerful, like an axe chopping a tree. This is more like a dance, a pulse of fluid movement.

This second time is slower, more intense. It means more than it ever had with Vinnie. I wish I'd known that before, that everything I did, every sacrifice I made for that man, it was all for nothing. Even now I'm not safe, thanks to the choices I made to be with him. With Rick, it's all so effortless. He came to me. I didn't have to fight to get him, there was no other woman on the scene to make things difficult. Just him and me, like this.

He groans then nuzzles his head into the back of my neck. I wrap my arms backward, holding him for a moment or two.

'Sorry,' he says, after a while. 'I let myself get carried away.'

'There's always the next time,' I tell him.

'I'm glad you're up for a next time.'

'And the rest.'

He hugs me for a while, then sits up. 'I'll make us some lunch. What do you want?'

'Sandwich?'

'I was going to wow you with my culinary skills. I can hardly show off with a sandwich, can I?'

'Oh, I don't know. See it as a challenge.'

He grins, climbs out of bed and pulls his pants on quickly. 'Right you are. By the way, I need to tell you about something later.'

I reach over to the bedside table for my bra. 'That sounds worrying. What?'

'Nothing like that. I do some web development work for the museum in Tannistock. Had an interesting conversation with one of their curators on the phone this morning about your smuggler's tunnel. It's got a fascinating history; it goes way further back than I knew. She invited us to go and visit her sometime. She's keen to hear more about what it's like.'

'Really? It's historic enough for a museum to know about it?'

'Hey, you know what small museums are like. Anything vaguely resembling good local history and they seize upon it with both hands. Anyway, it might be fun if you fancy it sometime.'

'Sounds great.' I yank on my jumper, smile as he sits beside me and hugs me.

'How's your hand doing?' he asks, taking it gently in his own. 'I noticed you winced when I grabbed it earlier. Is it sore?'

'A bit.'

'You should tell me if it gets worse. Infection's a devil to clear up once it takes hold. It can make you really ill if you're not careful.'

I think of the red patch on my palm extending steadily outwards, the milk-curdle pus seeping out of it. I don't want to share this with him though, don't want him to see me in that light, as something diseased and ugly. 'It's fine,' I tell him. 'Nothing to worry about.'

'All right. I believe you. You've got a trustworthy face.'

I smile sweetly and we both stand, gathering the rest of our clothes from the rug, the floorboards, the end of the bed. I like being thought of as trustworthy.

Even if it's not true. My mother's voice, not my own, ringing from somewhere in the past. It's wrong, or it is at this moment. Rick can trust me, because he deserves trustworthy behaviour. It's that simple. He earned it.

And Dad didn't? What did Dad do to deserve what you did to him, Heidi?

I silence the voice, because it's twisting the truth and it doesn't belong to me, even though it's in my head. I've earned this. I deserve some happiness after months of misery with a man that doesn't care nearly as much about me as he said he did.

CHAPTER EIGHTEEN

My phone starts ringing just after we finish lunch. First, just a couple of rings followed by silence. Then a call that I manage to answer, with only crackling down the other end. Thirdly, a garbled buzz, like someone talking underwater, a long way away.

Rick looks at me with concern as I get up from the sofa and start pacing around the room.

'Who is it?' he asks, just as the phone starts to ring again.

I stop by the living room window, stare at the farmyard beyond without really seeing it. 'Someone who really wants to talk to me,' I say, with a forced laugh. 'Or else, someone who's hellbent on driving me mad with their constant calling.'

'Not Vinnie?'

'No. I think it's his mum again. This is what it was like when she was trying to call before.'

'I thought she'd gone back home, never to return again?'

'So did I.' I study the screen of my phone, as though that'll somehow have the answers. 'Maybe it's not her. Maybe it's another crank caller.'

'Or one of your many admirers.' He sidles up behind me,

wrapping his arms around my waist. 'Have I got competition? Do I need to fight to prove my manliness?'

'I have to beat them off with a stick, you know. But what about your adoring females? Apart from Bea, of course.'

'What do you mean by that?'

'Nothing much, only that she's obsessed with you.'

He pulls away. 'What has she said?' There's a brittleness to his voice that wasn't there before.

'She hasn't said anything,' I say carefully, turning to him. 'But it's clear she thinks you belong to her. She's prickly with me; she'll say anything to get me out of the picture.'

'Did you tell her about us?'

'No, but she must have guessed. You spent the whole evening with me in The Fisherman's Rest the other night.'

'It's best if you don't say anything to her.' He releases me, sticks his hands in his pockets.

'Why?'

'It's complicated.'

'Tell me.'

'We can't get into it now.' He flinches as my phone rings again. 'Can you do something about that? It will drive us both mad.'

He wants me to stop asking questions. I bite my lip, study his face for answers but he's giving nothing away. Perhaps they were romantically involved. In fact, judging by the flush on his cheeks, that's the only conclusion to draw. I want to ask. I don't dare. I can't be that woman, the clingy needy creature. Those women never win.

'I've got to get back to work,' he says, waving vaguely towards the window. 'Those barns won't clean themselves out.'

'Do you need help?'

'It's okay. Look, why don't we meet up later? Go and visit that museum together and talk to Suzanne?'

'Suzanne?'

'The woman I was telling you about, who knows all about your smuggler's tunnel. It should be an interesting conversation; I'm happy to drive. Let's get a coffee and cake while we're out too, my treat. How does that sound?'

I soften, because it sounds good. It sounds like he's putting the effort in, fighting hard not to let the mention of Bea come between us. Those are the actions of a man who wants to move on from the past. I'm happy to go along with that.

I nod. 'I'll go home then, shall I?'

'You're welcome to stay here, but–'

'I can tell when I'm not wanted. You got your bit of action, now you're done with me, right?' I punch his arm to show I'm joking. 'It's fine. I've got things to do anyway.'

'Give me a call later, okay?'

'You call me. Make a girl feel wanted, please.'

He laughs. 'Right you are. Honestly, if I'd have known you were this high maintenance, I never would have shagged you.' He pulls me close, kisses me deeply, slips his hand over my waist, my torso, brushing the underside of my breast with the most teasing of touches.

'If I'd have known you were such a sleaze, I never would have shagged you either,' I whisper. 'You farmers, you're all the same.'

He presses a finger to my lips, then lowers me to the sofa. I can tell where this is going; now that we've started this, we can't get enough of each other. *He wants me so badly*, I think, as he tugs my trousers off again, throwing them over his shoulder. It's intoxicating.

Later, I leave his place and make my way home, through muck, through drizzle, through cold. But none of that matters anymore; none of it touches me. I'm happy, buoyant, back to *me* again. I don't need Miranda by my side to have a good time. I don't need the perfect family background, the ideal career, the wonderful home. I've got this; the good feelings, the confidence that I'm wanted. That's enough.

I spot the incongruous splash of red as soon as the house comes into sight. A car, sitting there on the driveway. A car I've seen before and hoped I wouldn't see again. Vivienne's back.

My hands clench into fists. It hurts. No bad thing, it sharpens me up in a heartbeat. There's no reason for her to have come back; I made my feelings clear when she left. She's got a nerve. More than a nerve, she's taking liberties. She's messing with the wrong woman.

The car door opens as I approach and Vivienne swings out of the driver's seat, hair dishevelled, expression halfway between harassed and furious.

'Where have you been?' she barks, as I open the side gate and walk down the path. 'I've been trying to call you.'

'I've been out.' I pull my keys out of my pocket, slot them into the front door. 'Why are you here?'

'What a way to greet me. Charming, especially after all the trouble I've had.'

'What trouble?'

'The road's blocked with a fallen tree, about an hour along, as soon as I took the turning for the A-road. Bloody thing must have come down in the storm. I couldn't see another route to take on my satnav.'

'There's another way out through the village. It's a long detour but it'll get you to the same place eventually. You can go that way.'

'I'm not going now, I'm exhausted. It'll be dark soon and I hate driving in the dark.'

I don't believe this. I look at her, trying to summon some compassion and managing only loathing.

'What about the pub in the village? They'll have an available room for the night, I'm sure.'

'You need lessons in hospitality. Surely you could put me up for another night or two?'

'A night or two?' I open the door and start to laugh. 'Why *or two*? You can leave the other way, tomorrow morning.'

'Can I stay tonight, then?'

I look at her, note her defeated expression, the air of desperation too. That helps, a bit. 'Come inside if you have to,' I say slowly, 'and we'll talk about it.'

She scurries to the boot, pulls all her bags out again, then throws one at me. I catch it with my wounded hand and gasp, it's either that or let it slam into my body. She doesn't notice. I haven't had such an urge to slap someone in a long time.

'I thought about everything while I was driving away,' she tells me, as we both enter the house. 'I'm disappointed about how things worked out earlier. We should be able to talk to each other as civilised adults. Vinnie would want us to.'

'Vinnie wouldn't care. We're splitting up.'

'He hasn't categorically said that to me.'

'I've just said it now. I've had enough of this.'

'But you've bought a house together. Let's not forget, it's technically my money.'

I stop in the hallway. Turn slowly to look at her. 'Your money? What do you mean?'

'Vinnie's impulsive with spending, you must have noticed. He loves to spoil people. It's a lovely trait, but not terribly useful when saving for major purchases like property.'

'You paid for half the deposit?'

'Over half, actually. He told me you put in ten thousand and he paid twenty. So the house is two-thirds mine, I suppose.'

She laughs but her eyes remain cold, watchful. I want to punch something, anything. Her preferably, but a wall would do. Vinnie lied to me, yet again. He said it was his money, his savings. Or he let me believe that, anyway. Now I learn that all he did was run to his mother. I should have known. Once a mummy's boy, always a mummy's boy.

Is that why you're really back here? I feel like asking. *To check out your investment? See how soon you can seize it for your own?*

She studies my face, reads what she needs to see there, then nods slightly. 'Shall we start again?' she says, putting a hand on my shoulder. 'Be civil and talk this through properly? As you're determined to split up with my son, we'll need to discuss the matter of this house. Other things too. Important things.'

The threat is unmistakable. *Important.* Important as in revealing, as in damaging. There are things I want to say, but I hold them in. If I lose my cool, I give her the upper hand. No chance.

She owns over half. Does that mean she could force me to sell at any point? I didn't look at the terms of the mortgage, I trusted Vinnie to go through the details. This house might be horrible, but it's all I've got right now. I haven't got anywhere else to go, and if I left, I'd be leaving Rick too.

'You look pale,' Vivienne says lightly. 'Are you all right?'

'I need some air, that's all.'

'Let's go for a stroll down to the beach. We can talk then; maybe you'll be more communicative outside this house. It does funny things to you, doesn't it? Strange place.'

'It's freezing out.'

'Come now, Vinnie mentioned you grew up by the sea.

You're used to this. We can discuss what will happen in the future. And carry on our conversation about Noelle too.'

'Noelle?'

'Yes. We were interrupted last night with that disturbance from outside. But the truth needs to come out, Heidi, don't you agree? Something strange has gone on, something I sense a mother should know. I can't get anything from Vinnie these days, but perhaps you'll be more reasonable.'

'For Christ's sake, Vivienne, what do you want from me?'

'It's not a matter of wanting, dear. It's a need. Time to start behaving like adults. Owning up to whatever's happened.'

She knows, I think, while simultaneously thinking she can't know. There's no way. She only thinks she knows, and I'll make sure to set her right.

My mind slips back to earlier in the day. Rick's breath on my neck, his body on mine. How I've gone from that to this, in such a short space of time, is a mystery. I can't process the difference, it's an ice bath after a hot shower. My hand burns with sudden, vicious energy. I look down, half-convinced I'll see burn-marks on the bandage. The first flickers of orange flame leaping upwards, tonguing a route outwards.

'You'll catch your death of cold out there,' I tell her, slumping on the stool at the breakfast bar.

She winks, a mocking gesture. 'Lucky I've got a thick coat with me, isn't it? No amount of icy weather can get through it.'

I don't bother arguing. I'm learning fast that what Vivienne wants, Vivienne gets.

'We may as well head out now,' she says, pausing in the hallway. 'Shall we?'

My stomach rolls. I feel sick. I think of the steep path down to the cove. I remember us, Vinnie and I, staggering down there in our wetsuits, not so long ago. Things were bad then, I thought as bad as they could get. I guess I was wrong. Badly wrong.

Beaches. The sea. As we make our way along the narrow path that winds down to the cove, I remember that other beach, that other time. How the undercurrent pulled the boat as Vinnie tried to bring it to the cove. How Noelle laughed and sketched him quickly. A masterpiece in two minutes. I wanted to rip it from the book. I wanted to make it mine.

'This path is rather steep,' Vivienne says, disturbing the quiet.

'You wanted to do this,' I remind her. Her back, clad in a thick coat, is broad, masculine. Stronger than she looks, maybe. I glance to my side, down to the sheer drop. It'd kill a person if they fell from this height. The sea is lethal in so many ways.

So lethal. Even in the sun. Even when everyone's laughing. Noelle asked me, 'Are you happy?' after we pulled the boat up the beach and the two of us settled on the sand. 'Are you happy, Heidi? Do you have everything you want in life?'

I told her yes.

She smiled and wrote something down. 'Lucky you,' she said. 'To have the confidence to take what you want. I don't know what I want half the time.'

Then Vinnie's shadow fell on both of us. 'There's a cave at the back,' he said. 'Dark in there. Much colder.'

'Do you think there's anything hidden in there?' Noelle shielded her eyes from the sun. 'I love the idea of things being hidden, waiting for the right person to come and find them.'

Vinnie shrugged and held a hand out to her. 'Let's go for a swim.'

'Let me look in the cave first,' she said. 'I want to leave my mark.'

'What, carve your initials in the stone?'

She gave me a look. 'Something like that.'

Vinnie pulled her to her feet. 'Then a swim, right?' He waited until she was by the cave's entrance, then whispered to me, 'She's not a good swimmer.'

He said it meaningfully. I know he did. And I nodded in response.

Vivienne stops and I nearly collide with her. It wrenches me out of the past. No bad thing.

'What I don't understand,' she shouts above the sea-wind, 'is how, if you were such good friends with Noelle, you didn't do more to find out what happened to her.'

Here it is, the final judgement, everything laid out in the open. Vivienne's old testament-prophet righteousness, hair a halo of steel-wire around her head, brow furrowed, face purple with cold. This is what this has all been building to, from the moment she arrived at my house.

Her house too, I remember. Her financial investment gives her power over me. I hate that.

'How do you know I didn't try to find out?' I reply.

'Vinnie told me neither of you wanted to. He refused to tell me anything more. It doesn't add up. Why wouldn't you check she was all right, after you'd broken her heart?'

'Vinnie broke her, not me.'

'What was that?' she shouts.

I point forwards, then behind me. 'Either get to the beach or let's go back. We're not having a conversation out here in a gale-force wind.'

'You're delaying things again. That's your tactic, isn't it, Heidi? You're skilled at slipping beneath the surface, keeping yourself hidden.'

My sigh is whisked from my lips the moment it departs. Below, the beach is barely visible. Grey waves thrash at the cliffs. The tips of jagged rocks peek every so often from the water, only to disappear again after. Keeping themselves hidden.

'This is stupid.' I turn to face her. 'There's not much point going any further, it's high tide.'

'No, let's carry on.'

She stumbles slightly as she continues. For a moment, the image is all too clear; her wrapped-up body sailing over the edge, crashing and thumping on the steep cliffside, slamming down on the piles of dark boulders that line the base.

I could go back. She couldn't stop me. But a part of me wants to continue. See how this plays out. She's right, we've circled around each other for too long now. I follow after her until we reach the bottom.

The water's already touching the edges of the path, leaving a dirty foam trail along the dark sand. It's ridiculous; all we can do is stand gingerly and stare, there's nowhere to walk, nowhere to explore. We're stranded. On our own. Not another soul in sight.

Just like the day when Dad told me he was leaving for Australia. The beach had been empty that day too and the sea wild, like this one.

'There's not much for me here, kid,' he had said without looking at me, zipping his wetsuit to the chin. 'You'll be okay, your mother too. I'll make sure of it. We'll still see each other. You can free-dive with me when you come and visit. We'll explore the Great Barrier Reef. We'll have an amazing time.'

Liar. I knew he'd never want me to visit him and he didn't. People leave. That's why you have to become a master at keeping hold of them, before they're lost for good. Or else make them regret leaving you forever.

'It's brisk, isn't it?' Vivienne announces.

'Vinnie made me swim in the sea, when we first moved in.'

'He loves an adventure.'

'He's impulsive, like a child.'

She raises an eyebrow. 'I'd call it spontaneous.'

I'd say self-centred and feckless. Dangerous traits indeed. But I keep these thoughts to myself. There's no point voicing them to a mother blinded with adoration for her son.

'So,' she continues, slipping her hands into her pockets, 'what really happened with Noelle, then?'

'What?'

'You know what I mean. What happened when she died?'

'How should I know? I wasn't there.'

One eyebrow rises. 'I don't think that's true, Heidi.'

'You've got no reason to say that.'

'Haven't I? Tell me your version of events, then.'

I take a step backwards. Vivienne's standing too close. Too large all of a sudden, too enveloping.

'Vinnie's been putting ideas in your head that aren't true,' I tell her. 'Trying to clear his own guilt. You need to ask him what happened, not me.'

'Oh, I have, and he's told me things. Worrying things. He says you're not to be trusted.'

'He's the one you shouldn't trust. He's a violent man.'

'Tell me your side of the story, then.'

I shake my head. 'Tell me what he said first.'

'He said you turned up on that weekend in Kent. On what was meant to be a romantic trip for the two of them. That you went with them on a boat trip. That you–'

'Whose version of events is that? And don't make out I forced myself on the pair of them.'

'Didn't you? You're a cuckoo, Heidi. You played the part of the good friend, the charming colleague. Then you broke them apart.'

'Is this what your visit is really about? To bully me into admitting things that aren't true?'

'You took what you wanted without a thought for anyone else. Poor Noelle.'

'Vinnie's blameless in all of this, is he?'

'He was weak and you took advantage of that. I believe Noelle's death is a result of you stealing her boyfriend. He was the love of her life. She wanted to marry him. You took that away from her and she took her life. Or worse.'

The tone is unmistakable. Threat.

'What do you mean by that?' I ask in a low voice.

'I think you know.'

'That's on Vinnie, not me.' I push her and she gasps, stepping back into the shallow water as the tide pulls towards us. 'He wanted her gone. As I said, he's dangerous. Psychopathic, perhaps.'

'That's my son you're talking about.'

I want to scream. She's not listening to me. It's driving me mad.

'You need to ask Vinnie whose idea it was to go out on a boat that day.' I emphasise each word in turn. 'Ask him why he insisted Noelle went swimming with him. Why he made her stay out there too long. Why he didn't take much time trying to find her after she went under.'

'So you were there, then. I knew it.'

'So what? You're not hearing what I'm saying, you–'

'So what? It proves you're a liar, Heidi. That you deliberately mislead people. But don't worry, I knew that anyway. Noelle texted me the night before and told me everything.'

'Told you what?'

There's a hint of a smile at her lips. Triumph. 'I'm going back now,' she tells me. 'I've got what I came for. I knew I would, in the end. I'll be calling the police as soon as possible and I hope they arrest you on the spot. You nasty piece of work.'

'What did Noelle tell you?'

'Move aside, Heidi. I won't be staying tonight now, you'll be pleased to hear. I'm sure I can find an alternative route home. Or somewhere else to stay.'

'That was your plan all along, wasn't it? You think you know the truth but you've got it all wrong. Now tell me before I get angry, what did Noelle's text say?'

'Is that meant to make me scared? Well, she had nothing nice to say about you, dearest. She painted quite the picture. The pushy slut that seduced Vinnie at work. Who pretended to be her friend. The bitch that smiled and smiled, while stabbing her in the back.'

'As if Noelle would ever have said that. Little Miss Perfect, she never had a bad word to say about anyone. Never an interesting word either.'

'Now the poison comes out.' Vivienne shakes her head. 'Did you want her dead, Heidi?'

'It was Vinnie, not me. He's the monster, your precious little boy. He held her under until she drowned, I saw him do it. I covered for him because I was terrified. Because I was an idiot and I loved him. There, are you happy with the real truth?'

I push past before she can reply. She loses her balance and steps into the sea, just as it races up to meet the path. It'd be a treat to see her land in the water and watch it soak her through. Even better, drag her back with it and claim her for its own.

Pull her downwards. Like Vinnie did to me that day. He denied grabbing my legs in the sea, but it's the sort of thing he would do. And I know who put the idea in his head in the first place.

Me. Because of what I told him about Dad. I should have kept my mouth shut.

I march up the path. Fight to keep my balance on the

slippery stones underfoot. Leave Vivienne still struggling to regain balance. I won't look back. I refuse.

Why did you do it? Dad screamed afterwards, right in my face, as soon we swam back to the safety of the beach. *I could have died, Heidi. Do you realise that?*

I was only fourteen. His lungs were bigger, he was stronger than me, he'd been free-diving for decades. It had only been a test. To see if I could hold on to him, or whether he really would swim away. Leave me alone forever.

So I grabbed him. Down on the seabed, among the darkness and silence. Around his waist, a tangle of limbs like an octopus. He thought I was hugging him to begin with. Smiled, though it was uncertain. Took my hands and prised me off gently, then started to swim away. So I clutched on to his thighs instead. I dug my flippers into the muddy sand to anchor my weight. Held on tight. He must have gasped in shock because bubbles plumed out of his mouth like little fish. I remember grinning. I couldn't stop, not even when he started shaking his head hard, slapping at me and pushing at my shoulders and my face. Not even when his mouth opened wider in a scream.

That was bad of me. I know it was bad. I just wanted to hold on to him in that moment and never let him go. He never should have wanted to leave in the first place. Leave me alone, in a wrecked old cottage in a dead-end village. With no hope of ever making anything better of myself.

I was a fool to tell people about this. Including Vinnie. Talk about giving people ideas.

I wish I hadn't bothered coming down here. There's no point to this. I'm wet and cold, had to listen to Vivienne spit accusations at me, based on a flimsy text and a few muttered comments from her son. After a minute or so, I hear pebbles being dislodged behind me. She's following, scrambling along in less than suitable footwear. She might trip and fall. She sounds hurried enough. She might reach me first, though, and pull me down with her. She could be capable of anything. No, not anything. Less than she imagines. She's all brash surface, hollow confidence, not much else; but I still feel vulnerable with her scuttling behind like a fat spider. I pick up my pace, taking care to keep as far away from the edge as possible.

'My legs are in agony,' Vivienne complains, voice drifting on the wind. 'This is dangerous. You're dangerous, Heidi.'

'No-one asked you to come down here with me,' I snap back.

She doesn't reply.

Finally, we reach the top. I'm wet through, hair slapping against my face. I turn and see that she looks no better, mascara making skull sockets of her eyes, fringe a mess of dripping frizz.

'Go through the back gate,' I tell her. 'Or follow the path round and return straight to your car, it's up to you.'

'My belongings are in your house.'

'I'll throw them out to you.'

She follows me through the little gate and slams it behind her. 'Don't you dare manhandle my things. As soon as I've got my phone from my bag I'll be calling the police. I'll suggest to Vinnie that he gives a statement too.'

'Shut up, Vivienne. I'm sick of your voice.'

She purses her lips. 'You're intolerable. I dread to think what you might be capable of. No wonder Vinnie left. He was probably fearful for his life.'

Oh, please. Vinnie's twice my height and weight, and ten times as brutish. I open my mouth to tell her so, then notice something jarring towards the side of the house. A mass of black that cuts through the grass, that shouldn't be there. It takes me a while. Perhaps I don't want to process what I'm looking at. The trapdoor to the smuggler's tunnel is open again.

No. Once, I can write off as a freak burst of wind, capable of lifting heavy wood. Twice? The wind's been strong, but not that strong. Or has it? Physics was never my strong point at school, nothing was if it didn't hold my attention straight away.

'What's that thing over there?' Vivienne stands next to me, squinting.

'Nothing.'

'That's what blew open the other night, isn't it? Some sort of trapdoor? I thought you'd closed it?'

'It's blown open again,' I tell her, in a drifting, faraway voice. It shouldn't be open. Someone opened it. *Or pushed from beneath. Someone wanting to get out, to take a closer look at the house.*

'Vinnie mentioned a tunnel,' Vivienne says. 'What a hideous thing. Before we get this place on the market, we'll get it boarded up again.'

'It's not going to be sold.'

'I'm the majority shareholder of the mortgage. If I say it'll be sold, it will be.'

'It's in Vinnie's name not yours.'

'And Vinnie would agree with me.'

I exhale deeply. I'm too tired for all of this. I just want it to be over. 'I went down into the tunnel the other day,' I tell her. 'That's how I injured my hand.'

'Why didn't you tell me that when I asked you before?'

I don't reply, only wander closer. It's magnetic. I don't want to approach but can't not. It's *bad* down there. I know this in the same way a child knows it, when fear pulses through every part of your body. Terrible things happen in dark, silent places.

The first five or so stairs are visible, then the rest disappear into impenetrable black, a darkness so thick it's tar-like, it swims and shifts before my eyes.

Vivienne stands at the edge and peers down, frowning. 'It goes down a long way,' she says.

'The woman who lived here years ago fell down those stairs.'

'That's dreadful. Why would you tell me that?'

'She died. They found her at the bottom, neck broken.'

'Is this another one of your lies?'

'It's the truth.'

'And you bought the place, knowing that happened? You really are messed up.'

I shrug. It doesn't matter anyway, whether she knows any of this or not. She shouldn't even be here.

She shouldn't be here. Some women just shouldn't be around, full-stop. They're a waste of space, they take up air.

'Do you want to go down and have a look?' I offer.

'Why would I want to do that?'

'You love uncovering the truth. Maybe you'll find some answers down there.'

'You're not talking sense.'

I place a hand on her shoulder, noting her flinch. 'Just a suggestion, nothing more,' I tell her. 'Nothing to worry about.'

'I should go now,' she says, faltering.

'That's the first thing we properly agree on,' I tell her with a smile.

CHAPTER NINETEEN

An hour later, I finally sit down on the kitchen stool. Exhausted. Vivienne's gone. Really gone this time, and the house feels freer without her presence. The driveway's empty of her car, her bags are no longer sitting in the hallway. *My* hallway, not hers. She's still a problem, a big problem, but she's out of my hair for now. The relief is intense.

I broke another nail closing the tunnel trapdoor. That's two nails down, eight to go. Like a cat's nine lives, only with one extra for good luck. I pick at the remnants of glue, then study the bandage around my hand. It's badly stained. The physical effort of the morning has broken the wound open again, made it weep. There's a numbness to it, my palm feels like it's become rock, weighing me down.

I need to leave. Vivienne's accusations have woken me up. Made me realise I need to act fast. Vinnie will be out to get me. He'll tell the police his version of events and they'll be on my doorstep before I have time to prepare. It'll be his word over mine. It needs to be my words that they believe.

Rick's place will do for a while. After that, I don't know. But I'll work something out. First of all, that trapdoor needs to stay shut. It can't be allowed to fly open again. I pull on a woolly hat and gloves then head outside again. Pile the pieces of broken shed on top of the trapdoor until it looks like a funeral-pyre. Nothing could dislodge that weight. I'm safe for now.

All the while, I hear Vivienne's voice in my head. *This is dangerous. You're dangerous, Heidi. Dangerous. Dangerous.* What would she know? I doubt she ever experienced a moment of real danger in her entire life. I go inside, strip off, have a shower. Stand under the water and let it wash over me while I close my eyes and breathe slowly. In and out. In and out. Like I used to as a child, when practising.

The trapdoor will open again, I hear, somewhere in the back of my head. *You can't stop it. Some secrets refuse to stay a secret, no matter how hard you try to keep them quiet.*

The shower-water chills to lukewarm, then cold. I jump out of the spray. It's always the way in this house, nothing stays comfortable for long. As I wrap my towel around me, my phone rings, a piercing trill in the silence. It's Rick. I answer quickly.

'Hey,' I say, scrabbling to pull on my clothes.

'Hello, you. What are you doing?' Rick's voice is richer than I remember. I smile, despite myself and despite everything that's happened today.

'I've been busy.'

'Me too. I've been talking to a client for over an hour. They wanted to tell me everything that's wrong with the website I built for them, despite the fact I built it exactly to spec. So frustrating.'

'Sounds it,' I reply. This feels good, normal. Two people, somewhere on their way to being boyfriend and girlfriend, chatting nonsense. I need more of this, much more.

'What are you doing now?'

I wander through to the bedroom and perch on the corner of the bed. 'Not a lot. I've just had a shower.'

'Sounds inviting. Well, if you're at a loose end, do you want to come with me to Tannistock? I know it's a bit late in the day, but I need to pick up some things. I thought perhaps we could go to the museum as well, speak to that woman there. We should get there before closing time.'

'What?'

'You know, the museum? The woman who wants to hear more about the tunnel? Suzanne, she's called.'

I close my eyes. The tunnel, yet again. Everything leads back to it. 'You're keen,' I reply lightly.

'Curious, more like. Aren't you?'

I bite my lip. I don't want to go to a museum. I don't want to talk to anyone. I want Rick to take me to bed again and do what he did to me before, and use that to forget about everything. I want to be free.

'Heidi, you still there? We don't have to go. We can do something another day.'

If I go with him, we'll probably end up back at his. That's enough of an incentive for me.

'Okay,' I agree. 'What time?'

'Fifteen minutes? I can come and pick you up. You did say Vinnie's mother was gone, didn't you?'

'She's gone. I'll see you in a bit.'

'Looking forward to it.'

After hanging up, I scramble into clothes, quickly put some lipstick on, a bit of blusher, some mascara too. I file the mess of my second nail. Maybe I can find a beauty salon in Tannistock, quickly pop in to get my nails fixed. This could be fun. Just like the old days, wandering the streets of London, espressos in cafés, early afternoon prosecco, buying a dress, a skirt, a beautiful pair of shoes. All things I used to do with Miranda. Rick will be just as good at keeping me company, I'm sure. Even better probably, because he's not a snake like her.

True to his word, his car pulls into the driveway quarter of an hour later. He toots his horn in a jaunty staccato to summon me, and I pull my coat on, quickly check my hair in the hallway mirror. High ponytail, good for emphasising the cheekbones. He won't be able to resist me.

You're dangerous, Heidi.

'Shut up, Vivienne,' I mutter, and open the front door.

Rick smiles from the front seat as I emerge. 'Glad you could join me,' he says as I settle beside him.

'Who could resist a trip to the museum?'

'Hold the sarcasm, please. This museum isn't too bad as far as local ones go.'

I tug on my seatbelt as he reverses off the drive. 'How are you?'

'Harassed. I need a break from work. Are you okay? You sounded odd on the phone earlier.'

'Did I?'

'Yes. Disconnected. Vague. I don't know.' He pats my leg, then brings his hand back to the steering wheel to navigate the tight corner. 'Maybe I just caught you unawares.'

'I didn't have any clothes on at the time.'

'Wish I'd known. I would have invited myself over sooner.'

We both laugh. I relax. It's good, being here. I can live in the moment. Stop seeing Vivienne's accusing expression in my head, stop seeing her stupid car, her stupid belongings too. None of it is in my house anymore, she's gone. I can relax for a while at least.

I glance across and study Rick's profile. His eyes are on the rearview mirror, concentrating. No, frowning. I look over my shoulder. There's a garish bubblegum-pink car behind us, following at what looks like a safe distance.

'Everything all right?' I ask.

His frown deepens. 'Yeah, I think so.'

'What's up?'

'It's nothing. Do you want the music on?'

'Is the car behind hassling you to hurry up?'

'No, nothing like that.'

'They've got zero taste when it comes to picking cars. Didn't it have those horrible false eyelash things glued to the headlights too?'

'Maybe.'

'It's probably got a sticker saying *powered by fairy-dust* in the back window.'

He doesn't answer, only presses his lips together. Strange. It feels like I said something wrong, but I don't know what. Either way, I don't like the shift in mood between us. I want this to be happy, fun, flirtatious. Not heavy. I can't do heavy today.

He switches the audio on. Abba pounds through the speakers, which lifts some of the tension. He motions for me to scan through his playlists, and I select *Disco Classics*.

'Can't beat a bit of Donna Summer,' I say, as the frenetic disco beat seeps through the car.

We travel onwards until the narrow country road widens to something resembling a main road. I peer down the turn-off road as we pass. There's no sign of a tree blocking the way, if such a tree existed in the first place. Vivienne was probably lying. But I don't want to think about her now. She's taken up enough of my precious time as it is.

The pink car is still behind us, but hanging back. Rick glances in the mirror, a lot. He's watching it. Something's up, but I don't want to ask what. I don't want us to fall the wrong side of happy again.

The sky's already darkening as we reach the outskirts of Tannistock. We drive along the main street, lined with narrow grey-brick houses, the occasional Georgian townhouse rendered in cream plaster. It's not so far from Nairbourne, but it feels like a million miles away. Tannistock's only a small town but it has people, energy, places to go. I miss all of that, so badly.

I'll be out of Nairbourne soon enough. I just need to tie up a few ends before I leave. And hopefully convince Rick that he wants to do something crazy and come with me. We're good together. It could work.

We pull into a narrow road that leads to a car park, which is almost empty. Rick parks in the corner under the streetlamp. It flickers on just as he pulls the handbrake. He looks in the rearview mirror again, then swears under his breath.

I look out of the back window, watch the pink car parking across the other side of the car park. It's illuminated in a pool of amber light from another streetlamp, which turns the pink paintwork fleshy. It's the same colour as a slab of meat being cooked slowly. Or a carcass lying under a harsh sun.

'Who is it?' I ask.

'Let's just ignore it for now,' he replies.

'You obviously know them.'

'Yeah, I do. But it shouldn't be a problem.'

'Really?'

'Really. Cross my heart and hope to die.' He opens the door, letting in the chill of the winter air. 'Let's go. The museum's just around the corner.'

I follow, but can't stop myself from checking the other car. No-one gets out. Rick glances across too, with a guarded look. Spine straight, chin up a fraction too high for natural confidence. Someone watching the pair of us. Surveillance. Police. Contracted killer, friend of Noelle's, friend of Vinnie's, friend of Vivienne's. Then I realise how ridiculous the thoughts are. It's a pink car with fake eyelashes on the headlights. No-one threatening would ever drive in a car like that. Rick will tell me when he's ready. He's open, honest. This silence and hurrying, it's just to get us away from here.

We slip down an alleyway. The darkening day makes long shadows of our bodies as we scurry along. Then we turn a corner onto a main street, join the flow of a few people carrying shopping bags, some with umbrellas up, pre-empting an impending rainfall.

Rick points ahead, to a small but imposing building with white pillars and two large arched windows. 'Told you it was close,' he says, attempting a smile.

'Have we got time to grab a drink?'

'Let's find this Suzanne person first. I'm not sure what time she finishes; we don't want to miss her.'

I don't argue, only trail after him through the heavy wooden doors into the little atrium, with a polished desk, a few shelves of knick-knacks for sale, and a young woman with plaited purple hair sitting in the corner. She looks about as thrilled to be here as I feel.

'We close in an hour,' she tells us, tapping her watch.

Rick smiles. 'No problem. We've popped in to chat to Suzanne, she's expecting us.'

The girl shrugs, then points along the nearest corridor. 'She's just finished the artefact session; you'll find her in the meeting room. Go down there, then turn right just before the end.'

I look longingly down the corridor on the other side of the room, where I can hear the vague clatter of cups being stacked, and detect a faint scent of fresh coffee. A café. That's what I want. Cosy chatter over a latte. Laughter, banter. Not this; wandering down long empty corridors. They're too much like tunnels.

Rick nudges me. 'Let's go and find her.'

'If this woman's just finished a session, she might need a breather. Why don't we—'

'It won't take long, come on.'

I find myself walking after him down the corridor. I haven't got the energy to protest. This all feels unreal anyway; it's something about the light. Washed-out, feeble, it reminds me of being underwater.

Why did you do it, Heidi? Why? Dad's mouth, releasing bubbles. Precious air escaping. I take a deep breath to compensate for the suffocating memory.

The thud of our shoes echo off the parquet flooring. The sound is good. It grounds me, shoves the thoughts right out of my head. It also makes me realise how empty this place is.

We turn into what must be the meeting room, though it looks more like a small classroom to me; two white tables with various objects displayed on them, several plastic chairs, one tall, narrow-shouldered woman chatting to an elderly man. We wait, lingering in the corner until we're noticed.

'Can I help you?' the woman asks eventually, nudging her glasses up her nose.

'Suzanne?' Rick extends a hand. 'I'm Rick Smith. We spoke on the phone the other day. About the smuggler's tunnel in Nairbourne.'

She grins. 'Ah! Rick the website guy.'

'That's me. We were in the area; thought we'd pop in to see if you were around?'

'I'm around, though I need to put this room back in order. Got to pack these artefacts back in their boxes.'

Rick nods, pulls out a seat for me and motions for us to sit. 'You carry on. This is my friend, Heidi. Or should I say, the owner of the tunnel in question.'

Friend. I wince, though try to hide it. I'm not sure how I want to be introduced, it's too soon for *girlfriend*, but still...

Suzanne switches her grin to me. 'The Nairbourne tunnel, eh? There are plenty of stories about it. Rick said you've been down there exploring? Found a fingernail in the wall or something like that?'

I nod and hide my hand under the table. I don't want her scrutinising it. She looks like the type to ask question after question until she gets the answers she wants.

'It's probably not the only fingernail in that tunnel,' she tells us, picking up a cracked ceramic pot and placing it gently in what looks like an empty ice-cream container. 'It was a common enough thing back then, a superstition of sorts. To keep the nixie away.'

'The nixie?' I repeat. 'How's that meant to work?'

'The old legend goes that if you can fool a nixie into believing another nixie is scratching her, she'll see it as competition. She'll run back to her patch of the sea to defend it. A bit like lions battling for territory. I'd be willing to bet money that there are other fingernails down there, if you go back down to look. The tradition was to line the walls with them.'

'That's horrible.'

'That tunnel was a horrible place back in the day, if you believe the stories.' Suzanne picks up a velvet purse, then a piece of lace, laying them in another box and closing the lid. 'I've studied a lot of local history over the years and the tunnel stands out for all the wrong reasons. It's perfect material for people who love the macabre.'

Rick laughs. 'We used to hear all sorts of spooky stories when I was a kid. Sounds like you know more than me, though.'

She turns to me. 'Are you sure you want to hear it? Given you actually live there?'

I shrug. 'Sure, why not? I doubt much of it's true.'

'These stories probably are. There are the smugglers of course. A bad lot. Much worse than your average smuggler. Not just stealing things but killing too. They ran quite the crime racket. The few people who dared to stand up to them got dragged down that tunnel, then goodness knows what happened to them. They weren't ever seen again, that's for sure.'

Rick and I glance at each other, thinking the same thing. The pile of bones. Rick said they belonged to animals. It's best for everyone to keep thinking that for now. *Bones. Murder.* I feel queasy, wonder why I agreed to this. It's too warm in here, the central heating is turned up far too high. I'm sweating under my coat but don't want to take it off. It feels protective, like armour.

'The smugglers sounded like fun,' Rick pats me on the shoulder. 'Did they carve out that tunnel?'

'That's the interesting thing,' Suzanne continues, packing the last of the items away. 'It was there a long time before them. No-one knows how long ago it was made, but we've got records of it dating back as far as the eleventh century.'

'You don't know who made it?'

'No-one does. We know it was used as a hiding place for various people fleeing from the Normans, but whether they dug it out or not, we're not sure. There's a tragic tale of a woman who lived down there in the early seventeenth century, called Alice Fellowes. She was an outcast. One of the few women from Cornwall to be tried and hung as a witch. The reports from the trial say they found bones down there, evidence of sacrifice and black sabbat practice. Piles of finger and toenails too, ironically. Her story often gets blended with the nixie's. The angry witch seeking revenge, dragging people to their deaths. History does love telling tales about the vengeful female.'

'Poor Alice,' Rick murmurs.

'Quite. So, what did you see down there, then?' Suzanne sits down abruptly, pulling the chair up close to the table with a screech. 'I'm all ears. I've always wanted to go down there to have a look.'

'We didn't see much,' I tell her.

'Apart from a pile of bones, a nail in the wall and a strange sense of dread,' Rick adds, throwing me a wry look. 'We both couldn't get out of there fast enough.'

'Well, if any place should be haunted, it's that tunnel.' She leans forward. 'This is a cheeky question, but would it be possible for me to go down there one day? From a local historian's perspective, it's endlessly fascinating. I'd love to take a few photos, have a look around the place.'

I shake my head, just as Rick nods. He frowns. 'Why not?' he asks me.

'It's not a good idea.' I can feel myself tensing. They're both staring at me. No-one should go down there anymore. It's a bad place. Bad things will happen if anyone ventures down there, I know it for sure.

'It's up to you,' Suzanne says, in an attempt to smooth over the uncomfortable silence. 'It's on your property, I'd never push you into it.'

'Excuse me?'

'I wouldn't force you, I mean. Do give it some thought, though. Various people have tried to gain access to go down there, but no-one's been able to for decades. Especially not since that poor woman lost her life when she fell down the stairs.'

I swallow hard. It's hot, too hot. I need a drink, something alcoholic. This conversation is taking me places I don't want to go.

'It's all very interesting,' Rick says with forced joviality. 'Has anyone written any books about it?'

'Not full books, but it's mentioned in several.'

'How about that?' His gaze travels over my face, trying to work me out. 'Your tunnel has celebrity status, Heidi.'

'I wish it was in someone else's back garden.'

Suzanne smiles sympathetically. 'That I can understand. That level of dark history, it's enough to make anyone want to board it up for good, right?'

I nod, all the while thinking, *Get me a drink. Get me out of here.* I've been through too much recently, and this isn't needed, not for the sort of life I want, which is about moving forward, not dwelling endlessly on the past. What's happened has happened, no-one can change that.

CHAPTER TWENTY

'Do you feel okay now?' Rick asks. It's quiet in the museum café, his words rise uncomfortably loud in the empty space. The light's probably doing nothing for me either. Everything's too white in here; white tables, white chairs, white walls, white blinds at the windows. The fluorescent bulbs overhead are working overtime to bounce harsh brightness off every surface, including my washed-out skin.

'I came over funny, that's all,' I tell him. 'The caffeine's helped.'

'You looked like you'd seen a ghost.'

'No, just heard a few stories about them instead.'

He nudges the last few crumbs of carrot cake onto his fork, then looks at me seriously. 'I thought you'd find it useful, knowing more about your home. But that was a bit much to take in, wasn't it?'

'Don't worry about it.'

'I don't want to give you sleepless nights.'

'Don't you?' I raise an eyebrow, which makes him laugh.

'I'm glad you brought that up, actually. I have to say, it surprised me.'

'What did?'

'You know. You coming over. *That* happening.'

'Are you referring to us having sex?'

He nods. 'That's the one.'

'Why did it surprise you?'

He shifts in his seat. 'It all happened so quickly. And with everything going on in your life, I presumed you wouldn't be interested. What with your brutal ex-boyfriend. And Vinnie's mother turning up unannounced. That sort of thing.'

'Let's not talk about them. They're not worth it.'

'I was surprised by my own actions as well,' he adds. 'Given that I've got complications too.'

His face is difficult to read. Instead, I watch his fork, twirling around and around his fingers; a nervous gesture. Something's not right. I look up. He's no longer looking at me, but at something over my shoulder. His expression fluctuates between surprise, anger and guilt.

I look behind me. Then I stare past the café door, along the corridor, right to the reception area. There's someone at the desk peering back at us. A mass of curls piled in a messy bun. Tall, bleach-denim dungarees and loose sweater underneath. The face; defiant, determined, ready to sting. *Bea.*

'Look who's here,' I mutter, then feel stupid for saying it. He already knows. The pink car was hers. It makes sense now. He implied it was casual between them. He's honest, trustworthy; that's the version of Rick I bought into. So why do I feel like I've been duped?

She's coming this way. Her shoes echo like a warrior drum beat, getting louder, louder; her shoulder-bag batting against her hip with every step. She looks strong, composed. Healthy. I feel feeble by comparison, a limp, unprotected thing with no means to protect itself. This isn't fair, whatever this is.

'Shit,' Rick whispers, as she pulls to a halt by our table. 'What are you doing here, Bea?'

She folds her arms, gives us both a long look. 'This looks cosy.'

'This is two friends, having a drink in a café,' Rick says.

'Friends?'

I can't disagree with her sceptical tone. When I last checked, friends didn't screw each other.

Rick sits straighter. 'Don't start, Bea.'

'Don't start what? Trying to get some clarity from you? Or trying to figure out what game you're playing?'

I stand up, then grab my coat and tug it on. 'I'll leave you both to it. Sounds like you need to talk.'

'What are you even doing here, Heidi?' She shakes her head. 'Haven't you got a boyfriend? Or has he really left for good?'

'You don't know anything about me.'

'I know that for some reason you dislike me. And that you're intent on stealing Rick from me too. Is that the sort of woman you are?'

I blush. That's Miranda, not me. She's the one who stole a man. I'm innocent in all of this.

You're dangerous, Heidi. I zip up my coat, quickly.

'Shall I wait for you by the car?' I ask Rick, turning away from Bea.

'You should know that Rick and I have been seeing each other for quite some time,' Bea says, standing in my way. 'He chased me, not the other way around. I was happy being just friends, ironically.'

'Come on, Bea,' Rick interrupts. 'That's not totally true.'

'You led me on, then ghosted me. I feel like a discarded toy. You've got bored of me and moved on, but didn't bother telling me.'

'I'm going now.' I start walking away. Rick grabs my hand. My injured palm shrieks in protest.

'Heidi, please don't be upset.'

'I'm not.' I smile sweetly at them both, ignoring the burn in my hand. I need to keep my cool here, and I won't let her intimidate me. She's in dungarees, for God's sake. 'I'll leave you both to chat properly.'

She knows she's lost, she's way out of her depth. I just need him to hammer home the final nail in the coffin.

'So, is it over between us?' she continues, turning back to Rick. 'Is this it?'

'Bloody hell, of course it's over,' I mumble as I start to leave. 'He slept with another woman, how much more of a hint do you need?'

She gasps. I pause. We both wait. Rick swallows hard, then rubs his face with his hands. He looks smaller suddenly. Hollowed-out, less than what he was before.

'You're right, Heidi,' he says eventually. 'It's best if I talk to Bea on my own. I'll meet you by the car in a few minutes.'

I frown, then straighten my features. 'Fine. See you there.'

I can't process this. They're a pair of strangers to me in this moment. Two thin faces, two lots of dark hair, two narrow builds. I'm the odd one out here, the one who doesn't fit the mould. I open my lips, wait for words to emerge, but nothing comes. So I turn and walk away. I refuse to look back. I'm worried that if I do, I'll see that they're already deep in private conversation. That they'll have dismissed me from their thoughts already. Rejected, again.

Bastards. Bastards. Bastards. Now it's my drum beat, my thumping heart, my pounding steps. I push open the heavy doors, ignoring the girl behind the desk on the way out. The cold air helps. It soothes my flushed cheeks, calms my racing heart a little.

The sky's a velvet navy-blue now, the moon's rising in the sky. I wonder, not for the first time, why when I look at it; all I ever see is a screaming face.

My feet are numb, my cheeks freezing, waiting in the car park in the dark. A huddle of teenagers congregates by the low wall on the other side, close to Bea's car. I stay in the shadows and hope they don't see me. I hope they're feeling destructive and kick a few dents in her ugly car for good measure.

I don't have to wait for long. After ten minutes, Rick emerges from the alleyway, coat tucked high over his jaw, arms wrapped around his chest. He sees me, raises a hand, then lowers it quickly.

'Did you have a nice chat?' I say, when he reaches me.

He unlocks the car, waits until we're both settled in our seats. 'Don't be like that,' he says, switching the engine on.

'Like what?'

'You know. Bitchy.'

'Bitchy?'

'I didn't mean it in that way,' he says. 'I don't know what I'm saying anymore. Forgive me, please.'

'What did you say to her?'

'Nothing much. We just discussed what was going on between us.'

'And what is going on between you? Because you gave me the impression it was nothing.'

He sighs, reverses the car. 'I know,' he says eventually. 'And I'm sorry. I should have told you. Everything happened too fast. Besides, you were still with Vinnie when you arrived in Nairbourne.'

'It's not the same thing.'

'We've both got baggage elsewhere, right? We hardly know each other really.'

'That didn't stop you ripping my clothes off.'

'And that was fun.' The car swings out into the main road, joining the line of commuter traffic. 'It was great, honestly.'

'But just fun, right?'

He pauses. 'Isn't that what you thought?'

I look away, out of the window. Past buildings lit by streetlamps. Past everything, all the way back to another version of myself. One who is leaving here without Bea having ruined everything. A version that has a chance to be happy, in spite of it all.

'Hey.' His tone is softer. Manipulative. 'Are you okay? I don't want this to change things between us. We're having a good time, aren't we?'

I fix a grin. Remember who I am. I won't let this break me. I run my nails across my legs, my slender legs, the legs that have turned many men's heads before this one. I lean across and pat him on the arm. 'Sure, we're having a good time. It's all just fun, as you said.'

His relief is palpable. 'I'm so glad we see eye to eye.'

'Of course. Don't worry about anything. I'm not like Bea. I won't chase after you like a lovesick puppy.'

'She's a good person. I'm just not sure I'm ready to give her the commitment she wants.'

We leave the outskirts of the town and head along a darker, narrower road, with no friendly streetlights to guide our way. *A good person.* Noelle had been a good person too. Good people spoil all the fun.

'I'm glad we've been so open with each other,' he says, switching his headlights on to full-beam. 'Aren't you? It feels like a real weight off my mind.'

I think of weights. My deadening, rock-heavy hand. Dead weights in dark places. Then stop.

'Honesty's the best policy,' I agree, running my uninjured hand over his crotch. 'I wonder how long it'll take you to show your true feelings if I keep doing this?'

He turns to me, smiles slowly. 'Not long at all.'

'That's good. Why don't you pull over?'

He finds a layby a minute or so later. Stops the engine then pulls me roughly towards him. A car passes us a few minutes later, slowing to squeeze by safely. I wonder, for a moment, if it's *her* in her pink car. Staring in, sickened by what she sees.

Do I feel anything about that? Not at this moment. Instead, I kiss him harder. Let's see who has the most fun here.

We end up back at mine, in my bed. I feel like I'm drowning. His arms and legs are all around me, tentacle-like on every part of me. Lips locked limpet-tight. The salt scent of sweat. But it's dispassionate. Disconnected. I rock back and forth on him, see his face half-lit by moonlight, and think *weak. Insubstantial.* Not the person I thought I knew. Not someone I really know at all.

We stop. I lie beside him, aware of the cold. He's so still, I wonder for a moment if I've killed him. Or if perhaps he's not even there at all. Maybe he's just a memory of the previous time we were together, when things were sweeter and more meaningful. But it's nothing like as poetic as that. We're just two people, lying in silence in the dark.

Like bodies in that damned smuggler's tunnel. I shiver.

His hand brushes my hip. It lacks confidence, enthusiasm too. 'You're a cool person,' he says quietly in my ear.

'Thanks.'

'I mean it. It's a relief. I thought you were going to flip your lid back in the museum. I wouldn't have blamed you either, with

Bea showing up like that. It's a rare type of person that can take that on the chin and move on from it.'

'Don't mention it.'

The weight of his arm lands across my chest. There's no affection to it, I realise that now. It's just gratitude; open thankfulness that I'm okay with this being sex and nothing else. Okay that when he's done with me, I'll *be cool* and let it go.

Sometimes, I'm such a traitor to myself, that I don't even know who I am anymore. I've lost grip of myself, again.

I sit up. 'I'm going to get a drink. Do you want anything?'

'I can think of a few things.' Again, the hand on my hip, stroking, stroking.

'You've had enough of that for now. If you don't want anything, do you think you can get your clothes on and go?'

He pauses. I smile in the darkness, before straightening my expression and switching on the bedside lamp.

'I don't mean to be rude,' I explain, grabbing my bra and slipping it over my arms. 'It's just I could do with a quiet evening. That's okay, isn't it?' *Given that we're both really cool people?* I want to add, but don't. Nothing more needs to be said.

Slowly he sits, nodding all the while like a confused dog. 'Sure, that's no problem at all,' he says, reaching to the floor for his clothes. 'I could do with a quiet one too. Work's been tough recently.'

'I knew you'd understand.'

We both dress quietly. I sidle a look at him. He's a good-looking guy, there's no doubt about that. But he's narrow, spare and limited in ways I hadn't really realised before. I made a mistake, getting tangled up so quickly with him, but I've learnt. I need to control my impulses. Sometimes they get the better of me.

He takes ages to wriggle back into his jeans. It's embarrassing watching him struggle. Finally, he stands, makes an attempt at smoothing down the duvet, then gives me a rueful smile.

'I'll hit the road, then,' he says. 'Give you some peace and quiet.'

'Cheers. And thanks for taking me to Tannistock today. It was a laugh.'

'Apart from Bea turning up.'

'No big deal. She doesn't mean anything to me, so how can it be?'

He chews his lip, nods, then moves towards the door. 'I can see myself out, if that's easier?'

'It's fine, I'm going downstairs for a drink anyway, remember?'

'Oh, yeah. Of course.'

I squeeze the top of his arm, then kiss his cheek. Step away and open the bedroom door, gesturing for him to go through. 'You're a fun guy, Rick.'

'Thanks. Maybe we can see each other soon? What are you up to on Saturday?'

'I don't know yet.' I let him go down the stairs first, then follow behind. 'I'll let you know.'

If I thought it was cold in the house, it's even colder when I open the front door. Sea-wind whistles through, lifting my hair, and for a moment, I think I see another car on the driveway. Vivienne's. Bea's maybe. Both women at my door, ready to get their revenge on me.

We kiss. It's a bumping of dry lips and not a lot else. Rick's fault, I realise, as he steps back. What we had could have been good, but he ruined it.

CHAPTER TWENTY-ONE

I shut the door and turn the heating up another notch, though it won't make a difference. Then I head straight to the fridge. There's a bottle of wine in there. I want to drink the whole lot, until my brain stops exploring all the dark places I don't want it to.

I sit on the sofa with the bottle, forgoing the glass. Stare at the night outside. There are evil things out there. Drifts of the past, lingering around that tunnel. Things from the sea, waiting for the right opportunity to make themselves known. Nixies, with claws outstretched. No amount of long forgotten fingernails stuck in stone will stop them if they want to get me.

I stretch my own fingers in response. They can do damage too. By holding others back. Holding them down.

I could have died, Heidi. Do you realise that?

'I didn't mean it,' I whisper aloud. I never meant to steal Dad's air away. Or to put him in danger. The hurt was too deep and heavy inside me. It turned into anger and I didn't think.

I could have killed him. My own father.

But I didn't. That's the key fact. *I didn't.* And we both moved forward from that. Just in opposite directions.

After ten minutes or so, the wine kicks in, as I'd expect, given I've already downed close to half. Everything's already warmer, getting steadily hazier and more unfocused. I care less about everything now, feel like I'm somewhere a few metres from my own body. Slowly, I pick at the bandage on my hand. Pluck and pluck at the sticky tape until the rough fabric starts to sag. Peel it away, sickened by the wetness. It shouldn't be so wet. I don't want to look. But I have to.

It's no longer a gash, but a hole. A deep, ragged hole, oozing dark. I touch it, draw back quickly. It's a jellyfish thing burrowed deep in my flesh, making its home there. Eating me from the inside out. The skin surrounding it is a furious red and it itches now it's exposed to the air, with a ferocity that makes me want to scrape it away.

I don't understand how it's got so bad, so quickly. Wounds don't get infected like this after such a short space of time.

'Noelle,' I whisper. Two discordant syllables. A protest. A noise that sounds like *hell*. Out there in the dark, I sense something pacing to and fro through the grass, watching me. Waiting to see what I'll do next.

She wasn't a good swimmer. Vinnie took her out swimming anyway. Insisted on it. Tugged her into the sea, laughing and laughing, his skin shining in the sun. That's the key detail; the thing the police should know. It was all his idea.

He threw her over his shoulder and carried her in. Hercules, playing with his pretty lover. Only I was his lover, not her. Or he said he loved me, anyway. I stayed behind on the beach, nibbled at the last piece of bread from the picnic and drank the last of the wine. Looked for her notebook but couldn't find it. It was for the best. Her talent was sickening.

I watched. She could swim just fine. She let him circle her, then laughed as he grabbed her. The water sparkled. The waves sighed and sighed. She was a princess clutching tightly to her rescuing knight. I don't know what that made me. I walked to the cave, kept my eyes on them from the shadows. She kissed him. I wondered if he was looking for me. Wondering where I disappeared to.

So hot that day. So cold now. Always so cold, no matter how much I drink. I'm different too. There are things I should feel more about, I *know* I should, but I can't.

Something moves outside the window, jerking my attention there in an instant. I don't want to look more closely. I want to not notice. If I refuse to see, then maybe whatever it is will leave me alone. My wound is weeping sludge, a tar-spill. I squeeze the skin around my palm, then bite back a yelp. Black blood glops out, slides past my thumb and onto the floor. The sight is enough to make my stomach roll. It hasn't spread into a small puddle as blood should; it's still circular, holding its own shape.

I drink more. My hand is a pit of hell and I'm not sure any amount of alcohol will make it feel less so.

A noise grates through the silence, a low grind of metal against metal. Then, hinges squealing, the sound of footsteps on the front mat, heavy and slow. *The nixie?* A half-formed word escapes my lips in a whisper; a gibberish sound of fear. *Noelle?*

This is it. Whatever's been stalking me, toying with me all this time; it's in the house. In the hallway. About to enter this room.

'Heidi?' It's a loud voice, terse. Rough. Masculine. Then, I hear a heavy thud, something being dropped on the floor.

It's Vinnie.

Relief washes through me. Then something with more bite. He's here, really here, after he's been gone for so long. He's come back, only he wasn't invited.

'Heidi?' He's behind me now, standing at the doorway perhaps. I don't dare look around. I can only stare at my palm, blink over and over, try to calm myself. The movement outside the window pauses. Alert, sensing an impending storm.

I can't escape this. So I turn and face him.

It's been days not weeks since he went away, but he's alien to me. Bigger than I remember him being, taking up more space. Broader of shoulder, thicker of neck, wider of jaw. Beard wilder. Hands larger, more capable of doing damage. A monster, not a god. I don't know why I didn't see it before.

'I wasn't expecting you,' I say. It's a rabbit voice, weak and unsure.

He grunts. 'I know you weren't. I didn't intend to come down.'

'Why are you here, then?'

'Because I need to know where she is.'

'Who?'

'You know who.'

'What happened?' he had screamed back then, on the beach. 'Why couldn't I find her, Heidi?' But now he doesn't mean Noelle. I rub my eyes and try to focus, shrinking into the safety of the sofa.

'Who are you talking about?' I ask.

'My mother. Where is she?'

I put the bottle of wine down carefully. 'How should I know?'

'She was here. I told her not to come, said it wasn't safe to be around you.'

'Around me?' I want to laugh. There's nothing safe about any of this. Him, this house, the tunnel, the sea that presses inwards towards us all day, every day. 'You've got a nerve.'

'In her last message, she said she was coming home. But she hasn't. She's not answering my calls, it's just ringing through to voicemail each time. Her neighbour says he hasn't seen her in a couple of days, that she's not answering the door either.'

'It's not my problem, Vinnie.'

'I'm making it your problem.'

I sit up. My head needs to be clear for this.

'You shouldn't have come back,' I tell him, standing. The room spins a little and I steady myself against the armrest.

'It's my house, I'll come and go as I like.'

'It's not your house. It's your mother's, apparently. When were you going to tell me that she paid your share of the deposit?'

'She gave the money to me, so it's mine. Don't change the subject. I need to know where she is.'

'She left. Drove off in a hurry. That's all I know.'

'You're lying. You lie about everything; you live in a fantasy world. Mum told me about Noelle's text, the day before she died.'

I brace myself, move closer to him. 'Get out or I'll call the police.'

He laughs. 'You won't call the police.'

'Leave, now. You left before; it should be easy for you.'

'Not before I take a look around.'

'Why?'

'I want to, that's why.'

'You're not looking around. Why don't you go back to your new girlfriend instead? I know all about Miranda, in case you hadn't guessed. Though she should probably be aware that you don't tend to stick with women for very long. Why is that, Vinnie?'

He frowns. 'It's not like that. Miranda's been a good friend.'

'I bet she has.'

'Where's my mother?'

'You're such a mummy's boy, aren't you?'

'Rich words indeed, from the woman who tried to drown her father.' He sneers at me. 'Miranda and I were talking about it the other night. Quite the little secret you've got there, Heidi.'

My mouth is frozen, with shock at first; deep, raw shock at the betrayal of them talking to each other about me. Then anger. The rage is directed at myself too. I'm an idiot for confiding in her, for believing I had a friend to trust. Alcohol's to blame. It loosened my tongue when I should have kept my mouth shut.

'What happened with Dad has nothing to do with anything,' I whisper.

'I think it does. It answers a lot of questions. I'd feel sorry for you, if you hadn't wrecked my life.'

'You wrecked mine first.'

The look he throws at me is pure, unfiltered contempt. It stings. He has no right to look at me like that. He's the traitor, the deserter. I step forward, but instead of meeting me, he retreats to the hallway then stamps up the stairs. I pause. Tilt my neck upwards and listen hard to his movements above. He's prowling from room to room, making the floorboards creak. I don't know what he thinks he'll find out there. He's always been a moron, I've just been too blind to see it.

I pick up the wine bottle, fetch a glass from the kitchen cupboard, pour and sip slowly. It's a waiting game now, in a few minutes he'll reappear and this'll continue. All I can do is gather my thoughts and regroup. He won't win. He can't, he just doesn't realise it yet.

Soon enough, his footsteps mark his journey back down the stairs. They're steadier now. The measured steps of someone calculating their next move.

'Did you find what you were looking for?' I ask as he enters the living room.

He shrugs. 'No, and I can tell by your face that doesn't surprise you. I bet you made her feel less than welcome, didn't you?'

'She and I talked. About you, in fact. It was nice and cosy.'

'I doubt that.' He takes a deep breath, then nods at the bottle beside me. 'Pour me one, please.'

'No. It's my wine.'

'Bought with our money in a joint account. Everything fifty–fifty, don't you remember that, Heidi? What a joke, eh. I'll be sleeping in the spare room tonight, by the way.'

'The spare room?'

'I don't think either of us would enjoy being in bed together again.'

'I wasn't inviting you to join me. I was questioning why you were staying here at all.'

'I don't have to justify myself to you. Not anymore.' He reaches into his jacket pocket for his phone then puts it to his ear, frowning.

'Calling Miranda, are you?'

'I'm trying Mum again.'

I keep my face neutral, though it's becoming an effort. 'It's horrible when someone doesn't answer the phone, isn't it?'

'Is that a dig? I didn't answer your calls because I needed time to think.'

'Maybe that's what your mother needs too?'

'She always picks up when it's me.' He hangs up, then nods to the hallway. 'I'm nipping to the shop to get some beers if you're not going to share that wine with me. Then I'm coming back and sleeping the night in the spare room. Because you don't get to tell me I can't, okay?'

I shrug. If he's leaving the house, even for a short space of time, that's something. That gives me time to make plans. He shakes his head at my lack of response, turns and walks out. A moment later, the front door slams and quiet takes over again. It's as though he was never here in the first place.

It's not safe, having him here. Not for many reasons. I turn the possibilities over in my mind, put the wine back in the fridge out of temptation's way. Barricading the door won't work. He'd smash windows, beat down the back door to prove a point that this place was his. I could leave, go to Rick's, but Vinnie might do something in my absence. Change the locks, call the police and tell them lies about me. Anything to ruin my life more than he already has.

I don't want to see Rick right now. But he could be useful. I take a moment to think it through, then reach for my phone.

'Hi, Rick,' I say, as soon as he picks up.

'Hello?' His greeting is guarded, hesitant too. I can hear another voice in the background, finishing a sentence perhaps.

'It's me.'

'I know that. What's up?'

I take a deep breath. Here goes. 'I'm in trouble, Rick. Vinnie's come back.'

'What? God, Heidi; that's not good.'

'He's behaving weirdly. Really unpredictable. I hate to pull you into this, but I'm scared.'

'Shouldn't you call the police?'

'He hasn't done anything yet. Besides, this is his house too. He hasn't broken any laws by being here.'

'But you said he was dangerous.'

I sigh. 'I know. I'm not sure what to do.'

'Leave. Come here.' Then, there's the voice in the background, definitely female, a questioning tone. The line is muffled, presumably with Rick's hand while he talks to them. *Bea*, it must be. Who else would be there at this time in the evening?

'Are you still there?' I ask.

'Yes, sorry. Bea's here, I was filling her in on the situation.'

I swallow my anger down, it's not helpful at the moment,

it'll only cloud things. Besides, Rick's irrelevant now. He's not who I thought he was.

'Heidi? You still there?'

'I'm here.'

'We'll come to you. We'll pretend to be friendly neighbours, popping over for a drink.'

'No, it's okay,' I say, just as Bea says something too, which I don't catch. I doubt it's anything nice.

'Seriously, it won't take us long to get there.'

'Vinnie's out now anyway, he's gone to get himself alcohol. He can't cope without his beer.'

'We'll come over in a bit, then. It's no problem, we'd both rather you were safe.'

It's *both* of them now, I see. Rick and Bea, the tight little unit, the perfect neighbourly couple. Amazing, given he was in my bed only a few hours earlier. I don't need them to come over. I only want them to have heard my fear, to report it to the right people when the time's right.

'I'm okay, for now,' I tell him. 'I'm hoping I can shut myself in my room, and Vinnie will leave me alone.'

'Why has he come back?'

'I don't know. He's accusing me of things which don't make sense. I think he's halfway to being drunk already, to be honest.'

'Please, let me come over. I'm worried.'

'I'll text you later, let you know how I'm getting on.'

'Make sure you do. If I don't hear from you, Bea and I are coming over.'

'I doubt Bea would want to.'

'She's worried too, Heidi. Did you hear that? She said *yes*.'

I want to be sick. Every word lands like a rock in the ocean. *Splash.* She's worried too. *Splash.* She said yes. *Splash.* Bea and I. Bea and I. Bea and I. Them, not me. The perfect pair.

'That's sweet of her,' I force myself to say. 'I'd better go, I heard his car on the driveway.'

'Call me if there are any problems, or if you're feeling scared. I still wish you'd call the police, though. They'll be able to help far more than we can.'

'I'll text you later.'

'In half an hour or so?'

'Sure. I've got to go.' I hang up. The scene is easy to imagine. Rick standing in the cosy farmhouse kitchen, phone still in hand. Her perched on one of the stools by the breakfast bar, expression caught between curiosity and irritation. Both of them discussing what to do for the best, which might or might not be right. Still, even that small phone conversation should be useful. It's all about planning the route ahead, clearing obstacles. Taking a deep enough breath before diving.

I pace the house, try to watch some television then switch it off a few minutes after. Find another one of Vinnie's tools, a claw bar, lying by the coffee-machine, and tuck it in the waistband of my jeans. It might come in useful, it might not. It's better to be on the safe side.

Vinnie returns soon after, a sheen of mist-moisture on his cheeks. He dumps a plastic bag of clinking bottles on the kitchen countertop, then starts unpacking them.

'What the hell have you done to your hand?' he asks after a while, raising his head to look at me.

'None of your business.'

'It looks horrible.'

'It was your fault.'

'Of course it was. Go on, enlighten me.'

'I injured it down in your bloody smuggler's tunnel. Someone, hundreds of years ago, had stuck a fingernail in the wall. It ripped my palm to pieces.'

He rummages in the kitchen drawer, then pulls out a beer

bottle opener. 'You went down there on your own? You really are mental, aren't you?'

'Who said I was alone?'

'Heidi, can we skip past the game-playing? I'm tired. I'm worried about my mother. I don't trust you as it is, so–'

'You don't trust me? Don't forget which of us is the killer, Vinnie.'

He stiffens. Stone-still, for so long I almost wonder if he's forgotten how to inhale. *I've gone too far*, I think, nerves tensing my muscles, making my heart race and my skin tingle. *Now he'll kill me. He wants to, I can tell.* I reach to my back, feel the reassuring coldness of the claw bar against my fingers.

'You promised you'd never call me that.' He places his beer bottle down slowly, fingers white against the glass.

'I promised a lot of stupid things that day. Covered for you when I shouldn't have.'

'I didn't kill her. You know I didn't.'

'Try telling Noelle that.'

'Stop saying her name.'

I sneer at him. 'That's your guilty conscience talking.'

'It wasn't me, Heidi. You were wrong to make me doubt myself. You're wrong now. I'd never have hurt her, not even accidentally.'

'You insisted she went in the water when she couldn't swim well. It's the same thing.'

'That's not what it was like. You know I tried to keep her above the water. I desperately tried to hold on.'

'Did you?'

'Yes, goddamnit. It was like she was being dragged away from me; I couldn't keep my grip.'

I laugh. 'It was you who dragged her under. Just like you tried to do to me when we first moved here. I felt your hands on my legs, pulling me down.'

'Liar. Why are you saying these things?'

'Recognise the truth. You're a killer. A violent man that disposes of people who get in his way. I only wish I'd known it sooner.'

He shakes his head, steps closer, crossing the expanse of floor between us with uncomfortable ease. 'Are you aware you're crazy?' he asks, standing close. 'Or do you really believe what you're saying is true?'

'That's right, try to gaslight me. You're wasting your breath. I know what happened.'

'No, you don't. Because you weren't anywhere near us, remember? You kept saying it, over and over again. *What happened, where did she go? I didn't see, I was too far away.*'

'I was too scared to say.'

'Bullshit. Where even were you?'

'I was in the cave, then I came to the water's edge when I heard you shout.'

'You looked wet to me, not dry.'

'Oh please. You're clutching at straws, Vinnie. It's pathetic.'

'Why are you saying all of this? Why now?'

'Because people need to know the truth.'

His mouth twists. 'You don't know the meaning of that word.' He's by my side, more quickly than I can react, grabbing me by the wrist. I gasp as he squeezes. A fresh clot of dark blood pools in the wound.

'Why were you down there?' he asks suddenly.

'What? What are you talking about?'

'In the smuggler's tunnel. You hated the thought of it before. You said you went down there with someone else. Who?'

'Let go, you're hurting me.'

'Not until you tell me.'

'It's none of your business.'

He draws nearer. His breath is hot, stale. 'Let's go down there now, shall we?'

I try to pull away but can't. His grip's too strong, and he's too far gone to be rationalised with. This is bad. I've pushed him too far, too quickly.

'Don't be stupid, it's dark,' I say.

'We've got a torch packed away somewhere upstairs.'

'We're not going down there.'

'Yes, we are. You and me both. Because I've got this crazy idea that you went down there with my mother.'

He pulls me across the floor. I stumble, manage to keep my footing. My phone's in the kitchen area; I can't reach it, not without getting him to let me go. I remember what Rick said, about coming over if he didn't hear from me. I don't know if that's a good thing or not. I don't know where any of this is going; only that I don't know how to play this. I'm in trouble.

My hand screeches pure pain as Vinnie tugs harder, cutting off the blood, making it throb. I shriek as he bashes it into his side on the way up the stairs, though there's a certain satisfaction in seeing my blood smear across the waist of his jeans. It won't look good if anyone else sees it. Evidence, working against him.

He pitches me forward into the bedroom, shuts the door, then points at the pile of boxes in the corner.

'Get searching.'

'No. We're not going into the tunnel. Not me, not you, not anyone.'

'Why did you take her down there, Heidi?'

'I don't know what you're talking about.'

'You do. You're hiding something. I know that look.'

'I didn't explore the tunnel with your mother.'

'I'm not necessarily saying you did.'

'Oh please. I was down there with a man, not her, okay?'

He swears under his breath, then starts rifling through the top box. I could pull the door open, run out and down the stairs, but I know he'd catch me before I reached the door. Besides, it needs to be him who leaves this house, not me.

We can't go down the tunnel, not like this. Not when I'm unprotected. Not when there are things down there that shouldn't be discovered. I sit on the bed, force myself to calm down, pat the claw bar pressing against my back, just to check. He eyes me with suspicion before returning to his rummaging.

'What are you doing?' He pauses his search, studies me carefully.

'Sitting here. Waiting for you to get a grip.' I'm amazed at how measured my voice sounds, given how much my pulse is pounding.

He glares at me for a moment or two longer, then returns to the boxes. I exhale slowly.

'Found it,' he says, pulling a weighty torch out and holding it aloft like a trophy. 'I knew it'd be in here somewhere. Come on.'

'Vinnie, be reasonable. It's dark out there, freezing cold too. Why don't we have a drink, talk things through like adults? We're not going to resolve anything by being like this with each other.'

'Nice try, Heidi. I'm wise to your games, though.'

You're wise to me? I wish I'd been wiser to him from the start, never got myself wrapped up in his mess. Look at where it's led me. To this, a nightmare stacked on piles of lies and secrets. Away from everything that makes me who I really am. Who I fought so hard to be.

He grabs at me again, but I'm better prepared. I lash out, catching him across the cheek with my nails. No blood drawn, but it's enough to make him shout.

'You shouldn't have done that.'

'Stop attacking me, then.'

'I haven't even started yet, believe me.' He lunges at me again, seizing my other wrist. At least it's not my damaged hand, that's some comfort. But the damage has been done. The wound's bleeding again, there's a blood-bubble swelling at the centre. It'll burst and spill soon. The infection runs deep.

Maybe they'll amputate it, I think, as he tugs me back down the stairs. Then the severed hand will have the chance to blow away on the wind like a leaf. Hit some poor person's window on a dark winter's night, make them imagine a nixie's after them too. Either that or a dead woman who refuses to let them be.

We walk downstairs, a mess of struggling limbs. He drags me through the living area into the utility room, then throws me my coat. There's no point in not putting it on. He'll force me out there anyway, whether I'm wrapped up warm or not. I pull the sleeve carefully over my hand, making sure not to accidentally knock the claw bar.

'After you,' he says with a mock bow, swinging the door open.

'You're mad,' I whisper.

He gives me a look of pure loathing. 'You have no idea just how mad I am, Heidi. Get outside. Now.'

CHAPTER TWENTY-TWO

I flinch. It's raining out there again, hard. I look down and see puddles in the waterlogged grass. Perilous weather. Vinnie thinks he knows what he's doing, but he really doesn't.

He nudges me hard. I step out and wetness pounds my face, drills against my coat, into my wound, turning the black blood-bubble into a sewage-stream. I don't say anything. This has gone past words. It's not over though, not by a long way. It could still play out in my favour, if I stay sharp.

'Why is the wood piled up on the trapdoor?' he asks, as he trains the light of the torch to the ground ahead. 'Were you trying to hide something?'

'It kept blowing open.'

'Oh please.'

'I'm serious. There's something wrong with this place. The whole house is messed up.'

'The only thing that's messed up is you.'

'Things keep happening. Taps turning themselves on. Water marks on the wall.'

He ignores me. Lurches ahead and starts throwing the wood

in all directions. I step back, ready to run. He turns, grabs me, then points to the remaining pile.

'Help me. Now.'

'No.'

'Of course not. I remember now. Because you're terrified by what's down here, aren't you? Look at you. So frightened you can hardly speak.'

I could pull the claw bar out now. Hit him with every bit of force I can gather. But if I got it wrong, and it'd be easy to in the dark, he'd turn on me. It's too much of a risk.

Finally, he kicks the last of the wood planks aside and flings the trapdoor open. It splinters down the middle. The damned thing won't ever stay closed now. Whatever's down there will be pleased.

A witch, looking for revenge. I look around and see hunched old women in every corner of the garden, crouched among the long grass, concealed in the shadows of the wall. Claws out, ready. Witch. It's a word that gets thrown around a lot, even nowadays. Manipulative witch. Sly witch. But witches get what they deserve in the end.

Vinnie trips and nearly pitches forward into the hole. The torch beam veers upwards in a crazed arc, then suddenly plummets, followed by a clatter of hard thumps. He's dropped it. He swears, clutches my arm before I can escape.

'The torch still works,' he says, with a laugh. 'Look. Down there. Light.'

I peer down, though I don't want to. See a thin path of light across the stone floor. I follow its route. See it shining on something it shouldn't.

Beware the witch.

He grips me tighter. 'Down you go.'

'Stop this,' I tell him. 'It's not safe.'

'There's something down there. I want to know what it is.'

It looks like it goes down a long way, Vivienne said when she squinted down into the darkness, just like Vinnie is doing now. Like mother, like son. So similar, so narrow-minded and judgemental. So stupid, when it comes down to it.

'Heidi?' There's an edge to his voice now. 'What am I looking at?'

'How should I know?' I look down, try to get a sense of where he's standing in relation to me. It's hard to tell. The wind's pulling his words this way and that, and the light from the house doesn't touch us here. But I need to know. I need to make plans. My mind rolls over the possibilities. I need long-term solutions, not temporary stopgaps. *Think, Heidi. Think.*

'Go on. Down you go.'

He's behind me, then. I don't know how he managed to get there. He can move quietly when he wants to. All it'd take is one push. I'd tumble and he'd close the trapdoor. I bet it'd stay closed this time.

Reluctantly, I stretch my foot out until I touch the first step. This is what insanity looks like; descending into this place in a storm. Every surface is slippery, every second that passes I brace myself for his hand at my back, helping to speed things along. I think of old women flying down in front of me, colliding with stone stairs, forehead cracking against rough rock walls. Neck twisting one way, spine the other.

I feel the claw bar against my waistband, pressing into me with every step. At least I still have that. While it's there, I've got a chance.

'What the hell?' he murmurs, following behind me. 'What is that thing on the floor?'

I told you we shouldn't come down here, I think.

'Tell me what that is. I know what it looks like, but I don't even want to imagine I'm right.'

I stay silent. I pick up my pace as much as I dare. There needs to be distance between us if I'm going to stay safe.

'Heidi? Answer me now. You *knew already*, didn't you?'

My foot reaches the bottom stair. I kick the torch, sending the beam skittering down the tunnel, or at least to the ragged wall that marks the first corner. Vinnie grunts as he misses a step and lurches forward. I hear a dull thud as he treads on something. Something that releases a groan.

No. It's not possible. Not after being down here for so many hours.

Not moving. Not breathing. I checked earlier, listened hard for a long time.

Shit. *Shit.*

'My God,' Vinnie whispers. I sense him moving in the dark, and I quickly reach for the torch, scooping it up, turning it in his direction with shaking hands. He blinks in the glare of the light, then bends downwards to the floor. Now he's crouching, hand outstretched, feeling for something.

Feeling for a pulse.

'Mum?' he whispers. 'Please say you can hear me.'

Vivienne groans again. She's really alive. She can't be though. She shouldn't be. This isn't part of the plan.

He looks up at me. 'You pushed her down here, didn't you?' His voice is flat, expressionless. I can't make out his features, they're twisted by shadows. But his posture tells me he's ready to take action. Fight or flight. Run and get help, or stay and hurt me. Badly.

I guess it's understandable, given that he's found his mother lying down here in the blackness. Damn her. It all took so much effort. Shoving her down here, gathering her belongings, driving her car to an empty field down the road, cleaning the house to remove all traces of her. All of it was for nothing, now that she's still breathing. Nobody should be able to survive that fall.

A witch indeed.

She groans a third time, then wheezes out a word or two. It's nothing that makes much sense, but that's not the point. She's coming to, regaining proper consciousness. I came down here after, checked her breathing, waited for a few minutes to make sure she was dead. But not well enough. This is the worst thing that could have happened.

Vivienne. Still a thorn in my side, even now.

I stand silent while Vinnie yanks his phone out, presses the screen then swears again. No signal, of course. It's patchy enough in the house, let alone down here.

'Mum, I'm going to call an ambulance,' he tells her, trying his phone a second time. He looks up at me, ghoulish in the torchlight. 'You bitch. You evil bitch. I *knew* it. I think I knew it all along, deep down.'

'Who said I pushed her?' I step back and reach for the claw bar with my other hand. 'She fell down. I knew nothing about it.'

'Oh really? So her belongings, her car, they all just vanished of their own accord, did they?'

I take another step back. I had to move the car, didn't plan on her being discovered. But now, it's incriminating. I need time to figure this out, and Vinnie's giving me none of that. His arrival has ruined everything.

'Why did you do it?' He stands up, looks upwards, then back at me. Of course he can't work out his priorities. Phone for help out there where he can get a signal, or get me first. There's murder in his eyes, that's for sure.

She forced my hand, I want to say. *She threatened to steal my house. Ruin my life.* She still can. She's alive, she'll fight hard to bring me down and so will he. Think. Think, then act. Fast.

'I need to go back up and you're coming with me,' he says hoarsely. 'There's no way I'm trusting you down here with her.'

'I'm not coming with you.'

'Don't you *dare* make this hard, after what you've done. I swear I'll...'

'What will you do, Vinnie? Kill me? I can tell you want to. That'll be another dead girlfriend to add to your list.'

'I'm not a killer. I wouldn't kill you. But I'm going to make sure you're locked away for this. I want everyone to know what you really are. Manipulative, lying, evil bitch.'

'You'll have to catch me first.'

'Don't play games. I'd catch you in a heartbeat.'

I switch the torch off. Blackness envelops us both, making me aware of how cold it is, how the stink of the sea circles in the enclosed space. There's another smell too, mingling with the ice-salt. A darker stench. Vivienne perhaps, lying there on the floor. Blood. Body fluids. How she's alive, I don't know. She's a tough old hag, I'll give her that.

'Heidi?' His voice is closer, he's moving in the dark. 'Stop this now. Put the torch back on.'

I tread backwards, keeping close to the wall. Let my fingers trail the surface, feeling for the curve of the corner, knowing that it leads to a longer stretch of tunnel, knowing that there are plenty of rough stones to trip over the unwary traveller. I know this, he doesn't. I have the advantage. For the first time, I feel this is my domain. That I belong here, with the sea on my skin and salt in my nose. I'm the one who's been infected with it, not him.

'Heidi? I can hear you breathing, you little idiot.'

I say nothing, only keep moving. I can sense him now, a hulking presence taking up too much space. He's muttering now, I can feel his rage. He wants to hurt me, regardless of what he says. He wants to rip me to pieces.

'I didn't kill Noelle,' he whispers, a dislocated voice in the black. 'You know I didn't. In fact, I think you know much more than you pretend to.'

Silence. It's a trick, to get me to reveal myself.

'What did you do that day, Heidi? I couldn't see you anywhere. You said you were in the cave, then ran to the edge of the sea, but that was a lie, wasn't it? You were under the water. You used to tell me how your dad taught you how to hold your breath, to dive down to the seabed. It was you, beneath the waves, pulling her under. You held her there, while I was trying to pull her up.'

Don't say anything, I remind myself. Let him speak, let this play out. It's too late to go back now anyway.

'I thought I saw a dark shadow moving through the water,' he carries on. 'A shark, I worried at the time, even though I know we don't get any dangerous ones over here. Then I decided it was a seal. But it was you, wasn't it? Hiding in the weeds at the bottom. Waiting for the right moment.'

Like a nixie. I want to laugh suddenly. A gasp escapes instead.

'I'm right, aren't I?' It's a tone of wonder, horror too. 'I even asked myself at the time, *Could she have been involved?* But I told myself no, because you were so strong, so confident, so sweet to Noelle too. You made me take the blame for it. You made me grateful to you for protecting me, not revealing the secret.'

And you were happy enough to keep it a secret, I want to shout. He could have gone to the police at any point and it would have been done. But he was a coward. Still is, even now.

'When Miranda told me the truth about what you did to your father, that's when I started to wonder. Is it true, Heidi? Did you really hold your dad underwater until he nearly drowned?'

No. Yes. It's complicated. Life always is. Love and hate can exist in exactly the same moment. Willing someone to hold you, but pushing them away. Wanting them to stay, while wanting them to die.

I tried to kill Dad. I admit it, but only to myself. I would have kept on holding on until his breath ran out but he wriggled free. I would have left him down there to rot. Then he never would have gone away, and it would have served him right.

He was a survivor. I want to laugh. That's me too, like father like daughter. I don't ever stop fighting. I won't stop now. I edge back again and dislodge a stone with my heel. It rattles too loudly, gives Vinnie a location to head towards.

His hand brushes my arm in the black. I jerk backwards but not quickly enough. Fingers wrap around me, then tug me in. I knock my shoulder hard against the wall and wince.

'Let me go,' I hiss.

'Not a chance. Once I've called the ambulance for Mum, I'm calling the police.'

'I'll tell them you did it.'

'I know you will. But Mum will back me up. She spoke to Noelle, the day before it happened. Noelle told her how worried she was when you turned up unannounced in Kent. How worried she was about being around you. How you wanted her out of the picture.'

'Big deal. That won't stand up in court.' I wrench away. He grabs me again and starts to pull me backwards.

'Stop struggling, else I really will hurt you. God knows I want to.'

Footsteps. It's a confused thought; unconnected with the reality of what's happening right now. But there it is again. The unmistakable sound of someone moving behind Vinnie, walking firmly. A torch beam now too, shining directly at us.

Vivienne? She hasn't got a torch. Then I realise who it is. It's enough to bring a smile to my face. Funny how fate twists and turns. Like this tunnel really, and the tales it's kept secret over the years. Now here's another story for it to keep stored up safely. Because one thing's for sure. I'll make sure nobody really knows the truth.

'Don't hurt me!' I shout, expressing each word clearly, then pulling away from him. 'Please, Vinnie, let me go!'

'Seriously, I'll break your arm and I'll do it gladly.'

'You're insane. Don't hurt me like you did her!'

Confusion pours from him, even as the torch light illuminates his head like a halo, even as he turns to face his unseen foe. Rick, standing there in the dancing beam of light. An unlikely hero, but I'll take anything right now.

'Who the hell are you?' Vinnie mumbles.

Rick lifts his torch. 'Let go of her now.'

It's a firm command. Confident. He's ready to vanquish this monster. Good. He swings the torch into my face and I shrink back, wiping my eyes. Quickly, I replace the claw bar in my waistband. It doesn't fit with the image of the frightened woman in distress, it can stay hidden now.

'Heidi, are you okay?' Bea's voice this time, from somewhere just behind Rick.

'I'm okay,' I reply, shaky, juddery. 'Please be careful. Vinnie's threatening to kill me. He's insane.'

'What?' Vinnie blinks in the glare of the light. So slow, like an animal awaiting slaughter, failing to understand its own impending death. He's lost. Hope rises inside me. I knew I'd get him in the end.

'Who's the woman at the bottom of the stairs?' Bea asks.

'It's his mother,' I explain quickly. 'There was an argument. She stood up against him, said she couldn't defend a killer even if was her son. So he pushed her down here.'

'Shit,' Rick whispers. He raises his torch like a club. It's his only weapon, I realise. What an idiot. I've told him before, Vinnie is a giant and he's a boy by comparison.

'She's lying.' Vinnie holds his hands up in protest. 'She pushed my mum down those stairs. She's psychotic. She killed my ex, she as good as admitted it, she—'

'Vinnie, it's over,' I interrupt. 'Even you can't lie your way out of this one. You've been caught. Now do the decent thing. Let me go. Haven't you tortured me enough?'

He pushes past Rick, then Bea. I see her eyes widen in the spotlight. Good. Shock is good. This is all playing out more perfectly than I could have hoped for.

'Where the hell's he going?' Rick flicks the torch to Vinnie's back, a target of light between his shoulder-blades, then trains it back on my face.

'He's probably making his escape. Just let him go.'

Vinnie growls in the darkness. 'I'm going to phone an ambulance. My mother's lying there, seriously injured. I haven't got the time for your vicious games, Heidi. If these two are suckered in by your performance, that's their choice. They'll learn soon enough.'

I feel a hand on my shoulder. It's narrow and light, I pick up a light scent of citrus perfume. Bea.

'We need to act,' she says softly. 'Rick, go after him. He can't get away, we have to report him to the police.'

'For Christ's sake!' Vinnie's voice booms around the narrow space. 'How can you be so stupid? Who are you, anyway?'

'Friends of hers,' Rick says hotly.

Bea laughs. I wish she hadn't, it's just enough to be incriminating.

'Friends, eh?' Vinnie's voice is louder again, he must have come nearer to where we're standing. 'Oh, I see. *Friends*. The same friend she couldn't stop texting when my poor mother was staying here the other night.'

'It doesn't matter what we are.' Rick's hands are shaking, I can tell from the judder of the beam of light, passing over Vinnie's face like a jumping creature.

'Let me guess, she latched on to you after I left. Heidi likes to have a man in her life. It makes her feel wanted. She's got daddy issues, haven't you noticed? Serious ones, given she tried to drown him as a girl. It probably escaped your notice, given you've only known her five minutes.'

He retreats again, a series of angry footsteps down the tunnel. The light passes from face to face; Bea's haunted stare, caught somewhere between horror and poorly concealed hurt. Rick's, narrow and tight, brow lowered. I dread to think what my own must look like; full of concentration, planning the next move, probably. But it's fine. So far, everything's okay.

'Let's get out of here,' Rick says. 'I don't trust him, not one bit.'

'I'm sorry to drag you both into this,' I say, as we edge carefully along the tunnel. 'I knew he was unpredictable, but I had no idea it was this bad. He's lost it, I think. Completely lost it.'

Bea says nothing. Her silence is unnerving, but perhaps it's just fear.

We turn the corner, and the light finds Vinnie again, hulked over his mother like a gargoyle, hand cupping her face. Rick steps forward, but stops as Vinnie holds up a finger.

'She's coming to again,' he says, glaring at us. 'She just said my name.'

'Get away from her.' Rick's voice sounds faltering, uncertain.

Vinnie ignores him. Leans down, ear tilted towards Vivienne's mouth. We wait. I wait, chest tight, nails digging into my wound. The pain helps. It brings me back to this moment, makes me alert to potential opportunities.

'Vinnie?' Two syllables, weak and broken, but undeniably from Vivienne. My stomach clenches. She's still alive, and worse, she's making sense. I press my fingers deeper until the blood starts to drip down my wrist.

'Mum?' Vinnie places a hand under her head, gently as a parent cradling a baby. 'I'm here. I'm going to get help.'

'My head. Hurts.'

'I know. Do you know where you are, how you got here?'

His top priority is to get evidence on me, not care for her. He won't rest until he's seen me suffer.

Vivienne gurgles something, struggles to clear her throat, cries out as he raises her head a little higher.

'I wouldn't do that,' Bea says. 'If her neck's broken, you might make it worse.'

'If her neck was broken, she'd be dead already,' I snap, then regret it. *Tread carefully*, I remind myself. *A single wrong move and you'll drown.*

'Her.' Vivienne's voice sounds stronger now, more alert. 'It's her.'

'Heidi, you mean?' Vinnie looks in my direction.

'Her. *Wicked*. Pushed me, hurt Noelle–' Her words falter, broken into pieces by a wracking wheeze.

Vinnie points at me in triumph. 'And there it is. You pushed her, Heidi. You're a killer. Now you've been found out.'

Rick's torch flies round in my direction. It's a light of interrogation, blinding me. I can't see anything, only white, piercing white. Like that sun, that day at the beach. It blinded me for a moment or two when I emerged from the water. Gasping for breath, a good distance from Vinnie, close to the shore. Arms aching, legs sore from Noelle's kicks and punches. Lungs burning. I hadn't held my breath that long in years.

I waded out to the beach, then turned and watched Vinnie still flailing around, hunting for her. It was exposing, being out of the water. I preferred slipping through the depths like a sea creature, winding in and out of the weeds.

He waved at me, screamed something. *Noelle. Gone under. Help.*

I took another breath, then dove back into the water to swim towards him. To help search for her, in the wrong places of course; I made sure I dragged her deep.

The supportive girlfriend. Ready to take over where the previous one left off.

'Heidi?' Rick's voice brings me back. He's confused, waiting for me to set things straight. I think of Noelle's face underwater, the eyes widening with shock. Then accusation. She struggled hard, even after taking in water. Thrashed like an eel until she went limp, let me go about making knots of the drifting weeds around her armpits, wrists, ankles. She held my gaze as she died. I knew then that it wasn't over, even after she was.

There's no escape from this. I've got no answer to Rick's look of dawning horror. Or Bea's stricken expression, hand covering her mouth. Or the weight of Vinnie's judgement, his delight at undoing me.

So, I turn away from the light. I choose darkness, and run back into the safety of the tunnel.

CHAPTER TWENTY-THREE

It's amazing, how a total absence of light can become a friend. My feet find their pace in the black. I turn the corner blindly, break into a jog with my hands outstretched, negotiating rough terrain, uneven walls. Weak light forms a broken pool ahead of me, thanks to a torch beam shone from behind. Someone's chasing me. Not sure which one of them.

'Stop!' It's Rick's voice. That's better than Vinnie; I stand a chance of outrunning him. I train my ears to the sound of his feet; two people following me, not one. Lighter footsteps. Bea. She shouldn't be involved in any of this. She shouldn't even be in my life, full-stop.

They're saying something to each other. It's terse, panicked. I can't make out what they're saying, but it's bound to be something to do with bringing me down. They're working as a team, a little duo. I think of Rick in my bed, only today. What a snake. Her too. The pair of them deserve each other. I can do much better.

'Heidi, stop this. We just want to talk, find out what's going on.'

Not a chance. My hands hit wet rock, I yelp as the impact

reverberates through my palms, down my wrists. Another corner maybe, though I don't remember one this early on when Rick and I explored it before.

Bea and Rick are muttering something to each other again. Their pace has slowed, they're thinking about what to do. That's a relief. It gives me time to feel these walls, see if there's somewhere I can hide. I pad my hands silently along the rock, to the right, then to the left. Something sharp connects with my thumb, and I feel the memory of it in my palm. A fingernail, embedded into the wall, maybe the same one, or different. Either way, the strength of it is unsettling. It shouldn't be this resistant to pressure, it should snap.

You won't get me this time, I think, moving past it. But you're welcome to claw the others, if you want. They're the intruders here now, not me.

I think of swimming, deep in the depths. Through weeds wrapping themselves around my limbs. It's dark down there too, if you go down far enough. It's amazing how weak the light is, even on the sunniest, warmest of days. A silent, watchful world that can't be trusted.

I remembered Dad, as I was holding Noelle down. I'd strained to keep him in the depths with me, but in the end he was too strong. He gripped my wrists to get me to release him, leaving bruises on my soft teenage skin for days after.

Noelle was easier, once I'd wrestled her away from Vinnie's grasp and dragged her down through the water. She was far weaker than Dad had been. Flimsily perfect, like the pages in that silly notebook of hers. Thin, insubstantial. What a naïve fool. Even now her body's been discovered, she's still a meaningless mystery. Until now. Everything hangs on me escaping. Then getting revenge later. I won't let Vinnie or Vivienne get away with this.

My outstretched hands leave the wall and enter

nothingness. It's another branch to the tunnel; confirmed when I fumble further and find a fresh rock-wall to the other side of me. I pause for a moment and listen.

They're still following, though more cautiously now. I can see the torchlight, a glare of light flitting this way and that. I can hear something else though; a rush and drag like a distant, breathing roar. The sea. I'm close to the end of this tunnel, to where the smugglers must have unloaded their stolen goods.

It gives me an idea. Which is just what I've been waiting for.

I creep along the tunnel, aware of the torchlight only a few metres from my feet. They're following quietly too, a cat and mouse chase that won't end well. I need to find the end of this tunnel before they catch up with me. Everything depends on it now. This needs to be tied up neatly.

Like Noelle, in all those weeds.

A circle of white appears in view. It's the moon, piercingly bright. Below it, there's the black of the sea, the noise of the waves, the bite of the wind. I keep moving further and the tunnel widens into the mouth of a cave. It's not a large space, but it's enough. I take my position by the rocks at the entrance, brace myself against the chill, then look down. All I can see are rocks, lots of them, half-buried in frothing sea-foam. There's ground to my right, probably the path that Rick mentioned to me before. It's narrow and overgrown, but just about passable. It must have been what those smugglers used long ago. Good to keep in mind if it gets to that point.

I look over my shoulder. The torchlight blinds me.

'Heidi, stop this.'

The moonlight casts weak light over Rick's features, turning him into a stone statue. He's handsome. Strong. It gives me a wrench to see him like this. Makes me think of our time in his bed before everything went wrong. So much has gone wrong in my life. It's amazing I'm still here and still battling on.

'It's all lies,' I whisper.

'Why did you run away?'

'Vinnie and his mum, they're trying to frame me. I panicked. I don't want him to hurt me anymore.'

Bea steps forward. 'Just come back with us. Please. I don't like you being by the edge like that. It's not safe.'

'What does it matter to you? You don't like me anyway.'

'I don't like what you did. That's different.'

She thinks she's clever, answering like that. The mature woman dealing with the hysterical child. She has nothing to be pleased about. All she's got is a home in a dead-end village, a job in a local shop, a lover who sleeps around. She's never escaped, never found herself a new, more exciting life. She's content to hang off a man like a parasite.

Just like Noelle. I groan at the thought. Always, it comes back to her. She was meant to stay down there in those weeds, not keep bobbing to the surface. Bea reminds me of her in many ways. Miss Perfect, Miss Nice. Miss Kindly, with entitlement running right through her.

Rick puts the torch carefully on the ground, then moves towards me.

I step back. 'What are you doing?'

'We're going to go back down the tunnel, Heidi. We're going to go up the stairs, then we're–'

'Don't talk to me like I'm a child. You weren't talking to me like a child when you were in my bed today.'

Bea's sharp intake of breath is quiet, but enough. Good. She should know.

We're a frozen tableau for a moment or two. Hardly enough time for me to think before he dives forward. He grabs at my shoulder, misses then grasps a clump of my hair instead. I yelp, push him away, tumble backwards, far too near to the edge. My heel tilts over sharp stone into nothing. I falter, arms pedalling, my whole body hangs in the balance. Bea screams. I must be falling, and I know those rocks lie below, waiting and ready for me.

I feel myself lurching forwards, then I'm steady again a second later. I'm safe, breathless but safe; but not through my own doing. Rick is clutching my injured hand, he stopped me from falling. Then the pain hits me, wave after wave running along my skin. He cringes, releases my hand and wipes his own down his top. That's two men smeared with my blood now. The infection must be spreading.

'You nearly killed me,' I whisper.

'No, I saved you.' He glances at Bea. 'You saw that, right?'

She nods. 'Just grab her, Rick. Or leave her here. We can't stay like this, it's too dangerous. Besides, the police might be here already. That Vinnie guy said he'd call them.'

Police. Of course Vinnie called them. Everything's breaking apart like the sea on those rocks. These two won't help me now, the trust is gone. There was a golden moment of confusion, but now it's cold suspicion, nothing else.

I lunge, sink my fingers into the fabric of Bea's coat, then grip hard. She stumbles and cries out. I take a breath. This needs to be fast, too fast for Rick to react to in time. My leg extends behind her, a perfect thing to trip over, then I push her hard. She flies backwards, a leaf-shape of flailing limb and hair. Twists to the side revealing her face in profile. Mouth a circle of shock, eyes reaching for some understanding and finding none. She's not falling cleanly, not like I nearly did only a minute or so earlier. Her twist lurches her to the right, past me. Then she disappears out of view.

Did she fall? She must have done. Why did she turn herself like that, though? I crane my neck out quickly, peer around, can't see her. She must have tumbled down and hit those rocks. It's not ideal, taking her out too. Too many deaths leave too big a trail. But she and Rick left me no other option than to fight my way out.

I reach for Rick, but he's too quick, arms already raised in defence.

'Bea!' he screams, a ragged howl over the beat of the sea below.

I lunge again. He ducks out of the way. I reach behind me for the claw bar, it's the only way left. Fumbling in my waistband, I draw it out and let the moonshine gleam along its length.

His eyes widen. 'You're insane.'

'That's not true. If you'd trusted me, none of this would have happened.'

'Bea!' He edges to the opening, peers down. 'You tripped her over, Heidi. Why the hell would you do that? She's never done anything to you.'

I don't reply. There's no time for chat, we're a long way past that. Besides, he made it clear that he wanted nothing more from me than a good time before returning to his *girlfriend*. His girlfriend who's now been torn up on the rocks. What a way to go.

I hold the claw bar out. Then, I slide slowly around him, inch by inch, blocking off the tunnel behind us. The last thing I need is for him to run. That really would put a spanner in the works.

'Look,' he says, wheedling, desperate too. 'This madness needs to stop. Put that thing down, please.'

I smile. A bit of begging never hurts, but it won't help him.

He moves back, not forward as I expected. I guessed he'd try to find a way to slip into the tunnel, catch me off guard and then disappear into the dark. But instead, he approaches the edge again, dangerously close to losing his footing and taking a tumble down there too. He's glancing to one side. I don't understand why, but it doesn't matter. All it takes is one push.

It's hard. I'm not a cold-blooded killer and I don't want to end anyone's life. Sometimes, though, extreme measures have to be taken to move forward in life. It's that simple. And I've come too far to drown now.

But it's difficult not to think of his body next to mine. The warmth of his breath at my neck. The easy way we laughed together, that evening in the pub. We'd been good together, for a short while. I really liked him, not just because he was good-looking, but because he liked me. Not Heidi the free-diver in training. Not Heidi the life and soul of every party, the sex-kitten in the office. The real me, whatever that is.

I've got to remember, if I weaken now, I lose. *Toughen up, Heidi.*

He watches me carefully. The moon's at his side, casting his profile into sharp relief. He's edging to his right. Taunting me, almost. Perhaps he thinks I haven't got it in me.

I move. It has to be now, though it's too close to the right-hand wall and doesn't give me enough room to get my full weight behind it. He jumps deftly to one side, just as I thrust my hands out towards him. He's always slight, speedy and unpredictable, right until this final moment. I lurch into nothing, pull myself back, then battle hard to get my balance.

Something wraps itself around my ankle. The claw bar falls from my hand and over the edge. I scream, then lose my footing completely.

It's her. Noelle. Cold fingers at my flesh. Clasping, tugging, refusing to let go.

Rick catches me again, just before I fall. For a moment, I rest in his arms. A mermaid, rescued by her lover. I look up into his face and remember lying with him like this before. Wrapped up safe in him, with nothing else to worry about in the world. The bliss of those few moments amongst all the chaos.

Then he throws me to the ground. My head hits stone. I reel, can't stop my eyes from closing. In the black of my eyelids, everything swims.

'Well done, Bea,' I hear him say. 'Thank God you're okay.'

Bea landed on the smuggler's path, not the rocks below. My ears start to ring with pressure. *The smugglers saved her and left me to rot.* Then I lose the pair of them as their voices fade to a distant radio whine, then to nothing.

Everything's silent and still. Like the bottom of a fathomless ocean.

I've sunk, I think, before I pass out completely.

I open my eyes. White light. Bright, it hurts to look at it. The bed's hard, covered with a plastic sheet not a cotton one. My head feels like someone's stuffed it with foam, I can't hold on to a single thought before it floats away again, until it's out of reach.

I wait a while, give myself time. I'm not at home. The room's the wrong shape, it's smaller and narrower. There are curtains to every side of me, faded blue and green striped fabric. I raise my head then lower it again. It hurts, right at the back. My eyes are swollen too and full of grit.

I move my uninjured hand to rub them and can't. It's stuck, attached to something at the side of the bed. I yank once, then again, harder. Something cold at my wrist. It doesn't make sense.

Remember. Come on, brain. It shouldn't be this hard.

I was in a cave. The cave, at the end of the smuggler's tunnel. It was dark down there, I remember panic, fear. Rick.

Bea. Waves below, rocks too. Then the images start coming to me more vividly. Bea grabbed my ankle, pulled me down, nearly killed me. Rick grabbed me, then threw me down to the ground. My head hit stone and his face swirled like a kaleidoscope.

I failed. Or not. I need to think harder, figure out how to play this. There are too many unknowns here. I'm in dangerous territory.

Someone pulls the curtain at the end of the bed back, with a rush of metal runners and colder air. It's a man in blue tunic and trousers, harassed expression, hair thinning at the top, see-through under the fluorescent light. He closes the curtain behind him, looks back to me and doesn't smile.

I try to sit up quickly. Only make it so far, then slide backwards against slippery pillows. I feel about eighty years old. Weak, feeble, not in full grasp of my own senses.

Who are you? I wait. Then realise I hadn't said it aloud, only in my own head. My lips are caked and I can't move them.

He approaches the bed and checks something on the machine beside me. 'You're awake, then. How do you feel?'

'My head's killing me.' My words are furry, almost incoherent. The room starts crackling at the edges as a fresh wave of pain throbs through my skull.

'We've sewn you up as best as we can. Your hand's another matter. A nasty infection, it's penetrated the muscle layers. You really should have gone to hospital far sooner. The amount of discharge coming from the wound surely indicated something serious?'

I shrug and try to sit up again. 'I had other things on my mind.'

He purses his lips. Disapproval. Distaste. He knows something, or thinks he does.

'Which hospital is this?' I ask.

'Truro.'

'Why can't I move my hand?'

He raises an eyebrow. 'See for yourself.'

I glance across. Lift my wrist. There's a metal band around it with a chain dangling below. Handcuffs. I'm trapped.

I finally make it to a semi-sitting position, force myself to concentrate. 'Why am I cuffed?'

'That's not for me to say. I'm here to look after your health. I need to take your readings then ask you a few general questions, okay?'

'Not okay. Where's Rick? What happened to Vinnie?'

'I don't know who they are. Now, could you sit up properly for me? I know it's difficult with the handcuff in place. Do your best, please.'

'Can't you just take it off?'

He shakes his head. 'I doubt the policeman out there would approve of that.'

Policeman? I crane my neck but the curtains block everything. I'm under arrest, being guarded. My mind races, remembers and remembers. Vinnie phoned the police. Vinnie's mother isn't dead after all. She must have told them I pushed her, and he would have backed her up.

I did push her, of course. I push the thought aside just as hard. She had it coming, she was never going to let me be. It's a miracle no-one killed the old hag years ago.

The doctor tilts my head downwards and starts examining the wound. I feel his fingers on my naked scalp, no hair to protect me. They shaved me there. It feels like a violation. I raise my bandaged hand to check the rest of my head. Only one patch then, which is something, though it probably looks ridiculous.

He checks my breathing. Uses a thin torch to check my eyes. Blood pressure, temperature. This is a chore for him. He's ready to leave for the day, to go home to his family, his happy little home somewhere in the suburbs. He'll forget all about me then, and I'll be left here alone.

It's the story of my life, men leaving. But now's not the time to get maudlin.

'How long do I have to stay here?' I ask.

'Hopefully not long. Unless that hand refuses to heal up, then we might have to try a different approach.'

'Can I go home after that?'

He gives me a look. 'You've been detained. Do you understand what that means?'

I think of cold hands underwater. Claws, scraping flesh. Dragging down, down into the darkness. Detainment. It's all the same, once you get down to it.

'I'd get some rest if I were you,' he says, standing. 'You'll benefit from it.'

I stay sitting. He waits a while, then shrugs. He's seen it all before. *You're no-one special*, he's thinking. It's written all over his face.

But he's wrong. I am. I've done things other people wouldn't dare, to keep driving myself forward. More than he ever has, probably. I watch as he locks the door behind him, then slowly slump down against the pillows.

I need to make plans. Get my story straight. No-one saw me push Vivienne. No-one saw me drown Noelle. Rick only thought he saw me push Bea, but it was dark. Shadows can twist the truth, make things seem how they aren't.

For now, I need to close my eyes. Rest. Then start fighting again.

CHAPTER TWENTY-FOUR

I wake to talking.

People talking in this room. Bright lights. Hum of noise. The hospital room. My prison, because I can't move.

It's a sensory overload. I startle, hit the top of my head on the metal bedhead, then gasp in pain. There are two people beside my bed. A woman sitting on a chair, a man standing behind her. Not doctors. They're dressed in dark uniform, both of them older, greyer, sterner. The police. Not now, this isn't the right time, not when I'm still tangled up in sleep and my vision's whirling and bubbling.

I sit up, as comfortably as my handcuff will allow. 'Were you watching me sleep?'

The woman glances up at the man, then back to me. 'I'm Inspector Landlow, Heidi. This is my colleague, Inspector Meadows. We were told you were feeling better now.'

'Not really.'

'Sorry to hear that. I was told your head injury wasn't too bad.'

'I was thrown roughly to the ground. It's amazing I'm not more seriously hurt.'

'Sounds like an eventful evening for all involved.'

I laugh. It's a hollow, biting sound. Not what I was going for. They need to feel sympathy for me, not suspicion.

'What's funny?' Inspector Meadows asks, sticking his hands in his pockets.

'Calling it eventful is an understatement,' I explain. 'Given my ex-boyfriend tried to kill me, then told my friends I'd shoved his mother down the stairs. It was the worst evening of my life.'

They look at each other again. There's doubt there, I can sense it. A crack in their wall of interrogation. I need to pull the crack wide until their whole case against me comes tumbling down. It's doable. It's Vinnie and his mother's word against mine. Rick might even be the solution to this, providing he tells them about how frightened I was of Vinnie before, how violent he was before he left. I can surface from this. I know I can.

Inspector Meadows clears his throat. 'Heidi, are you aware you're under arrest?'

'I'm sure Vinnie has painted a nasty picture of me. He's a liar, a killer too. He's the one you need to arrest.'

He ignores me. 'I need to explain your rights to you. You do not have to say anything, but it may harm your defence if you do not mention when questioned something which you rely later on in court. Anything you do say may be given in evidence.'

'What other rights do I have?' I ask.

'You can request legal advice, if you need to. There are various other rights that we can outline–'

'This is stupid. Vinnie planned all of this, he's set me up and you've all fallen for it.'

Inspector Landlow leans forward. 'Do you want to tell us about it, Heidi? We'd be happy to hear it.' She reaches inside a bag at her feet, pulls out a handheld recorder, then places it on the bed in front of me. 'Do you mind? It saves us having to have this conversation again down the station.'

I pause. I do mind, but I need to look compliant. Innocent. 'Fine,' I agree, trying a smile. 'I suppose.'

She smiles, pressing record. 'Thank you for being so cooperative. Interview with Heidi Rhys, the date is twenty-third November, 2022, time three thirty-two in the afternoon. Please, Heidi, in your own time.'

I take a moment to compose myself. Sleep's still got a hold of me. My head's aching, I feel less than prepared. But if I'm unwilling to talk, they'll draw conclusions. They need to see the wronged woman, the pretty little thing that trusted the wrong people. I want them to compare me to Vinnie. To remember his hulking presence, surly face, the power in his body. They'll naturally side with me, as long as I get the story right.

'Vinnie's a murderer,' I say, wrapping my free arm across my stomach. 'That's as good a place to start as any.'

Inspector Landlow frowns. 'That's a serious accusation. Who are you claiming Vinnie killed, Heidi?'

'Noelle. His previous girlfriend.' I swallow, rub my eyes. 'I know this is out of the blue. I should have come forward before, but I was scared. Vinnie said if I told anyone, he'd blame me. Make people believe I did it. So I've lived with the burden for months now.'

She nods. Is there sympathy in her eyes? There might be. My heart rises, just a little.

'Can you tell us about your relationship with Vinnie?' she asks.

'We had an affair. We used to work together; you know what it's like. When we first got together, I didn't know he had a girlfriend. By the time I found out, I was too much in love with him to pull away.'

'What was your relationship like with Noelle?'

'It was good. I liked her. That's what made it so horrible. I tried to stop seeing Vinnie, but he's persuasive. He doesn't take no for an answer. You've seen what he's like.'

I wait. They both wait too. They're difficult to read, but I think my words are having an effect.

'Vinnie said he loved me,' I tell them. 'I was stupid to fall for it. I should have known it was too soon and too messy. But I said yes because I was smitten with him. He told me to book a hotel room near where they were staying in Kent. He said he couldn't bear spending the whole weekend alone with her.'

'And you did?'

'Like I said, I was stupid.'

'When was this weekend, Heidi?'

'Early August. It felt wrong, right from the start. Vinnie was playing us off one another. Noelle was uncomfortable, suspicious. Who can blame her? It felt like a sick game. I didn't know how sick it was going to get, though.'

'Go on.'

'On the Sunday, we hired a boat and explored the coastline. It was hot, really hot. Noelle spent most of the time doodling in her little book. We found a tiny beach and had our picnic there, drank some wine too. Vinnie insisted Noelle join him in the water. She couldn't swim very well. He dragged her into the sea, way too deep. I walked off, I didn't want to watch them together. There was a little cave in the cliff. I went exploring. By the time I came out, all I could see was Vinnie on his own. No Noelle. Then her head burst out of the water. I could see she was in trouble and I started to run towards them. Then I saw him push her under.'

'Can I clarify, you actually witnessed Vinnie holding Noelle underneath the water?'

'I did. He pulled her under. Disappeared underwater himself too. That must have been when he tied her up in those weeds.'

'And you didn't call the police?'

Take it slow, I remind myself. They're listening hard, hanging off my every word. But they're still searching for ways to trip me up and I can't stumble, not now. This has to be convincing. I sniff, cast my eyes downwards, then back to them both.

'I was too shocked at first. I couldn't believe what I was seeing. I got my phone out but there was no signal. No way of leaving the cove either, except by boat. Vinnie eventually came out of the water. He looked exhausted, pale. Guilt-ridden. He told me Noelle had drowned.'

'And?'

'I asked him if that was the truth. He wouldn't meet my eye. He told me we had to keep this between the two of us.'

'And did you agree, Heidi?'

Nodding, I pat my eyes. 'He grabbed me and hugged me tight. Told me he'd done it for us. I felt horrible.'

I pause. They glance at each other again. I can't read their expressions, which is worrying. What I told them should arouse surprise at least, if not shock. Horror at the thought of cold-blooded murder.

'I doubt he's told you any of this,' I add. 'Vinnie's a good liar.'

Again, no response. They both nod for me to continue. My chest tightens.

I smile weakly, then continue. 'Things went sour between us both soon after that. I didn't want to move away from London, but he insisted. People were gossiping about him, all sorts of rumours were flying around. He was nervous about being found out.'

'And how did you feel about moving to Cornwall?'

'I hated the idea. But he wouldn't take no for an answer. He never does. He made me go swimming with him when we moved in, even though it was freezing. Tried to drag me under the water too, even though he denied it.'

'Would you describe yourself as a good swimmer, Heidi?' Inspector Meadows asks.

I pause. 'Average, I guess? Not good enough to fight against someone Vinnie's size. Luckily, he gave up trying after a while. Two deaths on his hands might have been one death too many for him.'

'What actually happened?'

'I felt his hands on my legs while I was in the sea, then he released me.'

'Was it definitely him?'

Yes, I think, though the truth is more like *no*. I was panicking that day, still searching for that female swimmer on the horizon. The swimmer who hadn't even been there. The sea was rough, freezing cold. It could have been cramp in my legs. But I prefer the *yes* answer. It serves me better.

'It was him,' I confirm.

'Why do you think he did that?'

'I don't know. Who can say what goes through a killer's mind?'

'Indeed,' Inspector Landlow says, crossing her legs. 'Keep going, this is interesting.'

'Interesting?' I study her, but she's unreadable. 'Why? What has Vinnie told you?'

'I didn't mean to put you off your flow. Please, carry on.'

They don't believe me. The realisation is a wrecking ball, smashing through any hope I had left. I'm in trouble. I scan their faces, see nothing there that gives me any comfort.

I should have asked for legal assistance. I should have used my right to remain silent. Above all else, I don't understand. Why don't they believe what I'm saying? There's no evidence to incriminate me, it's his word and his mother's word against mine. I look more like a victim than either of them.

Except you weren't pushed down a flight of stone steps, a quiet voice adds inside my head. I push that thought down too. It's not helping.

'There's not much else to tell,' I say carefully. 'We had a fight out in the garden. I told him I wanted to split up. He went wild, pushed me over, it was terrifying. I really thought he might kill me. Anyway, he left without even telling me, ran off to his mother's house, started spending time with my best friend, Miranda. Sounds like he started sleeping with her the moment he got there. Perhaps they'd been seeing each other before that.'

Inspector Landlow taps at the bed. 'And when did you start seeing Ricardo Smith?'

'Who? Rick?'

'Haven't you been spending a lot of time with Mr Smith? And sleeping with him too?' She watches me, impassive, poised.

Damn you, Rick. He told them. Of course he did.

'That was a mistake,' I clarify. 'I felt pressured by him. I was vulnerable.'

'Did you spend an evening drinking with Ricardo Smith in The Fisherman's Rest pub in Nairbourne?'

'Only as a friend. Nothing happened that night.'

Inspector Meadows touches his colleague's shoulder, just lightly. She turns, nods, then looks back to me.

'Shall we carry on?' she says lightly. 'Tell us about Vinnie's mother. What happened when she arrived at your house?'

I tap my fingers against my wounded palm, a steady rhythm to ground me. This needs to be told right.

'She turned up unannounced and was horrible from the start,' I say. 'Aggressive, threatening. Told me to leave Vinnie alone, which I was more than happy to do. She left in a rage, but came back later as the road was blocked. I don't think that was true though. Her car had satnav. She could have found another way out. But she wanted to come back to finish the job.'

'Finish the job?'

'She insisted we went for a stroll down to the cove. When we were down there, she started hurling insults at me, tried to shove me into the water. I stormed off. I couldn't bear being around her anymore. But she followed me back up to the house and wouldn't leave me alone. She started fighting me in the garden. I fought back. She's old but strong. Big, like her son. She tried to shove me down the smuggler's tunnel, but I slipped away under her arm. She lost her balance and fell down the steps.'

'She fell, and you left her there?'

'Of course not, I'm not heartless.'

'What then?'

'I went down, tried to help her but she wasn't breathing. I thought she was dead, I really did. If I'd known she was alive, I would have phoned for help straight away.'

'But you didn't phone for the police?'

This is the moment that everything turns on. I can't screw it up. It's not about proving my innocence; my chances of doing that are slim. It's about not giving them anything solid to pin on me. Pull it off and I'll sail away with minimal scars.

Here goes. I put my head in my hands and force out a sob. It sounds convincing. I add another, then wipe my face. 'I wish I'd called the police,' I murmur. 'I really do. But Rick was coming to pick me up, I had no time to react. I was in shock.'

'What about Vivienne's car? Her belongings?' Inspector Meadows asks.

Damn, I'd forgotten that. My mind works through the potential options. Think fast, faster than that.

'I think Vinnie must have moved the car when he arrived,' I

tell them. 'But I don't know for sure. I can't see who else it would have been.'

Why would he have done that? My mind races, comes up blank. I don't know why I said it, but what else could I say? Still, I wore gloves, wiped down the steering wheel, the gear stick, the door handle. There won't be any traces of me in that car, I'm sure of it.

'Ricardo said that there was no car on the drive when he came to pick you up.'

Shit. I keep my head down. I can't rush this, but I need to think of something and quickly.

'The car was parked to the side of the house,' I tell them. 'There's a good chance he wouldn't have noticed it. It was mid-afternoon, the sun was already setting.'

'The side of your house, you say?'

'Yes. I'm almost sure.'

Again, the glance between the two of them. Her fingers are tapping against her crossed knee, slow, deliberate. A shark with jaws wide, waiting for the right moment. I've walked into a trap. But they can't seal it shut. Not without evidence.

'What happened when Vinnie arrived?' Inspector Landlow asks.

'I don't know. I was distressed. This is distressing too, this interview. My head's really hurting.'

'Sorry to hear that, Heidi. We don't need too much more from you today. What time would you say Vinnie arrived?'

'Later in the evening? I didn't pay attention to the details. He left the house at one point, that's when he probably moved his mother's car. He forced me into our garden in the dark, tried to push me down the tunnel too.'

'But you managed to resist him?'

'I ran down the stairs. Saw Vivienne at the bottom. She was injured but alive, I noticed straight away. She started laughing.

Vinnie crouched down beside her and gave her a hug. Told her she'd given him the best present of all; a way to make sure I'd get imprisoned for life.'

'Then Ricardo and Beatrice arrived?'

'Rick and Bea, yes. Vinnie fed them a load of lies. I could see doubt in their eyes, so I ran down the tunnel. It was panic, pure and simple. They followed me. I should have stopped but I was too scared. We reached the cave leading out to the cove. Bea lunged at me but tripped and fell. Then Rick leapt on me and threw me to the floor. That's all I remember.'

I look up. It's not a water-tight story, I know that. There are pot-holes all over it, a few of them larger than others. But proof is the important thing and they don't have that. I need to keep my nerve.

'Thanks, Heidi.' Inspector Landlow smiles. It's not much, but it's something. 'Do you mind if I just ask a few questions before we finish?'

'If it helps. I really don't feel great, though.'

'It's appreciated. So, returning to Noelle's death for a moment. You said you were on the beach when she died, in a cave?'

'Exploring, yes.'

'And when you saw Vinnie push her under, you didn't try to enter the water yourself?'

'I'm a good swimmer, but not that good. And I panicked.'

'Wasn't your father a free-diving champion?'

My skin prickles. 'Why do you ask?'

'We were informed that he was. And that you're actually a very good free-diver yourself, capable of holding your breath for several minutes.'

'No. I don't have Dad's talent, sadly.'

'We've heard differently, from three separate sources.'

Nausea rises in my stomach. I run through the options.

Vinnie told them, obviously. Rick, I told him too. But who's the third? Miranda. It must be. She's betrayed me yet again.

'Why is that relevant, anyway?' I ask.

'Maybe it's not. What about your relationship with Noelle? You said you got on very well. Can you tell us more?'

I don't know where this is leading. I feel my body chilling, turning to lead. I'm sinking. I lift my hand and the handcuff pulls me back, reminding me that I'm trapped. The shark's jaws are closing slowly.

Keep your nerve, I remind myself. *They haven't got anything concrete to go on, and they never will, as long as you think first, speak after.* 'I told you already,' I say, keeping my voice even. 'We were friends, in spite of everything. I know that's messed up, but it's the truth. She trusted me.'

'She trusted you?'

'Yes, deeply.'

Inspector Meadows frowns. 'That's interesting. Maria, why don't you show Heidi what you've got in your bag?'

Inspector Landlow leans down with a practised air and starts rummaging. 'It's a good a time as any, I suppose,' she says, pulling out something small and square, encased in a plastic bag. 'I'll get my latex gloves on, hang on.'

She places the object on the bed. I can't help but stare. I know what it is. But it's not possible. It shouldn't be here. It should be swept out to sea or else disintegrated by sand and salt, blown away on the wind.

Noelle's little book.

'Do you recognise this?' Inspector Landlow asks, pulling a glove over one hand, then the other. She reaches over, opens the plastic bag, pulls the book out and holds it up.

'No,' I lie.

'Really? You pulled quite an expression when you saw it.'

'I've never seen it before.'

'Okay. Well, this was a little notebook that belonged to Noelle. I'm surprised you don't recognise it, as you mentioned you'd seen her writing and sketching in it earlier.'

'I didn't pay that much attention.'

Inspector Landlow shrugs. 'It was found in a small cave by the cove where her body was discovered. You were right. She was a talented artist and writer. There's lots in here, plenty of fascinating material.'

'Sad really, isn't it?' Inspector Meadows adds. 'What a waste.'

'Well, we've still got this,' she answers. 'It reads more like a diary than anything else, though there are some lovely sketches too. You're mentioned several times.'

I swallow hard. Noelle told me she just wrote poems, scribbled random thoughts, occasional pictures. She didn't keep a diary. They're lying, trying to catch me out.

'I'm going to read you a few excerpts,' Inspector Landlow says, leaning back against the chair. 'I'd like to hear what you think of it.'

'It doesn't mean anything,' I mutter.

'What was that?' She waits, then shrugs. 'Doesn't matter. Let's start with this one. "Vinnie thinks I don't know. He's so obvious, it's like a child playing hide-and-seek, feet sticking out of the bottom of the curtain, confident he can't be seen. Heidi, her name is. She's one of those women. Brash. Driven. The life and soul of the party. I can see the attraction, I guess. But she's no prettier than the other ones. Jayne. Phillipa. Willow. Uglier, actually. She's got a sly look to her. I'm done with this. All his grovelling when he comes scuttling back, all the bullshit about not being able to help himself. I'm a moron for trusting him. I wonder when he'll confess this time."'

I don't know what to say. It can't be true. Noelle didn't know. I know she didn't. She was far too gullible and naïve to know. As for the other women? I don't know. I don't know what to think anymore. Vinnie always told me I was special. What a bastard.

'What do you make of that, Heidi?' Inspector Meadows asks.

I shrug. 'I don't believe it. Those aren't her words.'

Inspector Landlow raises an eyebrow. 'Okay. What about this excerpt, then? "Spent the afternoon with Heidi, looking round the shops, having coffee. It's funny, she really believes I like her. She's poison. She sneers at me, mocks me, thinks I don't notice. She's already stolen my boyfriend; does she have to rub it in my face too? She's worthless. Him too. I could end this now. Get rid of him. Tell her what I really think of her. I'm done being the nice girlfriend that puts up and shuts up; I've done it for way too long. But I want to make it worse for them. Wait for the right moment then let the world know what they're really like. Selfish. Disgusting. In other words, perfect for each other.'"

This isn't Noelle. This can't be. She never would have written that. She fell for every line I ever fed her.

Did she? I think back to the way she used to look into space, that veiled expression on her face. I thought she was just zoning out. Maybe not. Maybe that was when she was hating me the most.

Inspector Landlow looks up at me then nods. 'Here's another entry, a bit later on. Presumably written when you were on your cosy coastal mini-break. "Heidi came. Unbelievable. All that shit Vinnie fed me about a fresh start, about wanting to try again, it's meaningless. The look on her face when we bumped into her in the hotel foyer; it was triumphant. Repulsive. The glee of a woman who thinks she's already won. What a delusional bitch. Her shine will wear off and he'll ditch her. He ditches all his little whores in the end. She's worse than the others, though. Bad. Rotten. There's something stinking at her core. She told me what she did to her father, after she'd had too many glasses of wine. Held him down below the waves to see how long he could really hold his breath for. Nearly killed him, she told me. That's a story she really should keep to herself. Naughty, nasty little Heidi. It's amazing how alcohol loosens the lips."'

'She made that up,' I whisper. 'Just because it's in that book doesn't mean it's the truth.'

'Correct,' Inspector Landlow says. 'However, we've got a report from a woman called Miranda Heath, someone you used to work with, claiming you told her the same thing. Vinnie too. Did they all make it up, Heidi?'

'They must have done.'

The two inspectors smile, a mirthless stretch of the lips, nothing more. Two predators with the scent of blood in their noses, my blood. They think they've got me. But this doesn't prove anything. It's just stories.

'You look like you're thinking hard.' Inspector Meadows perches on the corner of the bed. 'Care to share those thoughts?'

'I don't want to talk anymore. You're trying to frame me when I'm vulnerable. Nothing on this recording can be used against me, my head's spinning.'

Inspector Landlow nods. 'Sorry to hear that. This questioning wasn't official, by the way, Heidi. We just wanted to get you talking to us.' She picks up her recorder, switches it off, then slides it back into her bag. 'Inspector Meadows, I think we'd best leave Heidi in peace, don't you?'

He grimaces. 'I've only just sat down. But you're right, we should be going. Just one more thing though, if I may?'

She nods, as I shake my head. He ignores my reaction, focuses solely on hers. I feel like a child.

'I notice you've got very pretty nails there,' he says, gesturing to my hands. 'Are they real?'

'Excuse me?'

'Your nails. They're eye-catching, aren't they? My daughter's mad about false nails. The brighter the better.'

I look down at them. It's a weird tangent to go down, but it beats their questioning. 'They're false,' I tell him. 'Though some are broken. I'd kill to see a proper nail technician right now.'

'I can imagine.' He studies my hands thoughtfully. 'It's funny, when our forensics team were dredging the seabed, where Noelle was found, they discovered a false nail tangled up in the weeds by her left hand. Practically digging into her skin. Bright green it was, decorated with a sort of scale effect. Very attractive.'

My breath falters. The room is darker, smaller. Airless. No, no, no.

Not proof. Still not proof. I can't give up, not now.

I tighten my jaw. 'Probably one of hers. Or a passing swimmer.'

'Could be.' He stands again, smoothing down the bed cover. 'But Vinnie very kindly shared some photos that he took, on that little mini-break. There's a lovely photo of you and Noelle. In a bar, by the looks of it. With a bottle of wine between you both. Perhaps you remember him taking it?'

I don't answer. My lips are frozen, my tongue too big for my mouth. I fight to control my expression, but can't. There's no way to conceal this now.

'You've obviously forgotten,' Inspector Landlow says, with a smile.

'Maybe you had a bit too much of that wine,' Inspector Meadows adds. 'I couldn't see how much of the bottle was gone. However, your false nails were really clear in that photo. Beautiful bright green with scales painted on them. Would you say it's a coincidence, Heidi?'

I don't answer. They both nod, satisfied. This was the

intention all along. I've been netted. They've allowed me to bob to the surface with the illusion of freedom, only to drag me back down in the end. There's no escape, not from this. My palm throbs with sudden livid heat. At the end of it all, I'm undone by a single nail.

A nail. The irony is hard to ignore.

'We'll leave you for now,' Inspector Landlow says, picking up her bag and rising. 'Needless to say, we have just cause to hold you here, as you're now under arrest on suspicion of murder. Would you like to review your decision about requesting legal assistance?'

I close my eyes. Turn my world to black and let her words dally and dance around me, like bubbles in a stream. More words, from him, then from her again. But I don't hear them. I'm down here in the dark, far away.

CHAPTER TWENTY-FIVE

My hand heals, eventually. But it takes time and the scar is ugly. It's a whirlpool of twisted skin in the centre of my palm. The crescent curl of the fingernail's slash is still visible. A cruel reminder of what was done and who won in the end. It wasn't me. Not by a long way. I guess there's only so far a positive, forward-thinking attitude can take you in life. Sometimes the past grabs at you and refuses to free you from the darkness.

I sit in the back of the police van as it bounces along the road. There are bars on the windows in the back doors. Bars, bars, bars. That's all I've seen for the last few months in the cell they put me in. No bail granted before the trial. I'm too dangerous to release into the wild, apparently. The jury found me guilty in a matter of days. All thanks to one little fingernail and a dead woman's diary.

Fair play to Noelle. She managed to get me in the end.

There's not much to do on the journey back to London. The guards in the front don't turn to look at me once. The landscape outside changes from rolling fields to busier streets, then an endless stretch of grey motorway. I sit and wait. Stare at the bars. Think of the other sort of bars. Clapham cocktail bars, Shoreditch gin bars, West End wine bars. All those endless happy nights when I thought I'd finally burst through the surface and left my childhood behind.

Vinnie wasn't the first man to catch my eye during those years. He wasn't the first one I lured to me. But he was the worst. The one that dragged me down. What a waste of precious time he was.

He visited me before the trial. I had to sit there in drab prison clothes, no make-up, hair a mess. No fake nails either. He looked good, annoyingly. Healthier. Beard trimmed, waxed hair again, smart shirt and jeans. Must be Miranda's effect, or another woman. Another new shiny treasure for him to hoard for a while before moving on. I listened to his wheedling. He asked me to agree to sell the house. I said no. His wheedling turned harder, then threatening. He's applied for an order of sale now, whatever that is. I guess it means I'll never see that place again though. As a majority shareholder, he's in a good position to get what he wants. As per usual.

Funny to think I thought I loved him. Funnier to think I thought Rick and I had a future. Vivienne said that some people were better off alone. She might have been right. I should have stayed alone, the minute I wriggled free from my mother and ventured into the city. Alone is stronger. On my own, but always ready with claws out, just in case they're needed.

It's fine, I tell myself, as the van rattles onwards. *This is all fine.* I still have a future. I can still make something of myself.

As for this, right now? I never wanted to live by the sea anyway.

THE END

A NOTE FROM THE PUBLISHER

Thank you for reading this book. If you enjoyed it please do consider leaving a review on Amazon to help others find it too.

We hate typos. All of our books have been rigorously edited and proofread, but sometimes mistakes do slip through. If you have spotted a typo, please do let us know and we can get it amended within hours.

info@bloodhoundbooks.com